'The shimmering humour and life values Henderson
explores are certainly something you wouldn't want to miss'
– *The Star Online*

'An amiably weird take on family life' – *Daily Mail* **on**
The Last of the Bowmans

'A funny road trip story… but this brave debut novel also
tackles sensitive issues and does so in a confident manner'
– *We Love This Book*

'Deftly handled with an offbeat humour and a deal of
worldly compassion' – *Sunday Sport*

'J Paul Henderson is someone to watch out for'
– *The Bookbag*

'I found myself laughing out loud with the characters.
I really enjoyed this story' – *Book Depository*

ALSO BY J P HENDERSON

Last Bus to Coffeeville
The Last of the Bowmans
Larry and the Dog People

My name is

Herod 'Rod' Pinkney

and I'm in love

with a girl called

J P H E N D E R S O N

NO EXIT PRESS

First published in 2020 by No Exit Press,
an imprint of Oldcastle Books Ltd,
Harpenden, UK
noexit.co.uk

ISBN
978-0-85730-330-1 (print)
978-0-85730-331-8 (epub)

2 4 6 8 10 9 7 5 3 1

Typeset in 11.5pt Minion Pro by Avocet Typeset, Bideford, Devon, EX39 2BP
Printed and bound in Great Britain by Clays Ltd, Elcograf S.p.A.

'Tis better to have dreamt and woken up
Than never to have dreamt at all

ALT (*alt*)

Contents

The Start   11

Journal Entry   13

Continuation 1: Pinkney Industries   15

Journal Entry   39

Continuation 2: The Gallery Years   43

Journal Entry   67

Continuation 3: Edmundo and Nelly   71

Continuation 4: Donald   93

Journal Entry   121

Continuation 5: Miller v Lamprich   125

Continuation 6: The Parable of the Winnebago and the
Intercession of Mr Stenger   148

Continuation 7: Keeping Busy in the Time of an
Interregnum   175

Journal Entry   201

Continuation 8: The Battersea Square Concert   207

Continuation 9: Huntington Beach   232

Continuation 10: D-Day   259

Journal Entry   291

The Finish   295

The Start

In my opinion, the world can be divided into two types of people: one happy to talk about themselves, and the other not. I belong to the latter category.

Allow me to introduce myself. My name is Herod S Pinkney and I'm in love with a girl called Daisy Lamprich.

I think that's enough to be going on with.

7 June 2019

I showed the page you've just read to my agent, who collects glasses in a local pub called the Lansdowne. It's a short page, but it took me a long time to write. First words are important.

He read the typed sheet and nodded his head slowly. It was an interesting start, he said, but indicated that I would have to be a lot more forthcoming if I wanted a publisher to take an interest in my story.

'The reader wants to know about you, Rod, and what makes you tick,' he said. 'And it's too soon to start talking about Daisy. They're not going to take an interest in her until they've taken an interest in you. You have to hook them and reel them in; get them to invest in you as a person.'

We talked a while longer, but then the pub got busy and the landlord told him to get busy.

'Talk to the cripple in your own time,' he said.

You can gather that the landlord isn't a nice man, and if it wasn't for my agent working here I wouldn't give him my business. And it's not as if I am a cripple. Not everyone who drives a mobility scooter is an invalid.

I finished my drink and drove the short distance home. I live in a quiet street in Battersea, not far from the park, and it's been my home for some years. It's an end-terrace house, four storeys high since I had the basement dug, and desirable in every way. The front and side walls are covered in plants – living walls that make up for the small gardens to the front and rear of the property. I got the idea from the Athenaeum Hotel on Piccadilly, and even got the man who did their walls to do mine. The odd thing about him was that he didn't like heights. In the time he worked at my house he had two panic attacks and never smiled once. Edmundo takes care of the walls now. Edmundo takes care of most things.

Once settled, I poured myself a small whisky and mulled over what my agent had said. His name is Ric, by the way, though for the life of me I can't remember his last name. It's foreign sounding and full of consonants that don't usually sit together, which in his walk of life he considers an advantage.

'It makes me stand out from the crowd, Rod – a bit like your name makes you.'

I suppose he has a point, though personally I don't like my name and I'm happy to be a part of any crowd. I think it's good to fit in. That's why I ask people to call me Rod rather than Herod these days, though I only felt free to do so after my parents died. I suppose this would be a good time to tell you about them.

I think this is what Ric would want me to do.

Continuation 1

Pinkney Industries

My father was George Pinkney, the founder of Pinkney Industries. He was a burly man with a wide neck and size eleven feet. His jaw was square and his ears were flat to his head, as if pressed there by a laundress. He also had a thick moustache that hung over his top lip and he greased his hair to the point of waterproofing his head. He wore a suit and a tie every day of his working week, but on weekends and holidays favoured cravats.

My father was self-made and never tired of telling people this. I worked for him while he was alive, but I have little idea how he made his money. In truth, I think my father kept me in the dark intentionally. I got the impression he didn't like me, and he was forever telling me how much a poor substitute for Solomon I was. And that's what I was in the family: a substitute for a dead brother who'd shown more promise in his little finger than I did in my entirety – or so my father kept telling me.

Solomon died on his sixteenth birthday after diving into the shallow end of an outdoor swimming pool. If he was as bright as my father said he was, then you have to wonder why he failed to realise that the diving boards were at the other end of the pool for a reason. I kept this thought to myself, though. Life was hard enough just being a disappointment.

And because I was a disappointment to my father, I was also a disappointment to my mother. It could have been no other way. My mother worshipped my father, and it was this quality that endeared her to him. He expected no less of a spouse: a partner who would accede to his whims and decisions without question.

Most people considered my mother to be a beautiful woman, but I never saw this. Her full lips were always tightened when she spoke to me and her eyes invariably narrowed, and the smile that supposedly lit up the salons of London was never once in evidence. According to my Uncle Horace, who was married to her sister Thelma, my mother could have had her pick of London's eligible men but had chosen my father for his August nature. (I never quite understood this, because my father's birthday was in November.)

If my mother had wanted more children than the two she gave birth to, then she never said. It certainly wasn't something she would have confided in me. My father, however, had made it clear that he wanted only one child: a son he could mould in his own image and entrust with the family empire. Solomon was that child, not me. I was supposed to be another Solomon, but I wasn't.

I was born eighteen months after my brother died. By the time I was three, my father had already decided that I was never going to be another Solomon. For one thing, he said my face was too fat, and he was also annoyed by my sedentary nature.

'Every time I come into this house, Herod, you're sitting on your damned backside,' he'd say. 'What's wrong with you, boy? Do you want your buttocks to grow to the size of your face? Now give me three laps!'

(We had a large lounge.)

When I looked to my mother for support, she simply told me to do as my father bade, adding that Solomon had only sat down on a chair for meals. I never once believed this, but Solomon, though ever-present – his sports trophies and awards adorning the shelves and the walls of the lounge – was never there to question.

I started to sit in secret, whenever my parents were out of the room or, better still, out of the house, which happened often. I had to be careful around the cleaner and the babysitters, though, because my father gave them strict instructions to keep me on the move and to report back to him if they ever caught me sitting on a chair or stretched out on a sofa. My father was a firm believer in the power of money to make others do his bidding, and every time they informed on me they were paid a bonus.

The safest place to sit was the toilet, and this room became my home away from home when I lived at home. No one bothered me there, and I used to slip the bolt on the door to avoid being caught unawares, even though this was against the rules. My happiest times as a child were the hours I spent sitting on a toilet seat, reading a comic or just daydreaming – which was something else my father disapproved of.

Consequently, when my parents sent me away to boarding school at the age of seven, I was as happy as Larry. The school was situated in a small town in Wiltshire and discouraged parental visits during term time. This suited me fine, but what particularly pleased me was the school's expectation that I would sit in a classroom for most days of the week, and on wooden seats no less comfortable than the one in my parents' toilet. Learning became a pleasure, but for probably the wrong reason.

Although it was impossible to avoid all sport in a school

dedicated to building character on the playing field, I was excused from outdoor games in the spring and summer months because of my allergy to grass and tree pollens that occasionally gave rise to severe asthma attacks. The headmaster allowed me to substitute chess for the more physical games at this time of year, and I was much happier proclaiming my school spirit from a seated position.

I wasn't much good at chess and I used to lose matches to pupils much younger than me, but I never minded losing. Evidently, this was another quality that distinguished me – and not in a good way – from my late brother, who had also attended the school.

Teachers were never shy of telling me how much a shadow of Solomon I was, who, they said, was also more gifted than me scholastically. I wasn't stupid, but I did suffer from a form of dyslexia that wasn't diagnosed until after I'd left school. It's not so bad now, and with spellcheckers it's no longer a concern. I occasionally get words and numbers muddled but not often enough for it to be a problem, and as I no longer work for a living it hardly matters.

On the whole, my schooldays passed without incident and I made some good friends. The only thing I was teased about was my name: Herod.

'Why are you named after the man who killed all those children?' I was asked over and again. 'You know that Herod tried to kill Jesus, don't you?'

As a matter of fact, I didn't. Despite my father favouring biblical names for his sons, the Bible itself was banned from the house and not once did he or my mother take me to church. He was an atheist, I think, and if he was an atheist then so too was my mother. I think that's why religion came to interest me: if my father disbelieved in God then there was every cause for me to accept Him – even if it was only to annoy him and avoid the risk of running into him in the afterlife.

It was during a forced march along the Thames Embankment one school holiday that I asked him about my name. Why was I named after an ancient king who'd slaughtered hundreds of small children and tried to kill Jesus? And why the middle initial that seemingly didn't stand for anything? Why Herod S Pinkney?

'Because Herod was a great man,' my father answered, 'and I was hoping that by giving you his name, his qualities might rub off on you. And you can forget all that nonsense about him slaughtering hundreds of small children because that never happened, and if, for the sake of argument, it did happen, then there were no more than twenty put to death. There's no historical evidence to support such a notion, and if he didn't kill Jesus... well, that was his one failure.

'What you need to know about King Herod is that he was ambitious, ruthless, and one of the greatest builders of all time. He knew how to get things done and he wasn't prepared for anyone to stand in his way – not even his own family. If you want to succeed in life, Herod, then you need to have his qualities, especially when you have such a fat face.'

I used to get tired of my father telling me I had a fat face. I wasn't the only boy my age to have chubby cheeks, and I certainly don't have those cheeks today. In fact, and though I don't like to blow my own trumpet, most people consider me a handsome man, and I have no reason to doubt them.

But I'm digressing, which I'm not sure Ric would approve of.

'What about your middle initial, Rod? Why the "S"?' I can hear him asking.

Well, it turned out that the 'S' stood for Solomon, but my

birth certificate would only reflect this if I turned out to be like my brother, which, my father said, seemed increasingly unlikely.

'I named Solomon, Solomon, because of his knowing face,' he said. 'He looked wise beyond his years even the day he was born, as if he'd been thinking about things the entire time he'd been inside your mother's womb. I couldn't have wished for a more erudite looking boy.'

Again, I was reminded of the way Solomon died and I couldn't but wonder about his supposed wisdom. Apart from – well, actually, including his death, come to think of it – my older brother got all the breaks. Me, I got none. But at least I lived to tell the tale.

So life went on but nothing really changed. I did okay at school but not well enough to be accepted by either Oxford or Cambridge, and because my father wasn't prepared for a son of his to go to a redbrick university, I ended up going to work for him at Pinkney Industries.

Even though my father and I lived under the same roof, we went to his offices separately, him by car and me on a bicycle or by public transport. It was all right for him to sit in comfort, but not me. I had to use my legs.

And all the jobs he gave me at Pinkney Industries involved movement. If I wasn't working in the mailroom, delivering letters and packages to offices in a five-storey building with no lift, I was working for what these days would be known as a facilities department and tasked with rearranging office furniture every time my father decided to restructure the company, which was often and mostly, I suspect, to keep me busy.

I thought for a time that by starting me at the bottom, my father's aim was for me to learn all aspects of his business before promoting me to a position of greater responsibility, but in thinking this I was mistaken. My father's intention was for me to remain at the bottom in perpetuity.

Considering my education, I suggested over dinner one evening that I might be of more service to him doing something other than working in the mailroom and facilities departments, and surprisingly he agreed. He told me a vacancy had arisen in one of his American interests and that the job would be mine if I was willing to travel to the United States. I jumped at the chance, but in retrospect I should have known better than to accept his munificence at face value. The job in question turned out to be a deckhand on a Mississippi towboat, and it was the worst six months of my life.

When I returned from America I didn't have an ounce of fat on my body, and even my father had to admit there was less flab on my face than usual. And what was my reward? I was sent back to the facilities department!

If my father hadn't died unexpectedly from a heart attack, I would have probably been moving desks and changing light bulbs for the rest of my working life. As it was, he did die unexpectedly from a heart attack and was found slumped over his desk by the secretary who brought him his afternoon coffee.

I wasn't summoned to the scene because no one in the building knew I was his son. He'd never told anyone of our relationship and I'd never been allowed to mention it for fear, my father said, of people misinterpreting my employment as nepotism. During the time I worked at Pinkney Industries I was known as Brian Beasley. All things considered, I think most people would have construed my appointment as a punishment rather than an unfair leg-up, but, as always, I did as directed and said nothing.

I only heard the news of my father's death once I'd returned home and found my mother on the kitchen floor wailing. She was curled up in a foetal position, and it took time to unravel her and get her to a sitting position, and even longer to quieten her moaning. And when she did stop sobbing, she started to scream at me.

'Your father's dead, Herod, and it's your fault! He didn't die of natural causes, he died of disappointment: disappointment in you!'

It wasn't a promising start to the new family dynamic.

It's difficult to explain how I felt when my father died. No loved-one had passed away, but a familiar landscape *had* changed, as if a building I'd passed every day of my life had suddenly been demolished. There was a void, neither welcomed nor unwelcomed. That's all I can say on the matter.

I didn't cry then or at the funeral, which was large and unnecessarily showy, and though I tried to console my mother during the service, she pushed my arm away. There seemed to be no pleasing her that day: everything I did or said was somehow wrong. And over the weeks that followed, things between us didn't improve. She shut herself in her room and refused to talk to me and only emerged to meet with my father's solicitor or the financial director of the company.

One night I knocked on her bedroom door, and when she didn't answer I entered hesitantly. My mother was staring into space and ignored my intrusion.

'Mother,' I said. 'I'm worried about you. I want to support you but you won't let me. What can I do to help?'

She didn't turn or look at me, but in a voice that was both cold and monotonic replied that I could help her most by leaving the house and going to live with my Aunt Thelma.

'And don't even think about taking the car,' she added somewhat unnecessarily.

I didn't even know how to drive a car.

And so I went to live with my aunt. Aunt Thelma was my mother's sister who lived in Vauxhall, not far from my father's offices, and whose husband, Horace, managed a branch of Barclays. It was him who answered the door when I knocked, and the first thing he asked was what I was doing there with a suitcase. Before I had time to answer he shouted the same question to his wife. My mother, it turned out, had failed to mention my arrival to them.

The most I can say about my time with Aunt Thelma and Uncle Horace is that they were civil to me but that it was always a relief to leave their house on a morning and cycle to work, where I continued to report to the facilities department. Every day I expected to be summoned to the boardroom for a reassignment of duties, but three weeks went by and still nothing happened.

And then, the day before my birthday, Aunt Thelma told me that my mother had phoned and asked that I return home the following evening and join her for a celebratory meal. I was touched that my mother had remembered my birthday at such a sad time in her life, and I looked upon it as an omen: a new beginning for the two of us, and possibly news of my future at Pinkney Industries.

After finishing work the next day I went back to Aunt Thelma's and quickly changed into my best suit, and then, as it was my birthday, I hailed a taxi. I knocked on the door of my mother's house to show respect, and then opened it with my key. There was the sound of loud music, but the needle had stuck in a groove and it was difficult to make sense of what was playing. I called my mother's name (which was Mother, just as my father's name had always been Father), and lifted the needle from the vinyl disc spinning on the turntable. It was a recording of *We'll Meet Again* by Vera Lynn, which had been one of my father's favourites.

There was no sign of life in the downstairs rooms. The dining table hadn't been set and there was no hint of any food having been prepared in the kitchen. In short, there was no sign of the celebratory meal I'd been invited to.

I was about to climb the stairs when I noticed the French windows wide open. It was midsummer and the evening was warm, and it occurred to me that my mother might have arranged a table in the garden and that I'd find her there. In thinking this, I was half-right and half-wrong. There was no food on the garden table as I'd expected, but I did find my mother's body swinging from the branch of a large oak tree.

My mother's death, although obvious to me as self-destruction, was only ruled a suicide once the cleaner found a note under her pillow the following week. Until then, the police had been working under the assumption that it was me who'd hanged her from the tree, if for no other reason than to teach her a lesson for not cooking me a birthday meal.

I learned later that their suspicions had first been aroused when they arrived at the house and found me sitting in an easy chair eating a ham and cheese sandwich and seemingly unmoved by the discovery of my mother's body. My explanation, that I hadn't eaten lunch that day and was feeling faint, cut no ice with them.

'How can anyone think of their stomach at a time like this?' one of the policemen commented loud enough for me to hear.

They dug deeper and decided that I was a young man with a chip on his shoulder; a son resentful of parents who'd denied him the entitlement he deserved. My father, they noted, had placed me in a low-grade position within his company and left me there to stew, while my mother, believing me to have been a contributing factor in her husband's death, had banished me from the house and sent me to live with an aunt who, as it transpired, also wasn't enamoured of me. They argued that I had everything to gain from her death and nothing to lose, and that it was me, rather than my mother, who had placed the recording of *We'll Meet Again* on the turntable in an attempt to divert attention from myself and focus it on her frail mental disposition.

Honesty in such circumstances, I learned to my cost, is not to be encouraged. When asked if I'd loved my parents, I'd replied that I didn't think my parents had loved me, and when pressed on the point I had to admit that I probably hadn't. It didn't, however, make me a killer, I added.

'That's for us to decide,' the man leading the investigation replied, something they were only dissuaded from doing after my mother's letter came to light.

The letter was handwritten in green ink and addressed to me. She started by talking about Solomon and what a wonderful son he'd been, and then she listed the many ways in which I'd disappointed her and my father. In particular, she thought it a disgrace that I still couldn't spell properly after all the money they'd spent on my education.

She then came to the crux of her anguish: the death of my father. He'd been the love of her life, the reason for her being, and without him there was no point to life. She rued the fact that she hadn't been burnt alive on a pyre after he'd died – as they did in some parts of India (where my father also had interests) – and that such short-term agony would have been as nothing compared to the suffering she now endured. She was done with this world, done with me and done with Pinkney Industries. She was off to find George, her dear departed husband, who, she believed, couldn't have strayed all that far in the short time he'd been dead.

My mother's suicide wasn't unconscionable in itself, but choosing my birthday as the occasion for her death, and for me to find her body, was.

If my parents had shown me love while they'd been alive, and I'd been asked to choose between their affection and their money, then I would have gladly opted for their affection. But they didn't, and so in their absence I accepted their money. Overnight, I became a rich man.

Well, I say overnight, but it wasn't quite as simple as that. For one thing, there was a lot of paperwork to sort out, and for another, my Uncle Horace contested my mother's will, which had left everything to my late brother, Solomon.

Why her will had never been updated was a mystery to all, but that it hadn't was a stroke of luck for me, as I suspect she'd have preferred her estate to have gone to an animal shelter than pass to me. As it was, the house, her inherited savings and Pinkney Industries passed into my hands, and the next time I walked into my father's offices I was fêted like a king:

'Hello, Brian. What are you doing here?'

*

It quickly became apparent – both to me and my fellow directors – that I was out of my depth, and that under my tutelage the future of the company was anything but secure. I'm not trying to sing my own praises here, but I think I recognised this fact before they did.

I stuck it out for a month and then asked the financial director to step into my office. His name was Robert Green and he'd taken me under his wing during the short time I'd been there and shown me kindness. It was him, in fact, who'd mentioned that I might have dyslexia; certainly he could think of no other explanation for my strange memos.

We sat down and the secretary brought us coffee. He was about to take a bite of his biscuit when I asked him the question that had been puzzling me ever since I'd arrived at the offices.

'What is it that Pinkney Industries actually does, Robert? What do we manufacture?'

It turned out that we didn't manufacture anything, and that to his way of thinking the company's name had always been misleading. The company owned property, he said, made investments, bought and sold intangibles, and had as many interests overseas as it did in the United Kingdom.

'Without being condescending, Herod, it's a bit complicated.'

There was no kidding me there.

After more discussion we decided that it would be best – both for me and everyone whose livelihoods depended on Pinkney Industries – if I stood down as CEO and the company was divided into manageable chunks and liquidated. It was important to me that no employees lost their jobs in the transition – especially in the mailroom and facilities department – but although Robert couldn't guarantee this, he thought there was a greater chance of people losing their jobs in those departments if I continued to run the company.

We shook hands – his more capable than mine – and that, I'm afraid, was the beginning of the end for Pinkney Industries. That my father and, by default, my mother might be turning in their graves at this moment, concerned me not at all.

And then the day came when Robert invited me to the

office and handed me a cheque for eleven million pounds.

'The world's your oyster, Herod,' he said. 'Do you have any travel in mind?'

I told him I had, and that I was hoping to spend a few days in Bournemouth.

Robert walked with me to the car park and was surprised to see my bicycle standing in my father's reserved space.

'I thought you'd have driven here in your father's car,' he said.

I explained that I was having a few problems passing my driving test and had, in fact, already failed it twice: once for going through a No Entry sign, and another time for mistaking a line of parked cars for an active lane of traffic. The first failure I could understand, but the second I put down to the examiner being in a bad mood. It still jars me that he didn't mention my mistake for a full fifteen minutes, which was half the allotted time for the test.

Robert told me not to lose heart and I took his advice. A year later, and after only three more attempts, I got my licence.

Eleven million pounds was a lot of money, far too much for one person, and I decided to give half of my inheritance to a deserving cause. I wanted to make a difference to the country and to do it with one stroke: do something that would tackle poverty and improve the lives of those in need, alleviate suffering in all its forms and ensure that all citizens had access to good schools and a free health service.

I thought things over for a month, turned them in my mind again and again, and then, after breakfast one morning, I made the decision that I believed any person in my position would have made: I wrote a cheque for five and a half million pounds and donated it to the Conservative Party.

I then had to make decisions about my own life: where I

would live and what I would do. I had no attachment to the family home: I felt like an uninvited guest there, just as I had when I'd lived there with my parents. The house held no fond memories and, though the oak tree had been cut down, I could still sense my mother's body swaying from its invisible branch. It wasn't a question of whether I would stay but when I would leave, a matter that was resolved three months later when I stumbled on the property I now occupy.

I'd been visiting Miss Wimpole that day, a dyslexia therapist whose practice was in the borough of Battersea. Her rooms were several streets from where I live now but a good distance from the bus route, and it was while I was walking from the bus stop to her house that I passed the For Sale sign in its garden.

I already liked the area from past visits to Miss Wimpole, and as she'd intimated that we'd be seeing each other for at least three years, I thought it sensible to move closer to where she lived. I've always thought that convenience has a lot to offer in life.

Before I start telling you about the house, however, I should probably finish telling you about my therapist. Again, I think this is another thing Ric would want me to do.

Miss Wimpole was in her early sixties but looked older, as if a strong tailwind was blowing her through life. She was a spinster and wore cardigans and thick woollen skirts, and she had a cat called Pedro that never left the room. She'd been recommended to me by a general practitioner, and she spoke to me as if I was six – probably the age when most of her patients first visited.

'Well, dear, what makes you think you have dyslexia?' she asked me on my first visit.

I told her that I wasn't sure if I did or didn't because I'd never been able to find the word in the dictionary, but that Robert thought I had and that my mother had mentioned my inability to spell in her suicide note.

'Oh dear, dear, I'm so sorry to hear that,' she commiserated.

She then gave me some tests and decided that I was dyslexic – though by no means the worst case she'd encountered in her years of practice.

'But this doesn't mean you're stupid, dear, if that's what you've been thinking.'

I told her that I hadn't been thinking this, and that until she'd mentioned it the thought had never crossed my mind.

'Well, dismiss it immediately, dear,' she said, 'because you're not stupid: you just have a disability.'

The word disability unnerved me more than the word stupid, and Miss Wimpole noticed my concern. She patted me on the knee and gave a sympathetic smile.

'We don't have time for self-pity, dear: we have important work to do!'

And for the next three years we worked on what she called phonological skills, and though the underlying problem remained when we parted company – she retired from practice and went to live with her widowed sister in Cornwall – the degree of my symptoms had decreased considerably.

During the time I visited Miss Wimpole, the house in Battersea became my life. Although its structure was sound the interior had been sadly neglected, as if the previous owners had been blind to its decay. I didn't do any of the work myself, but instead hired a contractor to oversee the renovations. I told Mr Axelrod – a man in his fifties, and whose forearms were the size of my thighs – to simplify the house and to make it spacious and warm, and he succeeded beyond my expectations.

The wall dividing the kitchen from the dining room was demolished and a large glass double door was inserted into the wall separating the newly enlarged room from the lounge. The existing cast-iron radiators were replaced, installed for the first time in the upper rooms, and the fireplace chimney unblocked and swept. Lastly, though by no means least, the walls were stripped of their flowery wallpaper, completely re-plastered and painted in plain colours.

It was a year before the house was fully transformed, and during these months I lived in a single room, first on one floor and then on another, its changing location determined by the workers' schedule.

I might add here that living in a house under refurbishment is no easy matter, and it certainly hadn't been my intention to do this. My parents' house, though, had sold faster than anticipated, and to fit in with the new owner's timetable I was obliged to vacate the premises and fall in with the contractor's.

It might be puzzling that a man of my wealth, whose fortune had recently been increased by the sale of a substantial property, had chosen to squat in a building site rather than move to somewhere like the Ritz. It also puzzled Mr Axelrod, who asked me one day if I was hiding from someone.

The answer, however, is a simple one: I couldn't get used to the idea of being rich.

I'd never had money before, and the small wage paid by Pinkney Industries had barely covered the board and lodging demanded by my mother, and later my Aunt Thelma. I'd learned to scrape by, to value the pennies, and I'd witnessed my colleagues in the mailroom and facilities department doing the same. I didn't know how a man with money was supposed to behave, and so I chose to behave like a man without money, favouring public transport over taxis and small cafes over fancy restaurants. For me, this was the attraction of Battersea, which was a mixed area rather than a preserve of the wealthy. Its humdrum nature suited me, and I thought I'd fit in here.

The workmen left me a polished shell that now had to be furnished. Just as I'd placed the renovations in the hands of one person, I now gave responsibility for its furnishing to another.

Trudy Barnes was the wife of one of the plasterers, and I had no reason to doubt the recommendation of a man who'd smoothed my walls so beautifully. She was a dainty little thing, no more than five feet tall, but she scared the living daylights out of me. I supposed it was her artistic temperament that made her so prickly, though it was a disposition I'd never before associated with soft furnishings. Anyway, she got the job done, and although her choice of drapes was a touch on the garish side, I was pleased that she'd used the same carpet throughout.

I learned later, from the butcher in fact, that Trudy was colour-blind, and he supposed that this might be a drawback in her line of work. Later still, however, I heard from someone else that the butcher held a grudge against Trudy for returning a chicken she'd claimed was on the turn, and that I should take his opinion with a pinch of salt. It felt good to have stumbled upon a community where people took such an interest in each other.

I could live with Trudy's choices as they were, though, and over time, and once my parents' furniture was installed in the house, the curtains quietened to no more than a loud hum.

I didn't take all my parents' furniture, only the pieces I liked, but among them were the chairs and sofas I'd always been discouraged from using. The only keepsakes I held on to were photographs of my parents and Solomon – though more, I suspect, to prove to others that I hadn't grown up in an orphanage than for any sentimental reasons – and a selection of my father's cravats, which I'd always admired. I'm wearing one now, as a matter of fact: it's blue with white polka dots and made from the finest silk.

Next, I started to think about a job. I didn't need one, of course, but I was hoping that a pursuit of some kind would allow me to meet new people and, if all went to plan, make friends.

I'd lost contact with most of my old school mates – many of whom had gone on to university and now worked in the professions or had joined family businesses – and my social life was at best threadbare and had been so ever since I'd gone to work for my father. My wage in those days had been no more generous than that paid to any employee who worked in the mailroom or facilities department at Pinkney Industries, and certainly hadn't afforded me the luxury of mixing in the social circles of former friends – something I learned as a matter of course after accepting an invitation to meet with Gerald Smithson one Saturday night.

Although a year older than me, Gerald had also been a member of the school's chess club, and though we'd never been best friends, we'd always enjoyed each other's company. I bumped into him on Regent Street one day after hand-delivering a small package to an office located on one of its side streets, and it was difficult to know which of us was the more surprised. He was on his way to meet a client for lunch and running late, but suggested I join him and Charlie for a 'glass or two of the old vino' that Saturday night and make up a foursome. I happily accepted his proposal, and when I returned to the office I asked Trevor if he was free that evening.

Trevor also worked in the mailroom and was about the

only person in Pinkney Industries I was on good terms with. He was a keen snooker player and I'd accompany him to a local hall some lunchtimes. I never played the game myself – it involved too much standing for my liking – but I was more than happy to sit on a chair and watch him pot balls while I ate my sandwich.

Unfortunately for the evening ahead, Trevor had assumed that the foursome I'd mentioned related to a game of snooker, and when he emerged from the tube station on Kensington High Street that night he was carrying an uncased cue. My expectation for the evening was of four men having drinks together and shooting the breeze – the way we used to on the towboats – but in thinking this I'd been as mistaken as Trevor for supposing that we'd be shooting snooker balls.

It turned out that Gerald's friend, Charlie, was a girl, and that Gerald had been expecting me to arrive with another girl and not some 'greaser holding a pool cue', as he later put it. I had a bad feeling about the evening as soon as we walked into the wine bar and the management insisted on Trevor leaving his snooker cue in the umbrella stand by the door. And then, after we had joined Gerald and Charlie at their table, it quickly became apparent that neither of us had enough money for more than two drinks if we weren't to walk home that night.

Charlie, whose full name was Charlotte, was a pretty girl but distant, and for most of the evening she remained silent. Trevor, however, who would have done better following her example, showed no such reticence and spoke at length on the finer points of snooker, even after Gerald had made it clear to him that he wasn't interested in the game.

'That's because you don't understand it,' Trevor had countered before continuing.

It was difficult to get a word in edgeways with Trevor there, and it was often frustrating. When Gerald mentioned that he was an actuary, and I said that I didn't know what that was, Trevor explained that an actuary was a man who made watches for a living.

'Is that right, Gerald?' I asked, surprised by his choice of vocation.

Gerald said that it wasn't, and that anyone who thought this had probably been hit over the head with a snooker cue too many times. He compiled and analysed statistics used to calculate insurance risks and premiums, he said, and explained that Trevor had confused the word with Accurist, which was the name of a watch. He then pulled up the sleeve of his shirt and showed us his wristwatch, which proved to be just that: an Accurist.

'I was half-right, then, wasn't I?' Trevor said.

Nothing jelled that evening, and I was relieved when Gerald and Charlie left for the restaurant they'd booked.

'We reserved a table for four,' Gerald said, 'but I don't think they'll mind if I change the number. I'm one of their best customers.'

I still see Gerald from time to time, but I've lost touch with Trevor. Two weeks after our night out together, he was sacked from Pinkney Industries by no other person than my father, who'd found him asleep under his desk. To this day I have no idea why Trevor chose this particular location, other than that the carpet in my father's office had a thicker pile. Sometimes I watch out for him on television when they're broadcasting a snooker competition, but so far I haven't seen him.

Anyway, now that I had decided a career was the likeliest avenue to a social life, I was still faced with the problem of deciding its nature, and it made sense to seek the advice of a professional.

From my time trudging to and from Pinkney Industries, I was aware of an employment agency on Stamford Street – in the borough of Lambeth, just south of the river – and it was here that I made an appointment to see Adrian Crusher, its chief consultant.

Mr Crusher was a portly man in his early forties and he wore a distinctive dark, pinstriped suit. His hair was thick and black, and his shoulders were speckled with dandruff that he brushed away with his hand from time to time.

'I know all about it,' he said, when he saw me looking at the flakes.

I blushed when he said this and started to apologise, but he cut me short.

'Forget it, Mr Pinkney,' he said. 'Catherine the Great suffered from dandruff, and if it was good enough for her then it's no skin off my nose.'

I was impressed by his skilled use of words and I asked him if he was a writer. He said that he wasn't.

Mr Crusher read the handwritten notes I passed him and then scratched his head, causing a further fall of scurf.

'This is about the oddest employment history I've ever read,' he said, which, to be fair to Mr Crusher, was an accurate description.

Apart from my time as a deckhand on the Mississippi River, I'd worked only in a mailroom and a facilities department, and neither of these situations had seemingly prepared me for the duties of a managing director.

I explained the circumstances of my family and Pinkney Industries to Mr Crusher as best I could, and then mentioned that I was looking for a fresh start and counting on his direction. He then asked me a lot of questions about myself, what I liked and didn't like, and my expectations from life. I was unused to being interviewed and I found the discussion quite gruelling, and fitting that the man interrogating me was called Crusher. After about thirty minutes or so, he put down his pen, leaned back in his chair and clasped his hands behind his neck.

'Okay, Mr Pinkney, let me see if I've got this right – and please feel free to correct me if I haven't. One, you're independently wealthy and you own a large number of cravats. Two, you like sitting down but don't like talking about yourself. Three, you don't have any real interest in working for a living but believe that an occupation will allow you the opportunity of meeting new people and making friends, which currently you're without. And four, you have no ambition and aren't interested in money because you already have enough.'

I nodded in agreement after each point.

'In other words, Mr Pinkney – and in summary – if you could meet the right kind of person by simply riding around on a bus all day, you'd be more than happy to jump at the chance.'

Mr Crusher was good: he had me down to a T and I told him so.

'Very well then, I think I might have just the job for you.'

He then opened one of the lower drawers in his desk and pulled out a file.

18 June 2019

I was on my way to the Lansdowne to give Ric a copy of my first chapter, when I heard Lydia Walker calling my name. Lydia's my next-door neighbour and her husband, Donald, is one of my two best friends, the other being Edmundo. She's a large woman, solid rather than fat, and looks like a shot-putter. (Donald told me she worked construction in her youth, but I think he was joking when he said this. Sometimes it's difficult to tell with Donald.)

Lydia has a shrill voice that demands attention, and when I heard it I braked hard.

'Have you seen Donald, Rod? He's not answering his phone.'

I apologised that I hadn't, but suggested he might be busking with Edmundo (Donald plays the trombone and Edmundo, the panpipes). I've learned from experience that it's best to start any answer to Lydia with an apology. She's a difficult woman at the best of times and she takes offence at the slightest thing. You have to handle her with kid gloves; the way an expert on the Antiques Roadshow *would examine a piece of old glass.*

Lydia acknowledged my answer by closing the door, and only then, knowing that my apology had been accepted, did I feel free to continue my journey.

I was looking forward to seeing Ric and noticing his reaction to my calling the draft continuation 1 rather than chapter 1. His comment, that names had the power to differentiate, had stayed with me, and I was hoping that in a world of chaptered books my choice of word would catch the eye.

It might seem odd that Ric works in a pub and not in a conventional literary agency, but it's something that doesn't concern me. Ric has previously worked for agencies and still has the contacts, but it's a past that now shames him and he's happier collecting glasses.

'It's a world of egos, Rod, of overdressed shysters and as fake as a two-dollar bill. Agents and publishers aren't interested in real literature, just what sells and how much money it's going to make them. If shit sells then they'll publish it. It's as simple as that. Check out the bestseller lists if you don't believe me. And don't kid yourself that a book that wins the Booker Prize is any less shit than one that doesn't: it just means that it's a dull piece of shit!'

I liked it that Ric was so principled and that for the sake of literature he'd turned his back on the publishing industry and decided to plough his own furrow, which, at the time of our meeting and in his words, had proved to be about as barren as a 'fucking brick'. He was candid in telling me this – a quality I like in a person – but not overly concerned by his situation: it was simply a matter of time, he said, and of finding the right seed. And he was confident that my story, which he described as 'a quest for love in an uncertain age', would be his breakthrough: the first bestseller not to be shit!

I hope he's right, and I hope that my book has a happy ending.

It was Ric, in fact, who suggested I write the book. Before the new landlord moved in, I used to visit the Lansdowne often.

I'd take a book with me and sit in a corner, keep to myself rather than strike up a conversation. Ric had been clearing glasses from a nearby table and approached me when he saw me reading The Mackerel Plaza by Peter De Vries. It's a funny book about a recently widowed pastor, and Ric told me it was one of his favourites. We fell into conversation and over time became friendly, and the night I told him about Daisy and the circumstances of our meeting, he suggested I keep a journal.

'There's a book in this, Rod, a book that could well capture the nation's imagination. I used to be a literary agent and I know these things. I have the instincts...'

When I arrived at the Lansdowne I found Ric polishing horse brasses, and I asked him if he'd been promoted since my last visit. He said that he hadn't, and that he was only going the extra mile for the promise of a free meal that evening.

'I'm thinking of ordering sausage and mash, Rod. What do you think?'

I told him it was a good choice, and that it was difficult to go wrong with sausages.

Ric agreed, and then told me that his wife refused to keep sausages in the house and would only cook chicken. This news surprised me, because until this moment I'd had no idea that Ric was married. But he was, and it also turned out that he had two children: both girls and in their late teens. His wife worked in the City and was the acknowledged breadwinner of the family; earned enough, in fact, for them to eat wagyu steaks every night of the week if she'd so desired. But she didn't: in her mind meat was murder, but, fortunately for Ric, chicken was only manslaughter.

I handed Ric the envelope containing my manuscript and I was disappointed when he didn't open it. He said he had too much polish on his hands and he put it to one side.

'I'll read it when I get home, Rod. It's difficult to concentrate here – especially with this new landlord. He's a bastard, if you haven't noticed.'

Of course I had noticed this, but I was more interested in Ric's reaction to my calling the chapter continuation 1 than involving myself in a discussion of the landlord's qualities.

I asked Ric why he worked in a pub, collecting glasses and polishing horse brasses, when his wife earned so much money: why didn't he just stay home and watch television with her?

'There are too many hormones in that house, Rod, and it's an excuse for me to get out,' he replied. 'It's also important that I show willing; important that Suzie doesn't think I'm freeloading.'

He asked me then if I was staying for a drink, and when I said I was, he suggested I make it a short rather than a pint, which I usually favoured, because I had a book to write and that books didn't write themselves. I suppose it was his way of encouraging me, but I couldn't help feeling that Ric was becoming a bit of a taskmaster. I did as he suggested though, and ordered a small gin and tonic. I took it to a corner table and started to think about the next chapter: continuation 2.

Continuation 2

The Gallery Years

Adrian Crusher, the recruitment consultant I was telling you about earlier, arranged an interview for me at a small gallery in Mayfair owned by someone called Harry Stowell. I wore a green paisley cravat on the day of the interview and made sure that my shoes were well polished. I wanted to make a good impression and not let Mr Crusher down.

If I'm honest, it was a bit disconcerting meeting Harry for the first time, because it was difficult to know if I was being interviewed by an effeminate man or a masculine woman. The voice was between registers, and for much of the meeting I found myself staring at Harry's throat and trying to gauge the size of its Adam's apple. It was only after we'd arranged terms, and Harry had handed me a business card, that I realised I'd been talking to a woman.

Harriet Stowell was slim, almost hipless, and she wore tweed suits, white shirts and brightly coloured ties. Her hair was short – shorter than mine in fact – and dyed orange. She was in her mid-thirties and had inherited the gallery from an uncle who'd been an oil painter.

Harriet's preferred medium was creosote, which she occasionally mixed with tarmac, and she described her style as Industrial Naturalism. Oddly, considering the image conjured by such a description, she painted only landscapes and, though interesting, the canvases tended to smell and most of them remained unsold. She hung them on the walls of the gallery's upper floor and displayed the real money-makers – the works by more established and conventional artists – on the ground floor.

Harriet later told me that she'd warmed to me immediately. She'd liked my voice and my choice of neckwear and was struck by my cheekbones. In particular she liked my name, and though I told her I preferred to be called Rod, she insisted on addressing me – and introducing me to others – as Herod.

What had impressed her most, I suspect, was my willingness to work at the gallery for next to nothing and to submit to decreases in salary whenever business slowed or bills mounted.

'It's a pity there aren't more people like you in the world, Herod,' she'd said. 'It would be a much better place for gallery owners.'

I enjoyed working for Harriet, and I have fond memories of my time at the gallery. My duties were light, never more physical than hanging or removing paintings from the walls, and I would pass most days sitting in a chair and reading.

Harriet worked in her home studio for two days of the week, and other days would visit artists and arrange representation. These times I manned the gallery alone, answering the phone and welcoming prospective purchasers to the premises. I had little to say about the paintings they viewed – even the ones I understood – but no one appeared to mind. They had their own opinions and I was happy to agree with whatever they said. Occasionally someone bought a picture, for which I was paid a small commission, but most sales were made in the evening at events to celebrate the work of an individual artist or to launch a new collection.

Although Harry had liked my neckwear and shoes, she was less appreciative of the bits in-between, which, essentially, was the rest of my wardrobe. I favoured navy-blue blazers and grey flannels in those days, but Harry thought these too conformist. It was essential I look the part, she'd said, and a week later she drove me to the Whitechapel premises of her favourite tailor, a man who went by the name of One-Take Malone and who, if passed on the street, would have been mistaken for a tramp.

He was a small man, hunched, and his clothes were old and shabby: his trousers torn at the pocket and his worn waistcoat marked with blue chalk. A discoloured tape measure hung from his neck and there were pins squeezed between his lips; he had a pair of round pince-nez spectacles pinched to the bridge of his nose. Most notable, however – and peculiar – was the Imperial German spike helmet he wore on his head.

Mr Malone wasn't one for small-talk, and he was reluctant to talk about his helmet. He stared at me for a long time, walked slowly around me and then pronounced me a standard 38, as if somehow disappointed by the outcome. He then took the tape from his neck and spent the next fifteen minutes measuring every part of my body, meticulously detailing its dimensions on a scrap of paper he'd pulled from his pocket.

Harry explained that this would be my one and only fitting with Mr Malone: the One Take!

'Yes, Crispin is that good,' she said when she noticed my eyebrows rise.

Crispin, it turned out, was Mr Malone's first name, which surprised me as he looked nothing like any Crispin I'd met.

Although ostensibly the customer that day – the person

paying for the clothes and the intended wearer of them – I was allowed little say in the matter: it was Harry who chose the fabrics and Crispin who determined their cut. I wasn't unduly concerned by this arrangement as I had no experience of buying clothes and was still wearing some of Solomon's old trousers and jackets.

In retrospect, I think my passivity was a mistake, because when I collected the suits from Mr Malone the following month I found myself dressed in the same tweed and corduroy clothes favoured by Harry. I'm not saying that I didn't like the suits because I did – especially the buttons that were made from leather and were hemispherical in shape – but wearing the same clothes as Harry on a daily basis led to confusion and occasional embarrassment when a customer periodically mistook us for either siblings or lovers.

On one such occasion, an evening event, I distinctly overheard one man referring to us as 'those two lesbians'! If I had been a lesbian, I wouldn't have minded his comment, but I wasn't, and neither, in case you're wondering, was Harry, who in the short time I knew her had a string of steady boyfriends.

I know Ric will take issue with me for saying this, and tell me that I'm being contradictory: 'How can any woman have a *string* of *steady* boyfriends, Rod? It just doesn't make sense.'

But if you'd known Harry, then you'd understand what I mean. I'd have never described her as promiscuous – though I'm sure there were those who did – only that she had a short attention span and bored easily. Each span, however, was as sincere and intense as the one that preceded it and the one that followed. I think she fell in love too easily – something I've been accused of myself – but just as easily fell out of love, which is something I've never been guilty of. In fact, you could say that I've been a one-woman man long after there was no woman to be a one-woman man about, and this was certainly true of my relationship with Avril Longmire.

The reason for seeking a position, as I'd explained to Mr Crusher, was to widen my social circle and hopefully – though I hadn't mentioned this at the time – find a girlfriend, and this is exactly what happened when I went to work at the gallery.

Having spent my formative years at an all-boys school and in departments of Pinkney Industries equally male-dominated, I had little experience of talking to members of the opposite sex. Girls were a mystery to me, desirable but out of reach, and I was unsure of what to say to them or how to behave in their company.

I'd had no problem talking to Miss Wimpole or Trudy Barnes because there was every reason for me to talk to them, and besides, Miss Wimpole was an old woman and Trudy married, and so there was never any room for romantic misunderstanding or the questioning of my motives. Talking to girls without good cause, though, and purely in the hope of getting to know them on a more personal level, made me nervous, and if I was an interesting person – which at heart I believed I was – it never came across in my conversation.

Working at the gallery, however, and talking to Harry and her friends and to the customers who came to the gallery and to the evening events, changed me. Without knowing it I matured, and I was soon talking to girls my own age in the same carefree way that I'd talked to Trevor, though not about snooker.

It also helped that I was often complimented on my looks, which before this time I'd never considered, especially as my father had drummed it into my head that I had a fat face. I suppose it was a matter of confidence, of growing into my own skin, and for this, and in large part, I have Harry to thank.

Harry treated me as a friend rather than an employee, and she made a point of inviting me to any dinner or social party she gave. She recognised me as an ingénu, a man of wealth who lacked the social skills to survive in the world of the well-to-do without the intervention of another. And the world I now inhabited *was* one of affluence and high society: not once did a poor person walk through the gallery doors. Only the rich could afford the paintings on sale there or have the standing to be invited by Harry to one of her openings.

She herself, despite the occasional liquidity problem, was rich in assets and from a privileged background and the ideal person to tutor me in the ways of the advantaged. She taught me how to read a menu and decipher a wine list, who to tip and how much to tip them, and the difference between white and black tie events and the occasions that demanded morning dress or a lounge suit. Most important of all, however, and after noticing my awkwardness at an early event, she took it upon herself to school me in the ways of courtship.

We were in a restaurant at the time, ostensibly practising my food and wine skills, when she broached the subject.

'Have you ever kissed a girl, Herod?' she asked out of the blue.

I blushed and admitted that I hadn't, that I was having a hard enough time just talking to them. She smiled when I said this, but in a caring rather than an amused way, and she told me to take heart. She then took a sip of her wine – a Sancerre from memory – and gave me the following advice.

'When you're talking to a girl, Herod, you should never try to be anyone but yourself. At the same time you should forget about yourself and think only of her. Listen to what *she* has to say rather than talk about yourself; empathise and take an interest.

'If you like her then ask her out, but don't lose sleep if she says no because it's obvious then that she's not the one for you. But if she does agree to see you again, you must smile and act happy around her, look into her eyes and make her feel special. Take her to places she's never been before and do things that she wants to do, even when you don't. Be patient with her and let her know that you're there for her – that you'll always be there for her.

'And pay attention to the small things: what she likes and doesn't like, her favourite drink, her favourite flower, and pay for everything – everything! Don't ever let her pay for you, however insistent she is, because she won't mean it. It will be a test, and she'll be waiting for you to fail.

'And don't – and I can't emphasise this strongly enough, Herod – don't ever continue to go out with a girl for the sake of having a girlfriend. Relationships are two-way and there should be give-and-take on both sides. If she lacks consideration for you then end the relationship and move on, find someone else…'

'This salmon is excellent, by the way,' she said.

We fell silent while a waiter took our plates and another served the beef. The sommelier brought the bottle of Château d'Yquem I'd selected and poured a small amount into my glass. I examined the label on the wine bottle as Harry had instructed me to do, smelt its bouquet and then tasted it. I told the sommelier that the wine was excellent – even though I had no idea if it was or wasn't – and after he'd left I asked Harry how soon after meeting a girl I should kiss her? Harry said that the girl would make this more than clear to me, and then moved into territory I was least expecting – the bedroom!

'And be considerate of her in bed, Herod: respect that she has needs more complicated than your own and probably more time-consuming. And whatever else you do while attending to these needs, don't ever look at your watch or glance at the bedside clock! You have to put in the effort and not rush to the finishing line.'

I didn't really understand what Harry meant by this, but I didn't like to ask for an explanation because the people at the next table appeared to be eavesdropping. In time, however, in privacy, and in the company of Avril Longmire, everything became clear.

Avril Longmire wasn't the first girl I dated, but she was the first girl I fell in love with. I met her at a 'Shadow and Smudge' event organised by Harry to showcase the work of two charcoal artists she represented, both of whom were drunk that evening and leaving their fingerprints everywhere. As usual, I was the wine waiter, circulating the room and offering glasses of champagne to prospective buyers.

Having previously established that Harry was wearing tweeds that night, I'd dressed in a fawn corduroy suit and tucked a red polka dot handkerchief into my breast pocket. It was for show rather than use, and I was surprised when a young girl I hadn't seen at the gallery before snatched it from its pouch and sneezed into it.

'I'm sorry about that,' she said. 'I think I'm allergic to charcoal.'

She then pressed the handkerchief back into my pocket and took a glass of champagne from the tray.

'My name's Avril, by the way.'

I told her that mine was Rod, but that most people at the gallery referred to me as Herod.

'I hope you won't,' I added.

Avril was a student at the Royal College of Art and had been passed an invitation to the event by a tutor in the fine art department who'd been unable to attend.

'Art's fine, as long as it's fine,' she'd smiled. 'Tell me, Rod, do you believe in fate?'

I said that I was open-minded on the subject, but happy to have been there when she'd needed a handkerchief.

I asked her then about the things she liked to paint and she told me triangles: she painted only triangles. She explained that pyramid composition was the most fundamental of all compositions, and that triangles, in one way or another, were present in everything and everywhere.

'I'm not sure I'd agree with her there,' Harry said when I mentioned this to her the next day. 'Pyramid composition came into vogue during the Renaissance period but I'm not sure it has much relevance today. It certainly doesn't feature in any of my paintings. It's more likely she's fixating on her genitalia – either that or the Holy Trinity.'

She suggested that if I was seeing her again – which I was – then I should hedge my bets and take both a packet of condoms and a Bible with me.

Of course, I did no such thing. Harry had a habit of reducing everything either to sex or religion, a by-product, no doubt, of her time at a Catholic boarding school. I couldn't say for certain that she was wrong, because in the conversation I'd had with Avril the previous evening neither of us had raised the subjects of either sex or religion. And why would we? Why would anyone on first meeting? Well, maybe Harry would, but there was no other person I could think of. Certainly Miss Wimpole wouldn't have done so, and I doubt Trudy Barnes did when she first met her husband-to-be.

And so, when I met Avril for the second time, in a small Kensington restaurant close to the Royal College, I took with me no more than my wallet and a spare handkerchief.

I don't think anyone would have described Avril as

beautiful, but she was strangely good-looking. Oddly, as she was slim, she already had the makings of a double chin that had seemingly developed from her habit of pressing the flesh under her jaw into her neck. I don't know why she did this, the same way I never understood why she tilted her head and pulled her face out of shape when she thought about things. She also had creases around her neck, as if she was ageing like a tree, and large ears that stuck out at right angles whenever she tied her hair back. All in all, though, it was an appearance I found pleasing, and one that gave me confidence in my own looks.

In retrospect, I realise that I fell in love with Avril from the inside out rather than the outside in, which, in my experience, is a recipe for disaster: making allowances for a person's poor character in consideration of their appearance is never a good idea. In other words, I fell in love with Avril first as a person and *then* realised how beautiful she was. It was love for the right reasons.

Avril was from Surrey, and her family lived in a large detached house close to Godalming. Her father was a solicitor who practised in Guildford, while her mother stayed at home and took care of Avril's younger sister, Addy, who went to a local school. The Longmires were nice people, and Avril and I spent many a happy weekend in their company. It was my first real experience of family life, and I came to see myself as their future son-in-law, an outcome that I'm sure would have pleased them.

We were a couple for almost two years. At first we'd meet weekly and then, as our feelings for each other grew, as many nights of the week as my duties at the gallery and her schedule at the art college allowed. Much of this time we spent at my house in Battersea, simple evenings in and home-cooked meals. Avril liked the house, its simplicity of line and overall spaciousness, but was less certain of the curtains and the silence of its walls.

'I can't believe you work in an art gallery and have no paintings, Rod. Does Harry know this?'

I said that Harry didn't, that she'd never visited my house, and that I'd yet to see a picture at the gallery I'd want to hang on my walls. I was happy though, when Avril suggested she bring me some of hers.

She gave me two paintings, both of which still hang on the lounge walls. One was a large red triangle measuring four feet by four, and the other, a multicoloured portrait of myself measuring six feet by four. The portrait is my favourite. It has my head in the top centre of the vertical space and my shoulders and body at its base, and my features are delineated not by lines but by a mass of small, intricate triangles. In truth, the portrait looks nothing like me, but I hold on to it for sentimental reasons and for the memory of what happened after we'd hung the picture.

'Was that good for you?' I asked Avril, lying next to her in bed and feeling rather pleased with myself.

'If I'm honest, Rod, I don't think that would have been good for anyone. We need to do a lot of practising!'

She'd then burst out laughing and kissed me on the nose.

The months that followed were the happiest of my life. I told Avril that I loved her and wanted to spend the rest of my life with her, and she told me that she had strong feelings for me, too. And then one day, while sidestepping the pigeons in Trafalgar Square, I asked her to marry me and she said that she probably would, but not for the moment because she had to pop over to Alice Springs.

By this time, Avril had finished her studies at the Royal

College of Art and was working as a research assistant at the Victoria and Albert Museum. She'd found it difficult to make a living as an artist, and I'd been unable to persuade Harry to display her triangles in the gallery. To tell the truth, I think Harry thought that Avril was a bit nuts – at least, that was the word she used most often when she referred to Avril:

'How's that nutty girlfriend of yours doing, Herod? Still painting vaginas?'

Some days when she said this, I felt like handing in my notice.

Although I'd made it more than clear to Avril that I had enough money for her never to need to work, she told me in equally certain terms that she valued her independence too much to be bankrolled by another person – however dear that person might be to her – and that she still hoped to make her mark as an artist. And she'd just stumbled on something big while working at the museum, something far too big for her to ignore. She'd heard about the circles and dots that Australian aborigines drew in the sand and on their bodies, and she saw a strong parallel between their work – 9,000 miles away – and her own triangles.

'I can learn from them, Rod, and I can encourage them to put their dots on to canvas and maybe incorporate my triangles into their compositions. I could go down in history as the person who brought aboriginal art to the mainstream and my time at the college won't have been wasted.

'I need to do this, Rod, and if you love me you'll let me take this trip. It would only be for a short time and we can marry when I return. You do love me, don't you, Rod?'

Well, of course I loved her, and because I loved her, I not only wished her well in Australia, but also paid for her plane ticket.

Avril promised to write every day and to telephone whenever possible. She said that our love was too special to be affected by separation and could only grow stronger. I believed her, and when the day came for me to take her to the airport, I knew it for sure.

It was the week before Christmas – the time of year when friends and relatives usually come together – and there was a haunting instrumental version of *God Rest Ye Merry Gentlemen* playing over the tannoy. I was overwhelmed by the sadness of the occasion and started to cry. Avril stayed strong – more for my sake than hers, I suspect – and consoled me as best she could, handing me her handkerchief when mine was too damp to be of further use.

And then they announced her flight and we walked to the point of departure and kissed for the last time.

'I love you, Avril,' I said, 'more than you'll ever know.'

She squeezed my hand and told me that she had the strongest feelings for me, too. And then she was gone.

It was the last I ever saw of her.

Avril wrote only occasionally, but her letters had an air of despondency that cheered me immeasurably. The aborigines, by all accounts, were a stand-offish people who were unwilling to share their designs with her. Every time she got close to discovering them they would smooth the sand and walk away.

'You wouldn't believe how precious these numbskulls are about their stupid drawings,' she wrote in one letter. 'They say the dots and circles have a deep and sacred purpose and that they aren't intended for the eyes of white people. What nonsense is this? We wouldn't turn them away from our churches, would we? All we'd do is ask them to put some clothes on.'

When I opened the next letter I was fully expecting Avril to tell me that she was on her way home and the day I should meet her at the airport. But she didn't, and she sounded worryingly upbeat. She said that she'd made a friend and was going to spend some time at a sheep station in Western Australia and would I please stop phoning her parents.

And then, a month later, a bombshell arrived through the post: Avril was marrying a man called Bob Fawcett and would be remaining in Australia to paint sheep – because sheep, in one way or another, were present in everything and everywhere – and that she was sorry if this news hurt me because it made her want to jump for joy.

And so that was that.

But in many ways, it wasn't. I couldn't stop thinking about Avril or wondering how things might have been. A series of 'what ifs' and 'if onlys' looped through my mind, and I had to avoid the places we'd frequented as a couple. I found myself walking down streets and recalling entire conversations word for word, and occasionally having to wipe a tear from my eye.

The break-up became my sole topic of conversation, and although friends were at first sympathetic to my situation, they quickly tired of hearing about it. I moped around the gallery, there in person but never in spirit, and eventually Harry could stand no more of it and lost her patience.

'Look, Herod, you're not the first person to break up with a girl and you won't be the last. It's a risk we all take when we fall in love. Pitying yourself won't help anything. Chalk it up to experience and get back on the horse. That's what I do.'

I commented that her relationships were probably less meaningful than the one I'd had with Avril, and that it was easier for her to get on with life whenever she broke up with a boyfriend because she did it so often.

'My life's over, Harry, and I'm not even thirty! I don't think I'll ever love another woman.'

'Well in that case, Herod, you'd better learn how to fuck yourself then!' she'd snapped.

Harry was right, of course, and it embarrasses me now when I think back to this time. A year passed before I asked another girl out, but eventually I did fall in love again and for the first time with a girl called Gloria Stubbington-Hawes.

Gloria didn't like walking places – a quality I like in a person – and she rode a Triumph motorbike that belonged to her brother. She had a jaw that was strong enough to break a man's fist and permanently flat hair. Occasionally she suffered from depression and these times I liked her best. I think the melancholy was nature's way of reining her in, of making it easier for people to be with her, because when she wasn't feeling blue she was often unbearable, dismissive of others' feelings and certainly too full of herself to have room for me in her life.

We broke up countless times over a four-year period, but ended on good terms. If we bumped into each other on the street today, I'm sure that we'd hug – certainly so if she was feeling depressed that day.

Harry liked her, however, admired her spirit and plainly preferred her to Avril. She would have been pleased that it was Gloria who accompanied me to her funeral.

Harry died at the age of forty-two after falling down the steps that led to the first floor of the gallery. She'd been carrying one of her paintings at the time, one she'd promised me for my birthday, and she'd either been overcome by its fumes or lost her footing.

I found her the next morning – the morning of my birthday – lying at the bottom of the staircase with her head poking through the canvas. Her body was cold and she had a strange grimace on her face, and her favourite tweed trousers were torn at the knee.

I dialled for an ambulance and waited on the pavement, reluctant to stay in the gallery. I reasoned that if I couldn't see her body then the accident might never have happened and there'd be a better chance of her being alive when I returned to the room.

The ambulance arrived within ten minutes, and one of its crew sat me down in a chair and made me a mug of sweet tea. He said I was in a state of shock, a condition that wasn't improved when the policeman who'd led the investigation into my mother's death walked into the gallery.

'We meet again, Mr Pinkney. What happened this time? Did you run out of rope?'

It soon became clear that in his mind the circumstances of our second meeting were no different from those of our first. It was my birthday, and as usually happened on my birthday I'd found a woman's body. I was sitting comfortably in a chair, as if unmoved by the event, and if not eating a ham and cheese sandwich on this occasion was at least drinking a cup of tea. I was the same young man he'd met previously, the one with a chip on his shoulder who resented people who kept him in low-grade positions, and I'd smashed the canvas over Harry's head for no other reason than to teach her a lesson for painting me such an awful picture for my birthday.

The matter of Harry's death, however, was quickly resolved, and the policeman was again left with no scalp to attach to his belt. The coroner found that Harry had fallen down the stairs the previous evening at a time when I was at the cinema with Gloria, and her death was ruled misadventure.

The funeral took place three weeks later in a small church in

West Sussex, in the village where Harry had been born. It was full to capacity and many of the mourners were my friends. It was a sad occasion and I shed more tears in the church that day than I had saying goodbye to Avril at Heathrow Airport. Apart from my parents – whose deaths somehow didn't count – I'd never lost anyone close, and Harry's departure hit me hard, especially when the new owners of the gallery turned it into a restaurant and offered me a job as a waiter.

When Harry had been alive, the gallery had been a meeting place for friends as much as a place of business and a second home for me. Without her it was just another building and there was no reason to stay, especially when the proprietors' offer of employment had been made solely for the purposes of continuity and in the hope of attracting ex-patrons to the restaurant. The idea of being on my feet all day also didn't appeal, and so I politely declined their offer and decided instead to spend my days at home, building a library and learning about God – things I'd been intending to do for some time.

*

As a child I'd avoided books, grappled with them at school and not once read for pleasure. Reading had always been a struggle – and unsurprisingly so when you consider my undiagnosed dyslexia. But thanks to Miss Wimpole, and empty days at the gallery that had allowed me the time to practise phonological skills and to work on assignments, reading had become a new-found passion and I was determined to make up for lost time.

Mostly I read fiction, about things that weren't rather than encyclopaedic fact that was. I liked adventure stories and mysteries and books with happy endings, and my favourite author was Enid Blyton. I was a big fan of *The Famous Five* and they had some of the best adventures. One of the characters was called George, but her real name was Georgina and she dressed like a boy. Because Harry's real name was Harriet and she dressed like a man, I drew a parallel and wondered if Mrs Blyton had met Harry and based George's character on her.

When I mentioned this to Harry she said it was the most stupid thing I'd ever said and suggested that I show more enterprise and read books on the human condition. When I told her that I had no interest in reading about skin diseases and would be sticking to fiction, she said that this was the second most stupid thing I'd ever said.

When I say that I wanted to build a library, I don't mean this literally. I had no intentions of buying a plot of land and asking Mr Axelrod to fashion an athenaeum for the people of Battersea. I was rich but I was no Andrew Carnegie, and besides, Battersea already had a library.

No, my ambition was more modest and of a personal nature, and was eventually defined by a series of shelves that ran from floor to ceiling in one of the upstairs bedrooms. I'd have preferred the bookshelves to be in the lounge, but the walls there were already taken by Avril's large paintings and the one Harry had intended as my birthday gift. (I'd had the torn canvas repaired, as well as cured, and it now takes a trained eye to see where her head had pushed through.)

I placed the books in alphabetical order by author, and my childhood comics face down on the bottom shelf. I bought books that I wanted to read and those that others said I should read, and the shelves quickly filled. When the bookcase was full, I started to pile new purchases on the floors of other bedrooms until – and this was some time later – they too were filled with books. It was then I decided to extend the basement and display all the books in one place. It was the best idea I ever had, because if the Bulgarian workers hadn't found Donald in the course of their excavations, it's unlikely that the two of us would have met.

As previously mentioned, I also wanted to spend my new freedom learning about God, though probably for the wrong reason. My father had been an atheist and I was intent on putting as much distance between him and me as possible and not bumping into him in the afterlife, which I believed to exist. If he, as an atheist, was residing in hell – as those of a more religious nature had assured me he was – then it was paramount that I went to heaven. But to get to heaven I had to believe in God and accept Jesus as my saviour, and for this to happen I was in need of a few pointers.

I started by buying a Bible – the Revised Standard Version – but found it hard going and gave up on page four at the point where Seth becomes the father of Enosh. I had nothing against either man, but I had no idea what they were doing there. I wished that Enid Blyton had written the Bible because, if she had, it would have been a lot easier to read and I'd have probably understood the adventures better.

It was clear that I was never going to get to know God by reading His words in a vacuum, so I decided to find someone who could explain them to me in plain English.

If I'd learnt anything from mixing with the rich, it was this: if you had a problem – whether it related to a legal case, a medical condition or the cut of your trousers – then you went to the top man in the field. By this reasoning, I should have asked for an appointment with the head of the Church of England, but I was reluctant to drive all the way to Canterbury and ready to admit that the archbishop had probably more pressing matters on his plate than to grant me an audience. I thought it best to lower my sights and make do with a bishop, and the one that came to mind was Lucius B Williams.

Bishop Williams was the pastor of a church called the Assembly of Christ, which was situated at the end of my street but on the other side of the road. I passed the church every time I went to the Lansdowne and I remembered his name from the notice board.

One Sunday morning, shortly before Easter, I paid the Assembly of Christ a visit. My intention had been to sit at the back of the church and remain anonymous and only make myself known to the pastor if I liked his demeanour. The plan unravelled, however, when it quickly became apparent that I was the only white person in the room and all the back pews, where anonymity was possible, were filled.

I was about to leave and reconsider my strategy, when an usher took me by the arm and led me to a seat closer to the front. The congregants there were very welcoming. They rose to their feet, shook me by the hand and told me their names. They were dressed in smart, dark clothes and all the men wore ties. I regretted wearing the same tweeds and cravat I'd worn to the Lansdowne the previous evening, and I hoped that my attire wouldn't cause them offence.

The service that followed was noisy. The hymns were sung with gusto and there was a lot of clapping and whooping and everyone – including Bishop Williams – appeared to be having the time of their lives.

The bishop was a man of medium height but appeared to weigh a ton. He was dressed in a long flowing robe, a purple shirt and a white clerical collar, and he clasped what appeared to be a large duster in his left hand. Surprisingly, for a man his size, he jumped around a lot when he preached, and he used the flannel to dab the sweat from his brow. He played with the words of his sermon, effortlessly juggled them and patterned them into rhymes that brought the congregation to its feet.

I was as mesmerised by his performance as the rest of the congregation, but unsure of his message. After the service ended I approached him, apologised for my appearance and asked if I might have a quiet word. He said he'd be happy to have a conversation with me and asked me to wait in the church while he went to the door and said goodbye to his parishioners.

When he returned, we sat down on the same pew and faced each other. He told me how pleased he was to see me at the service that morning and hoped that I wouldn't become a stranger. He then asked me what it was I wished to talk to him about.

I explained that my father had been an atheist and christened me Herod, because he'd admired the king and wanted me to grow up to be like him.

This news surprised the bishop because he'd never known anyone to like Herod or want a son to take after him, and he was immediately supportive.

I told him that now my father was dead, I was hoping to find God and learn about Jesus, but that I was having difficulty understanding the Bible and in need of some guidance.

After a further ten minutes of conversation, Bishop Lucius decided I was lacking the necessary foundation for belief, and he suggested that I join the children's Sunday school. The children in the church, who had been sitting together on the two front pews, had left the service after the second hymn and retired to another room. There, the bishop told me, they listened to a short story from the Bible and then re-enacted the episode – through the medium of small figurines, miniature animals and palm trees – in two large sand boxes. He thought

I would benefit from this approach and I agreed with him. So the following Sunday morning, and dressed in a formal suit and wearing a tie, I joined the children in the anteroom and played in the sand for the next nine months.

The chairs in the room were a bit on the small side, wooden and uncomfortable, but otherwise I enjoyed my time in Sunday school and I made some good friends, especially Leta and Dewain, who were brother and sister.

I heard stories about David killing Goliath and the flood that destroyed the world, the discovery of baby Moses in the bulrushes and the parting of the Red Sea, Jonah being swallowed by a whale and the Babylonians throwing Daniel into a lion's den. These were adventures as thrilling as any I'd read, and though the tales in the New Testament were less interesting, there was no doubting that Jesus was the nicest of men and one that I'd have been happy to meet for a drink in the Lansdowne.

Eventually though – and to my disappointment – it came time for me to leave the children and remain in the church with the grown-ups and listen to the bishop's sermons.

I liked Bishop Williams, but I found him hard to fathom. God had been easy to understand in the anteroom, but in the church He became a lot more complicated, and to this day I have no clear understanding of the Holy Trinity or the doctrine of atonement.

I believed myself to be a Christian but I was less certain of Christianity, and I could never understand why Christians felt it necessary to sit on seats as hard and uncomfortable as fixed benches. Out of loyalty to Bishop Williams I continued to attend the morning service for a further three years, but it was a half-hearted attendance and I often wished I was elsewhere. When the bishop was unexpectedly recalled to

Jamaica and the BBC started to air *The Rockford Files* on a Sunday morning, I said a quiet goodbye to the Assembly of Christ and instead joined the viewers of *Songs of Praise*.

I'd like to say that my faith today is as intact as it was then, but I'm afraid that it isn't. For reasons that will become clear, I lost my belief in the same place that the Bulgarian workers found Donald.

I no longer worry about meeting my father in the afterlife, though, because I no longer believe there is a hereafter. No, when I die, I'll be cremated and my ashes will be scattered and that, I'm afraid, will be the end of Herod S Pinkney.

26 June 2019

It's good news! Ric has read both continuations and given them his approval. He's also allowing me to call them continuations rather than chapters, but he suggests that I might want to qualify the caption with a short description. Continuation 1, for instance, might be adjusted to Pinkney Industries and continuation 2, to The Gallery Years. He told me to give some thought to this idea.

My main concern was to know if he thought the reader would have invested in me as a person by now and, if so, was this the time to bring Daisy into the story?

'Rod,' he said, 'the reader will have taken to you as they would a stray kitten. Their hearts will have gone out to you!'

But what about those readers who didn't like cats, I persisted: would they have warmed to me?

'Of course they'll have warmed to you,' Ric laughed. 'I was talking metaphorically – but this is a case in point. You're an innocent, Rod, a literalist, and there's no side to you. You'd happily accept that a homeopathist was a gay pharmacist if someone told you so, and this is the kind of thing that will endear you to a reader. Readers like simple people.'

I was pleased that Ric thought the reader would fall in

love with the book, but I was less happy with his reasoning. I didn't look upon myself as a simpleton, and I certainly wasn't expecting people to feel sorry for me. And, as for thinking that homoeopathists were gay people, well, the thought had never once crossed my mind. I don't even know what a homoeopathist is. I let things go, though, because I was reluctant to upset him before asking again about bringing Daisy into the story.

We were sitting in a small cafe and Ric wasn't expected at the Lansdowne for another thirty minutes. I'd just ordered two more coffees, and I asked him if he wanted a piece of cake with his. He joined me at the counter to survey the pastries and then pointed to the carrot cake. I ordered him a slice and then chose a piece of caramel shortbread for myself, which the waitress brought to the table.

I waited while he ate his cake and was about to ask him about Daisy when he leaned forward and confided that things at home weren't all that good.

'It's my own fault, Rod. I should have brushed my teeth before I kissed Suzie after eating those sausages. You wouldn't have believed her reaction. It was as if I'd dragged her by the hair through a slaughterhouse! We got into a real argument then. I told her I was my own man and could eat sausages any day of the week if I wanted to, but she contradicted me and said that I wasn't my own man – that I was her man – and that I should remember this if I didn't want to sleep in the spare room.

'The sooner you finish this book and we both start earning some money, the better, Rod. Once I start bringing home the bacon – not literally, of course – the more likely she is to mellow. I think this is what the argument was about, really: not that I'd eaten sausages, but the fact that I'd spent her money on them, which I hadn't. I got the meal in return for polishing the horse brasses – and you can vouch for me on this because you were there at the time.'

I sympathised with Ric and asked him if he wanted me to write a letter to Suzie about the sausages, but he said no: it was best if I kept out of it, and that Suzie would get annoyed if she knew he'd been talking about her behind her back.

I then – rather cleverly for a simpleton, I thought – took advantage of his hope for a timely completion of the book and introduced the subject of Daisy: could I bring her into the story?

'It's still a bit soon for that, Rod. I'm not expecting you to write about every year of your life, and I'm happy for you to fast-forward, but we do need a solid bridge between the time you stopped going to church and the occasion you met her.

'But we're not far from this happening: another couple of continuations and you'll be there. The thing about telling a story is that you have to let it unfold naturally and of its own accord, and for this to happen, the writer has to be patient.'

That night, I thought about what Ric had said and started to compose a bridge. It wasn't easy, but after numerous rewrites and several glasses of brandy, I came up with a real winner:

And so time passed.

When I read the sentence the following day, however, I was less sure. I liked its pith, but I was ready to admit that it lacked flesh and probably ran counter to Ric's admonition that a story had to evolve of its own accord.

I decided to try again. If I was to explain my present circumstances as fully as Ric suggested, then it was obvious I had a lot more writing to do.

Continuation 3

Edmundo and Nelly

My life, as it is today, came into being after I started using dental floss and had the basement excavated – though these two events were distanced by some years.

I visited the dentist infrequently, and I'd only made an appointment to see Mr Hamburg after a letter arrived from the practice asking me to confirm that I wasn't dead. Although he was pleased to see me alive when I walked through his door, Mr Hamburg was less happy with the large deposits of plaque he found on my teeth.

'Teeth don't grow on trees, Mr Pinkney, and if you want to keep yours then you'll need to start taking better care of them. If you're happy to run the risk of gum disease and tooth decay, then fine; but if you're not, then I strongly recommend that you start flossing. Now, what's it to be?'

I'd been flushing the used dental floss down the toilet for about three years before I had to call a plumber, or, more accurately, ask Nelly if she knew of one. Nelly had been cleaning my house for about two years by then and I trusted her implicitly. How could the word of an ex-nun not be trusted?

I'd found her name on a postcard taped to the window of

a local newsagent and her advertisement caught my eye: *Ex-nun: Hates Dirt*. I hated dirt, too, though not enough to do anything about it on a regular basis, and it seemed fitting that a man of my station should better the life of someone of a lower station by allowing them to deal with it.

Nelly de la Puente looked like a friendly beach ball. She was small, almost as wide as she was tall, and she appeared to be in her late fifties; her dark hair was peppered with flecks of grey and her smiling, if deeply lined, face was makeup-free. She sang while she cleaned the house – hymns I recognised and Spanish songs I didn't – and bustled from one room to another as if late for an appointment. She came to me on Tuesdays and Thursdays, one day dusting and vacuuming, and the other day washing and ironing clothes. She also ran small errands for me and took my suits to the dry-cleaners and posted letters.

Nelly would take a short break in the morning and another in the afternoon and stand at the back door of the house and smoke a cigarette while she drank her coffee. She brought sandwiches for her lunch and ate them in the kitchen, and at these times I would join her. Occasionally she would pull a small bottle of bourbon from her bag and offer me a sip, but I always declined: not out of any implied judgement, but because drinking at lunchtime always made me fall asleep in the afternoon.

'It wouldn't if you chewed coca leaves,' she laughed.

Mostly we talked of inconsequential matters, weather and traffic and things like that. I wasn't in the habit of talking about myself and so I couldn't complain when another person chose to do the same. If I'm honest, though, I'd have loved to have known why she'd stopped being a nun and started drinking whisky and smoking cigarettes, and if she'd had any personal experience of chewing coca leaves.

In the hope of drawing her out on the subject, I mentioned to her one day that she had an interesting surname. She agreed that it was and said that my name was an interesting name too, but then returned to the conversation we'd been having about the Albert Bridge: did it require a fresh coat of paint? In fact, until the day I asked her if she knew of a good plumber, she'd never once mentioned that she was married.

Her husband came by the next morning and introduced himself as Edmundo de la Puente, husband of Nelly and an expert in the ways of toilets. He was a rangy man, as tall and slim as Nelly was short and round, but of a similar age to his wife. His complexion was dark and he spoke English falteringly, as if the words he sought were coated in grease and forever slipping from his grasp. What struck me most about Edmundo, though, was the look of worry on his face, as if he was about to walk into a trap. I gave him my warmest smile and told him to cheer up and that it might never happen.

'It already has, Señor Pinkney,' he said. 'It already has.'

Edmundo didn't elaborate on his words at the time, but in the months that followed and in dribs and drabs, and only after he'd accepted me as a friend. And by telling me his story, he also told me Nelly's.

I can't duplicate the way Edmundo talks on paper, and nor would I want to. So what follows is the story of Edmundo and Nelly in my voice. All you have to do is pretend that I'm Peruvian and speaking English with a thick Spanish accent. (To give the impression of it being a real-time conversation, I've also interposed my name into the paragraphs from time to time.)

*

'I was born in Ayacucho, Rod; an isolated city in the central Andes of Peru, known as the Corner of the Dead. Once it was an attractive city, but it had fallen into decay. Its inhabitants were poor and malnourished and largely Indian, and life expectancy no more than forty-five years. My father was one of the few doctors in the city.

'When I left school I enrolled at the city's university, one of the oldest in Latin America, and entered the engineering programme. It was here that I met the man who would become known as Chairman Gonzalo, the feared leader of The Communist Party of Peru by the Shining Path of José Carlos Mariátegui – a mouthful I know. In future I will shorten it.

'His name in those days was Abimael Guzmán, and he was the head of the university's philosophy department. He was a tidy man, well-shaven, and he always wore a dark jacket. He was gentle-mannered, more an owlish intellectual than a potential terrorist, but time and experience changed him.

'I was introduced to him by a friend in the engineering department and I quickly fell under his sway. When Professor Guzmán changed, I changed, and when he left the university in the mid-seventies and went underground, I followed his example. It was during this time, hiding out in Lima, that I met and became friendly with Nelly – or Sister Driscoll as she was known at the time – a teacher in the shanty towns that surrounded the city.

'Abimael Guzmán opened my eyes to the unfairness of Peruvian society and its exploitation of the peasantry. Indians were treated as inferiors by white people and they were without power. Their lands were stolen by rich landowners and the church, and they lost their lives to malnutrition, tuberculosis and pneumonia. The only party in Peru to offer them hope was the Shining Path.

'The aim of our party, Rod, was to replace the sham democracy of Peru with a communist utopia – and this, the Chairman believed, could only be accomplished by force: by following the example of Mao Tse-tung.

'He envisaged a revolution that would start in the countryside and move to the city, and where better a place to start than the mountains around Ayacucho? The Shining Path became the protectors of the peasants there, and also their avengers: it punished the unfair landlords, the rustlers who stole their cattle, and the corrupt police officers who extorted money from them.

'We struck the first blow for freedom in May 1980, when five of us walked into the voter registration office of Chuschi and tied up the registrar. No one but us took this action seriously, and our subsequent exploits were similarly ignored. I think the government looked upon us as a group of political pranksters rather than an actual threat, and considering we were armed only with stick rifles and a few starter pistols, I suppose you can understand this.

'But then we got hold of dynamite – lots of dynamite! – and we started to blow up bridges, electricity installations and the tourist trains that plied their way to Machu Picchu. We also attacked courthouses, police stations and briefly occupied small towns, and this made the government sit up. It had no choice but to take us seriously now, and it responded by declaring a state of emergency and razing the villages that helped and protected our fighters. This pleased us a lot and gave our revolution legs.

'But for the Chairman it wasn't enough. He believed that moderation would be the death of the Shining Path, and that the best way to win the support of the people was by fear and intimidation: cruelty, he said, would win the day for us! This was music to the ears of the Indians who fought alongside us and they were happy to oblige his wishes. Pent-up resentment, once unleashed, is a formidable tool, Rod.

'And so the killing started: mayors and elected officials at first, and then trade union officials and small businessmen, and then cooks, post office officials and mine guards and then… well, anyone, really.

'But the nature of the violence changed and its cruelty and brutality increased: throats were slit and people were stoned, bowstringed and burned. One poor tourist had her eye gouged and replaced with a cork; a mission leader was crucified, castrated and disembowelled; and a child – his throat cut – was held by the feet before his parents while the blood drained from his tiny body. It was not the revolution I had signed up for, Rod, and I started to have misgivings.

'I had joined the Shining Path for its ideals: Justice for the Disadvantaged! Food for the Hungry! Respect for the Powerless! But all we sowed in those years of struggle was misery. We lost popular support – if indeed we ever had any – and even the peasants turned against us.

'And who could have blamed them? The Shining Path was no less severe on them as it was on the rest of Peruvian society: they were killed for minor offences and axed to death if they refused to cooperate with us. We also prohibited them from holding parties and drinking alcohol, and we closed the small markets they depended upon because we viewed them as examples of capitalism.

'The Chairman was captured in September 1992, arrested in an apartment above a dance studio in Lima, but by this time I was already living in England with Nelly.

'My wife, Rod, if she has not already told you, was born in Wells-next-the-Sea, a small port in north Norfolk, and had grown up eating fish and chips. She had entered the convent and taken religious vows to serve Christ and lose weight, and working as a missionary in Peru gave her the opportunity for both.

'She had hoped to improve conditions for the Indians through hard work and prayer, but she came to the view that such an outcome was more likely if she instead gave logistical support to the Shining Path, and this, she believed, is what Jesus would have done.

'The violence and cruelty meted out by the Shining Path, however, robbed her of this illusion – just as it had robbed me of mine. She came to view the Chairman as a ruthless zealot, a horseman of the Apocalypse, and the Shining Path as a cult of destruction. She had also noticed that the Indians who supported the party were more ready to accept Abimael Guzmán as their saviour than Christ, and in the jungle areas they believed him to be supernatural: a man who could escape capture by transforming himself into a snake or a bird.

'I have blood on my hands, Rod, but revolutionary blood and not the blood of innocents. I did not stab or axe any civilian to death, and I never had the chance to shoot an adversary because I never had a gun. Hardly anyone in the Shining Path had a gun: we had maybe 750 firearms among us.

'But I threw sticks of dynamite at soldiers and policemen, and I am ready to accept that I have killed. Now I hope that I did not, but at the time I was hoping that I would.

'The Shining Path was not an organisation you could easily leave, Rod. If anyone had got wind of our plan to escape, Nelly and I would have been bludgeoned to death and our bodies left unburied. And if we had stayed in Peru, where my name was now known to the authorities, we would have been similarly punished, or at least imprisoned. Our only route of escape was if Nelly renounced her vows and I returned with her to England as her husband.

'It was Nelly's decision to do this, Rod, and I will always love her for making this sacrifice. If I am speaking truthfully, though, which I am, I had already fallen in love with her as a woman, but I had never been able to act upon my feelings while she was a nun. It would have dishonoured us both.

'So she renounced her vows and we were married by a padre sympathetic to the aims, if not the methods, of the Shining Path. The ceremony was simple and necessarily secret, and our honeymoon was spent under the stars. Once we had our papers, and Nelly's family had wired the necessary money, we travelled south and slipped over the border into Chile and made our way to Santiago. From there we flew to Madrid and then to London, and we travelled to Nelly's home town on four different buses.

'We stayed in Wells-next-the-Sea and walked along the beach and ate fish and chips for three months. That Nelly was no longer a nun disappointed her parents, as did her choice of partner, who spoke no English and screamed out in his sleep – something I still do.

'A town as small as Wells offered few prospects to a couple as odd as us, and so we moved to London and sought our fortunes in anonymity. In time Nelly became a cleaner and I became a man who does odd jobs for people, a vocation that has allowed me to meet your good self, Rod. I am honoured to know you.'

The last sentence of Edmundo's story moved me, and I was left humbled by the thought of all the horrors and privations he'd endured solely for the pleasure of meeting me.

I knew then that our friendship was special and that it would last the course of our lives.

*

Edmundo, on the day he'd first called at my house, had unblocked the toilet in less than an hour and left the bathroom as clean as he'd found it. It was then that we'd sat and drank the first of our many coffees together, but the only time we drank Nescafé.

I asked Edmundo if he could do other things, besides unblocking toilets, and he told me he could – but only if they didn't require certification. I'd asked him then if he was comfortable with heights and he replied that he was, that most people from the High Andes were comfortable with heights and that it was difficult to live there if you weren't. We'd then gone outside and I'd pointed to the living walls. I told him that the man who looked after them had moved to Sweden and the company he'd recommended was proving unreliable.

'No problem, Mr Pinkney' – this was pre-Rod days – 'I have ladders and I can tell weeds from flowers.'

And so Edmundo became my vertical gardener, and in the years that followed my plumber, electrician, plasterer and painter, and my first port of call in any household emergency.

I encouraged him to drop by the house anytime he was in the area, and on his second visit – and only a week after he'd unblocked the toilet – he brought me two small gifts: a packet of Peruvian ground coffee and a cafetière. I think it was a hint as much as a present, but the best hint a person has given me.

When it became clear to Nelly that Edmundo had told me their story, she became less taciturn and we occasionally sang hymns together. I told her that I'd attended the Assembly of Christ for a time, but now watched *Songs of Praise* on a Sunday because its service allowed me to sit in an easy chair and not on a hard pew.

Nelly had laughed when she heard this, and joked that she was built for hard seats, and that every time she sat down on a chair it was like sitting on a cushion. I didn't know whether to laugh or not when she said this because a woman's weight is always dangerous ground for a man to tread, and not one of us knows where the landmines are buried.

I changed the subject and asked her if it was true – as Edmundo had intimated – that there were thirty-three churches in Ayacucho, one for each year of Christ's life?

'I've never counted them, Rod' – Nelly had also started to call me Rod by this time – 'but if there are, I doubt any one of them understands the meaning of His teachings!

'Edmundo and I attend the Sacred Heart these days and we like it there. If you ever care to join us one Sunday, you'd be more than welcome. I can't promise you the seats will be any more comfortable than those of the Assembly of Christ, though.'

I thanked her for her invitation, and then gave her one of my own: would she and Edmundo like to come to my house for dinner one Saturday?

Although Nelly and Edmundo worked for me, I considered them friends more than employees and I wanted them to know this. When Nelly told me they'd be pleased to have dinner with me and a date was agreed upon, I decided to cook them a meal that would remind them of the country they were no longer allowed to enter.

Edmundo, in particular, was saddened by this state of affairs, and had often expressed sorrow that he'd been unable to attend the funerals of his parents. He was a middle child, with an older brother and a younger sister, and he missed his native family. Occasionally they would visit him and Nelly in London, but these times were few and far enough apart for his nephews and nieces to have grown into strangers.

Although Edmundo was resigned to a life of exile, I knew from our conversations that he yearned for his country of birth – its air and familiar smells, the chatter of its people and its mountains. The least I could do when he came to dinner was prepare a meal that would transport him to the realms of the High Andes and, albeit for a short while, reunite him with his beloved homeland.

I came up with the idea of cooking guinea pigs after reading a travel article in the *National Geographic*. The writer had stated that cuy – which was the Peruvian word for guinea pig – was a 'must' for any traveller to that country, and that no other meat was more emblematic of its cuisine. Indeed, an indication of its importance to the Peruvian diet was the fact that the guinea pig had its own national holiday, and the replica of Leonardo da Vinci's *Last Supper*, hanging in the cathedral at Cusco, even depicted Christ and his twelve disciples sharing a dish of cuy.

The guinea pig, the article continued, was cooked whole – its head, teeth and ears left intact – and could be either barbecued, baked or, if flattened by a heavy stone, also fried.

I decided to ask the butcher for his advice: how did his customers prepare their guinea pigs?

'I don't sell guinea pigs, Mr Pinkney. I've got some guinea fowl in the back, if that's what you're after.'

I showed him the article in the *National Geographic* and he read the paragraphs on cuy and then scratched his head.

'It says here that they taste like rabbit or wildfowl, so guinea fowl might still do the trick. I've also got a few rabbits, if you'd prefer those.'

I explained that, for the sake of my dinner guests, it had to be the real Peruvian McCoy, and I asked him if he knew of any other butcher in the area who might stock guinea pigs. He said that he didn't, but suggested I might want to try a pet shop.

'If you manage to find any, I'll be more than happy to skin them for you, Mr Pinkney. I could also try flattening them if you decide to fry them.'

It struck me that the butcher was a true professional and I thanked him for his helpfulness. I told him that, in the event I did source a supply of guinea pigs, we had a deal! I then set off for the nearest pet store with my fingers crossed.

I was in luck when I got there because the pet shop had six in stock, which varied in price from £15–30. With hindsight, I should have just bought them all instead of asking how many cavies would satisfy the appetites of three people, because when I did ask this question the owners threatened to call the police, and it would have been my luck that the policeman to arrive would have been the same one who already suspected me of killing my mother and Harry.

I was taken aback by the vehemence of their response and I apologised for any unintended offence I might have given. I then surprised myself – and certainly them – by suggesting that they never go to Peru for a holiday because the police in that country ate more guinea pigs than the rest of the nation put together – even though I didn't know this for a fact.

I don't like confrontation and usually keep thoughts like this to myself, but because the owners had been so unnecessarily rude to me and because, at heart, I knew I was better than they were, I expressed them forcefully.

The encounter unsettled me, and I worried that word of me trying to buy guinea pigs for the purpose of nutrition would spread through the pet shop community. I decided to lower my sights rather than suffer any further embarrassment, and when I returned home that afternoon I went online and researched Peruvian foods that, hopefully, would be easier to find.

Eventually, I settled on ceviche as a starter and a hearty beef stir-fry with a side of salsa criolla for the main. Most of the ingredients I could find in Battersea, but I had to travel to New Covent Garden Market in Nine Elms for the ají and Peruvian chilli peppers.

I'd driven my father's Jaguar for about three years before I part-exchanged it for a Saab. Oddly, in that it hadn't been driven by him for at least four years, the Jaguar still smelled of his pomade when I sold it, and the new-car aroma of the Saab came as a relief. I remained loyal to the Swedish manufacturer while I drove and bought a new car from them every two years.

I enjoyed driving, but parking in London was becoming increasingly difficult. I found myself having to leave the car in places far from my intended destination and having to walk longer and longer distances, which defeated the whole point of having a car. The day came when I decided enough was enough and I sold the Saab. I now travel by taxi and pay cab drivers to drop me at the door. It's money I can afford and, for the convenience, money well spent.

The driver who took me to New Covent Garden waited at its entrance with the meter running while I went looking for the peppers, and on the return journey I asked him to make a short detour. The location of the market was close to the site of Pinkney Industries, and I was curious to see it one more time. It was solely a trip down Memory Lane and I had no intention of introducing myself to the new owners.

This proved fortunate, because when we arrived at the location it turned out that the building had been destroyed by fire. The ground-floor windows were boarded and buddleias and weeds sprouted from the charred masonry. The iron-barred gate was swung closed and padlocked, and there was a sign warning potential intruders that the grounds were protected by guard dogs. A larger billboard announced that the site was soon to be redeveloped into luxury apartments and directed enquiries to a named estate agent.

The driver stopped the taxi and I climbed out for a closer look. The building held no warm memories for me, but I did wonder what had happened to the people who'd worked there. I also thought of my father for the first time in years. Pinkney Industries had been his pride and joy while he'd been alive, and he would have been as gutted as the building if he'd witnessed it that day. For a moment I felt sorry for him, but the moment soon passed. My father wouldn't have wanted my pity and nor, when he was alive, did he show me any. It was fitting that his legacy was a ruined shell.

Although I don't prepare my own meals today, I used to be a dab hand in the kitchen and entertained often. On the day I was expecting Edmundo and Nelly, I started to prepare the ceviche and salsa criolla immediately after I'd finished eating breakfast: I marinated the sea bass in citrus juices and added lime juice to the sliced red onions and avocados. The stir-fry would be cooked at the time, but I double-checked that I had all the ingredients: beef, tomatoes, corn cobs, yellow potatoes, onions, rice, and the ají and Peruvian chilli peppers I'd obtained from New Covent Garden.

I'd also bought three types of Peruvian wine – Tannat, Malbec and Chardonnay – six bottles of imported beer (Cusquena) and, for Nelly, a bottle of Rebel Yell bourbon. I put the white wine in the refrigerator and then looked at the clock: it was midday and there was time to read the paper.

The only day of the week I buy a newspaper is Saturday. I buy the *Daily Telegraph*, but not for its editorials. If I'm honest, I think the paper is a bit po-faced and publishes too many photographs of Helen Mirren, but theirs is the only crossword I can finish. It was Miss Wimpole who'd first encouraged me to solve crossword puzzles, but just the straightforward and not the cryptic ones. She'd told me that it was a good way of making new friends, which was her pet name for words.

'Words aren't your enemy, dear: they're your friends!' she'd say.

The first time I completed the *Telegraph*'s cryptic crossword – after fifteen years of trying and the purchase of a thesaurus – I had it framed in thick white wood and hung on the wall of my bedroom, just above my head. These days I can usually complete it in less than three days, and sometimes I send off my answers to the newspaper in the hope of winning a pen. So far I haven't had any luck, but I'm thinking of telling the compiler that I'm a recovering dyslexic in the hope that this information, in the event of a tie, will tip the balance in my favour. Even though I don't need a new pen, it's become a matter of principle that I win one.

I read the sections of the newspaper that interested me and decided to leave the crossword for the following day when I could give it my full attention. I still had more preparation to do and I didn't want to leave things until the last minute and then feel rushed. I set the dining table and took the ceviche and salsa criolla from the refrigerator, then cut the beef and vegetables into large chunks, as the recipe advised. By the time the doorbell rang at seven o'clock, I was ready and waiting, sitting in my favourite chair and relaxing with a small glass of sherry.

I hadn't mentioned to Nelly and Edmundo that I was

preparing a Peruvian meal that evening for fear they'd come dressed in ponchos and chullo hats and be stopped by the police en route. I know the police have a hard time of it these days, but I doubt that racial profiling is the answer to the nation's problems, even though the *Daily Telegraph* thinks it is.

I've never met the editor of that newspaper, but I'd wager he wouldn't bat an eyelid if he heard of an elderly Peruvian couple being frisked for cocaine on the streets of Battersea. Tell him that the police had stopped and searched Helen Mirren on her way to an awards ceremony, though, and we'd never hear the end of it. He'd write editorials and want questions raised in the Houses of Parliament and demand an intervention by the prime minister!

The evening, I'm glad to say, was the success I'd hoped it would be. Nelly and Edmundo were touched that I'd gone to so much trouble on their behalf, especially after I recounted the story of the guinea pigs and my trouble at the pet store.

Edmundo and I started the evening with beer, and I poured a large measure of bourbon for Nelly. Over the course of the ceviche, which I served with corn on the cob, we drank the bottle of Chardonnay and consumed the Tannat and most of the Malbec with the stir-fry. Edmundo said that he'd never met anyone as nice as me and that he'd be the first to rally to my cause if I ever raised the standard of rebellion against the British government.

Although Nelly admitted that she *had* met a person nicer than me – pointing to Edmundo and nudging him in the ribs – she was ready to admit that I was by far the nicest person she cleaned house for, and wondered, considering my niceness, why I'd never married.

I told her it was a long story but that I hadn't given up hope. 'There's someone out there for me, Nelly, but who that someone is, I have no idea. All I know for sure is that she won't be an Australian motorcyclist.'

Nelly said that she had no idea what I was talking about and, after consuming so much alcohol, I had to admit that I wasn't entirely clear on the matter myself. We all burst out laughing and Edmundo started to hiccup. What a night it was proving to be.

'Let me tell you about the time I was served with a restraining order!' I said.

The girl I was seeing at the time, and whose lawyer served the order, was called Isabel Green, and she was a divorcée of unusual good looks. Her complexion was the purest white, as though she was sickening for something and had just thrown up in a bucket, and was in sharp contrast to her short, bobbed hair that was as black as a minister's coat and styled with a fringe. She had blue eyes the size of saucers and lips the colour of cherries, and her smile was as warm as any radiator on the market. Until you knew her better, it was difficult to understand why any man would divorce Isabel Green.

Isabel had a daughter called Annabel, who was six at the time, and they came as a pair. You weren't allowed to love one without loving the other, and neither could Isabel love any man not loved by her daughter. We were an inseparable trio for almost a year, but I always found it easier to love Annabel than her mother, who was more self-absorbed and often in a bad mood.

Annabel would offer me a glass of lemonade and a choice of biscuit when I called at the house, and we shared jokes that Isabel found silly. I'd have been happy if she had become my daughter, but I was less certain of having her mother for a wife, and I suspect that my relationship with Isabel only lasted as long as it did for the sake of Annabel.

But then we went to Chester and our trio disbanded – not for any musical differences, but on the grounds of health and safety.

It was Isabel's idea that we spend a weekend there: a friend of hers had recently moved to the city and she wanted the two of them to spend time together. We arrived on the Friday and checked into the Grosvenor for two nights. Over dinner that night, Isabel asked me if I'd mind taking Annabel to the zoo the next day while she discussed grown-up matters with a friend in need of an ear.

I was happy to agree to this, and the next morning Annabel and I set off for the zoo. In my experience one zoo is no more special than another, but to share its wonder with a small child is something entirely different. It was one of the most unforgettable days of my life, and a day that became even more memorable when I had to take Annabel to the A&E department with a suspected fractured skull.

We were exploring the old city at the time of the accident, and Annabel had been perched on my shoulders. We'd just entered the Rows, a shopping district with covered arcades, and I'd forgotten to make the necessary adjustment to take into account the lower ceilings. Consequently, when we climbed the steps and entered the arcade, Annabel's head didn't quite make it and her forehead slammed into a wooden timber dating from medieval times. She wasn't knocked unconscious, but she was left feeling woozy, and as a local shopkeeper had suggested she might have sustained a skull fracture – though why a jeweller would have known this, I didn't know – I thought it best to err on the side of caution and call for an ambulance.

The next call I made was to the number Isabel had given me, and I was surprised when a man answered the phone.

I introduced myself and explained that I was at the hospital with Annabel, and then Isabel came on the phone and started to scream at me:

'I can't leave you for two minutes with my daughter…!'

That kind of thing.

She'd calmed down by the time we returned to the hotel, but the evening was uncomfortable and certainly not the time to ask about the man who'd answered the phone.

We left early the next morning and interrupted our journey at Leicester, where I took Isabel to another A&E department with a possible eye injury.

Annabel had been eating an apple at the time, and though I don't like littering I was less happy to have the smell of a browning apple in my car for a further hundred miles. I explained to Annabel that throwing an apple core on to a grassy verge wasn't really littering because the core was organic and, if not eaten by a family of voles or a lonesome hedgehog, would degrade of its own accord. I took the apple from Annabel and asked Isabel to lower the passenger window while I readied my aim. Instead of leaning back in her seat after she'd done this, though, Isabel inexplicably leaned forward and opened the glove compartment and the apple core smacked her hard in the face.

She howled, Annabel screamed, and I drove to the hospital.

When I dropped them at their house in Richmond, Isabel told me that there was no point in me coming in as she never wanted to see me again, and that this was as good a time to stop seeing me as any.

'You're a likeable person, Rod, but you're unintentionally dangerous and it's safer for both me and Annabel if we don't see you again. I'm happy to talk to you on the phone, but that's as close to you as I want to get.'

I told her she was overreacting and that we should talk about things once she'd had a chance to calm down and that I'd drop by later in the week.

'No, you won't!' she'd said. 'And I'm going to make sure that you don't!'

I was served with the restraining order three days later, though I think it was called something else in those days and was in no way as serious as it is today. Certainly my solicitor wasn't worried by the letter, and he wrote back saying that his client (me) had neither the desire nor the inclination to travel to Richmond. At my insistence, and to ensure that no long-term damage had been sustained by either skull or eye, he also suggested that they make appointments with specialists of their choosing and that his client (me) would pay for these consultations.

'You are a gentleman, Rod, a man out of time,' Edmundo said. 'Such decency should be rewarded with a song!'

He then left the room, still hiccupping, and went in search of his coat.

'Did you ever see Isabel again?' Nelly asked.

I told her I hadn't, but years later had bumped into Annabel on the pavement outside Harrods.

'It's Uncle Rod, isn't it? I'd know that cravat anywhere!' Annabel had said.

We'd hugged each other and then gone to the Harrods Café for a coffee and to catch up on each other's news: Annabel's skull was fine and she was newly married; her mother's eye was also fine and she was newly divorced; and I was still unattached and living in Battersea with no known ailments.

'I think my mother would welcome a call from you,' Annabel had smiled when we parted.

'I hope you didn't call her!' Nelly said.

I told her I hadn't, that past experience dictated against such action.

'What about Annabel? Did you ever see her again?'

Sadly, I hadn't. I'd kissed her goodbye in the Harrods Café and she'd headed off for the home appliances department.

'For all I know she might still be there,' I said. 'She was looking for a kettle.'

Edmundo returned with a set of panpipes and wet his whistle with a small measure of the remaining Malbec.

'Tonight, you have entertained us royally, my friend. You are the Sapa Inca of Battersea, Rod, a man of no less stature than Pachacutec himself, and we will repay your kind hospitality by playing you the music of our land.'

On hearing this, Nelly pushed back her chair from the table and went to stand by him. Edmundo cleared his throat, hiccupped, and then blew into the pipes.

The melody he played was pensive, sad, and Nelly stared tenderly at the glass of Rebel Yell in her hand. Edmundo paused for a moment, and when he repeated the refrain Nelly began to sing. She had a clear voice and sang the words in Spanish, a song I remembered from her vacuuming the lounge.

It struck me that Edmundo might have been a professional panpipes player if he'd decided against earning a living. Even though handicapped by his hiccups – which occasionally caused unintended whooshing noises – he played the instrument like a maestro. But the more he played, the less he hiccupped, and for their finale Nelly sang a song in English and one that I recognised. I applauded them loudest for this tune, and once they'd finished I asked them if they knew of any other Simon and Garfunkel hits that had been translated into Spanish.

Nelly explained that the song they'd just sung was *El Condor Pasa* and that it was a famous Peruvian melody about a giant bird and not composed by Simon and Garfunkel: Paul Simon had simply added the lyrics.

Well, when she told me this, I could have been knocked down by a feather, and I told her this.

We were sitting at the table again, and my comment about the feather must have triggered the thought of dusting in Nelly's mind because she then mentioned the books in the upstairs rooms that, in her words, were gathering dust.

'Why do you have so many books, Rod? Why not just give them away when you've read them? It's the only part of cleaning your house I don't enjoy.'

I told her it was because the books were a history of my life as a reader – just as my vinyl records and CDs, also stored in the upstairs rooms, were a history of my tastes in music. Ideally, I told her, I'd have liked the books and records to be in one place, but that I didn't have a room large enough.

'Have you ever thought of having your basement extended?' Edmundo asked. 'A lot of people have their cellars excavated these days, and it adds a new tier to the house. It is ironic, do you not think, that in a city synonymous with capitalism, upward mobility is now achieved by going downwards?'

It might well have been ironic, but I liked the idea!

Continuation 4

Donald

The task of transforming the cellar into a larger basement area started four months later. The firm I hired was called the Bulgarian Basement Company and its slogan – *Basements are in our Blood* – had caught my eye in the *Yellow Pages*.

The company had made its name building bunkers in the People's Republic of Bulgaria during the Cold War, and it was this that had tipped the balance in their favour. I was also swayed by the owner's assurance that no Englishmen would be employed on the project and that the basement's completion would therefore be timely and not constrained by either labour disputes or safety considerations.

The company was owned and run by Dimo Lazarov, a man in his mid-fifties whose clothes were old friends rather than fashion statements. He visited the house twice: once, to survey the property and to discuss options, and the second time to talk through the detailed plans he'd drafted.

Originally I'd been thinking of having just the existing cellar converted into a room, but at Dimo's suggestion – and because he was such a personable and polite man – I agreed to have the basement increased to the size of the building's full footprint, which Dimo estimated would take from five to six months and leave me with three new living spaces and a bathroom.

As part of the company's design and build service, Dimo also promised to obtain the necessary planning permission and building regulations approval, as well as securing a party-wall agreement with my adjoining neighbours.

'You strike me as a man beloved of the world, Mr Pinkney, so I presume you are in high standing with your neighbours?'

I had to admit that I had no idea who my neighbours were, even though they'd been living next door to me for seven years. I'd called several times when they'd first moved into the house – to make myself known and to welcome them to the area – but my presence had never been acknowledged, and the bottle of wine I'd left on their doorstep as a welcoming gift had remained untouched for two months before I reclaimed it.

My next-door-but-one neighbours were similarly mystified by the identity of the new owners, and all anyone in the street could say for sure was that they appeared to enjoy their own company.

'Leave it with me, Mr Pinkney,' Dimo said. 'If they don't sign the consent form, I'll send Boiko round to see them. Boiko can be persuasive!'

Three weeks later I received a phone call from Dimo telling me that my neighbours – whose names were Donald and Lydia Walker – had agreed to the conversion, and that Boiko and his boys would start work on the basement on the first day of the following month.

Boiko Chavdarov was Dimo's right-hand man and brother-in-law, and a person who commanded fear and respect in unequal measures – the larger measure being fear. He was a 200lb machine of hard muscle and had a jagged scar running the length of his right cheek. His eyes were small and narrow, and he had the thickest and most independent hair of any man I'd met, a mop that refused to be parted or combed in any one direction.

Boiko was the only man on site to speak English, and on the first day of operations he took me to one side and told me that if it was all right by me – which, considering his bearing, it obviously was – he'd prefer it if I didn't interfere with their work. His team of workers was self-contained, he explained, and had no requirement for mugs of tea or coffee that in his opinion were the bane of British productivity, and that his men would bring their own meat sandwiches for lunch. Boiko said that he'd talk to me only when necessary, and he suggested that I vacate the downstairs area during the months of upheaval and make myself comfortable in the upper storeys of the house.

Having alerted me to the inconvenience I was about to endure, Boiko wisely left it to Dimo, the company's more acceptable face – and the one without a jagged scar running its length – to reassure the immediate neighbourhood. Dimo knocked on doors and leafleted residencies, apologised for any disruption the work might cause and patiently answered questions. Unfailingly, he also detailed the advantages of having a cellar transformed by the Bulgarian Basement Company, and emphasised the value such extensions added to a property.

I can't tell you the ins and outs of what Boiko and his team did to transform the underground chamber into a living area – their methods of underpinning, waterproofing and insulating the space, for instance – only that on their first day of work they hung a thick plastic curtain at the bottom and top of the steps leading to the cellar, and then knocked out the small street-facing window to allow for the conveyance of displaced soil and rubble to the outside surface by means of a mechanical belt.

The waste in the front garden was then shovelled into barrows, wheeled up a plank into a large skip that was emptied and replaced as required, and in this way the basement took shape. Work would start at eight in the morning and continue like clockwork until six in the evening, when the same minivan that brought the workers would arrive to take them home.

It was towards the end of the second month of excavations that they found Donald. I was in an upstairs room listening to *Trout Mask Replica* at the time, and it took a while before I realised the commotion was downstairs and not integral to the recording, which I'd been struggling with for some weeks.

'Mr Piccaninny! Mr Piccaninny!' Boiko shouted up the stairs. 'We have unearthed a wild man! Do you want me to kill him?'

I was used to Boiko addressing me as Mr Piccaninny – a name I was happy to answer to in his presence – but I was bemused by the rest of his sentence, which appeared to make no sense at all: did I want him to kill a wild animal?

I turned off the music and went downstairs with no more expectation of finding a wild animal in the hallway than I would a circus elephant, and I was consequently taken aback when I found Boiko holding Charles Manson in a headlock and another worker supporting his feet.

The man in their grasp was slim and pale, no more than five feet six inches and appeared to be in his early sixties. He had a full beard and greying shoulder-length hair swept back from his forehead, and he was wearing a pair of old jeans and a red Christmas sweater populated by white reindeer.

'He claims to be your neighbour, Mr Piccaninny, and that he's a friend of the criminal Richard Nixon! Say the word and I'll break his neck and dump his body in the skip. No one but us will ever know.'

The man who looked like Charles Manson tried to say something, but Boiko tightened his grip and cut off his air supply.

'Let him speak, Boiko,' I said. 'We need to know who he is.'

Boiko relaxed his hold, but rather than telling us his name, the man started to shout at Boiko.

'Richard Nixon was not a criminal and I'll square up to any drongo who says otherwise! Nixon was – and still is – the greatest president the United States has ever had! Donald J Walker fought for him in Vietnam and Donald J Walker will sure as hell fight for him in Battersea!'

On hearing this Boiko again cut off his air supply and banged his head against the wall.

'Stop, Boiko!' I said. 'I think this man is my next-door neighbour!'

If not always a good judge of a woman's character, I like to think that I'm a better judge of a man's. It was true that Donald bore an uncanny resemblance to the murderer Charles Manson, but there the comparison ended, and once his eyes had acclimated to the light and it was clear there was no madness in them, I started to relax in his company. I made coffee and put some biscuits on a plate, then joined him at the kitchen table.

'That fellah, Mr Piccaninny: the one who had me in a headlock?' Donald gasped, still recovering from his ordeal. 'Would he really have killed me?'

In truth, I didn't know the answer to this question because I had no idea whether Boiko would or wouldn't have killed him if I'd given him the go-ahead, but I sought to reassure Donald by telling him that Boiko's bark was a lot worse than his bite – even though, this too, I didn't know for a fact. I mentioned then that my name was Pinkney and not Piccaninny as Boiko had referred to me, but for him to call me Rod. He then held out his hand and formally introduced himself as Donald J Walker and insisted that I call him Donald.

'You're probably wondering what I was doing in Vietnam, Rod, and that's perfectly understandable,' he said.

Strangely enough, the thought had never crossed my mind, and I was more interested in knowing what he'd been doing under my house. But, before I had a chance to ask him this, Donald pulled a metal comb from his shirt pocket, ran it through his hair several times, and then started to tell me about his years in Vietnam and his reasons for being there. His voice was deep and with no traceable accent, but his vernacular was often Australian and he had a tendency to refer to himself in the third person, as if in awe of the person he'd become. He also spoke at length.

One thing you can say about Donald is that he's never short of breath when it comes to talking about himself.

*

'I grew up in the Black Country, Rod, in a town called Brierley Hill. You've probably never heard of it, and there's no reason why you should. It's not a destination place, more a place that people leave, but if you had a hankering for steelworks it was like living in pig heaven.

'I wasn't a fan of the landscape myself, but my old man loved its brutality and thought it built character. He managed a division of a large meat products company in the town and he expected me to follow in his footsteps after I finished school. When I didn't, and took a temporary clerking position instead, he gave me a right gobful and told me I had a kangaroo loose in the top paddock.

'By that time, though, I'd already decided I was going to fight in Vietnam and so there'd have been no point in me taking a permanent job. Donald J Walker was a small fellah, Rod, but he liked to think he was tough and he wanted the chance to prove it. He had the opportunity of going to Rhodesia and helping his uncle defend a tobacco farm, but he wanted to be a real soldier and fight in a real war and the only war worthy of the name – and one he believed in – was the war in Southeast Asia.

'If it had been left to me, I'd have travelled to the United States and enlisted there, but this would have involved me renouncing my British citizenship and my old man was against this and he got madder than a cut snake when I suggested the idea. He was anti-American, always had been, and kept telling me that the Yanks only turned up to wars at half-time and then stole the glory. The only option remaining – and one my old man agreed to – was for me to immigrate to Australia and join its army.

'And so I took advantage of the Assisted Passage Scheme they had in those days and became one of those Ten Pound Pom fellahs; sailed from Southampton on a ship called the *Fairstar* and arrived in Melbourne in the summer of 1964. I worked construction while the Australian military considered my application, and completed my basic training at Puckapunyal. From there – and largely on account of my bulldozing skills – I was assigned to 3 Field Troop of the Royal Australian Engineers.

'If I'm honest, Rod, Donald J Walker was disappointed by

this placement. He'd joined up to be a jungle fighter and not some lever puller and he made this known – told them in no uncertain terms that he wanted a fair suck of the bottle. One thing I learned about the army that day is that it doesn't give a damn about a fellah's feelings. It's like Judge Judy says to the people who come before her: if you want to talk feelings, go see Dr Phil!'

(Dr Phil, I later learned, was a television therapist.)

Fortunately for Donald, the work of an engineer turned out to be a lot more interesting than just building roads and bridges – it also involved breaking things, and their expertise in dismantling booby traps, defusing bombs and exploring and destroying the Vietcong's secret tunnels made them an essential part of any search-and-destroy mission. Mostly the tunnels were boltholes, leading from village huts to nearby gullies or canals, and ran for no more than a few yards, but the tunnels discovered in the area known as the Ho Bo Woods were something entirely different.

The Ho Bo Woods was in a district of Vietnam called Cu Chi, and at one time had been famous for its rice paddies, orchards and rubber plantations. The Americans, however, having decided that the area was the headquarters of the Southern Vietcong and a likely staging post for the North Vietnamese army, had bombed the Woods to within an inch of its life and then sprayed the surviving inch with a chemical known as Agent Orange. Curiously, considering its newly acquired desolation, the area continued to be a hive of Vietcong activity and the Americans had to put boots on the ground – theirs and the Australians'. And so, on the first morning of 1966, they re-carpeted the area with their finest bombs and sent in the troops.

'It should have been a walk in the park after all that

pummelling, but it was the furthest thing from a piece of piss,' Donald said. 'We came under fire almost immediately and the bullets were coming from nowhere. A couple of fellahs were killed outright and the rest of us had to take refuge in a gulley. We stayed put there for a good two hours before one of the fellahs saw smoke rising from an anthill and figured that the firing was coming from there. We tossed a bunch of grenades and things went quiet, but it was too late in the day to do much else and so we decided to get some kip. The next day, though, and once it was light, we blew up what was left of the mound and found ourselves standing at the entrance to a bloody city!

'It was then I got busy in Vietnam, Rod – busier than a cat burying shit! From that day forward, and when it came to tunnels, Donald J Walker became the go-to guy!'

Before leaving the area, Donald and two other members of 3 Field Troop investigated and mapped more than 1,000 metres of tunnels and recovered weapons, equipment and documents, which were then passed to the Americans. The passages they explored proved to be the tip of an iceberg that stretched for 600 kilometres below the surface, and an entryway to a subterranean realm of classrooms, workshops, hospitals and living accommodations, and home at any one time to thousands of Vietcong.

The tunnel in the Ho Bo Woods was the first of many tunnels Donald would investigate, and as his expertise grew and reputation spread, the US Army took an interest in the man from Brierley Hill.

Having already decided that it was better to mine tunnels for information than simply destroy them with explosives, the US Army was in the process of forming its own team of tunnel warriors. They needed men of experience, however, men who were already trained in the craft, and the most renowned of these was the strange Englishman fighting with the Australian forces. Accordingly, Donald was seconded to the US Army's 1st Engineering Battalion and for the rest of his stay in Vietnam was stationed at Lai Khe, where he trained and joined American soldiers in the art of tunnel warfare, never once afraid to lead from the front or by example.

The US Army recognised that it could never force a man down a tunnel, so the tunnel rats were all volunteers. Donald described them as an odd bunch of 'pikers': men who didn't fit in with other people socially and preferred to 'drink with the flies'. Mostly they kept to themselves and read books or stared at things. They didn't do drugs or go to clubs, and they weren't much for conversation. Some, like Donald, were there to prove themselves, but others were there for the killing, the kind who would have probably been in jail if not in the army.

The tunnels they explored were at most two feet wide and no more than two and a half feet high, and no one tunnel was ever the same. There would be a straight drop immediately after the entrance, and the passages would regularly change direction, but apart from this the layout was anyone's guess. Sometimes there were anterooms to the side or trapdoors under the floor leading to other passages, and some tunnels had as many as six levels.

'There was no greater testing ground for a soldier than the tunnels of Cu Chi, Rod. When you climbed into a tunnel you were venturing into the unknown. You had no idea where the mines and booby traps were hidden, and there was no guessing how many Vietcong might be down there. It was old-fashioned one-on-one combat and all you had was a knife and a pistol. You'd crawl along, feeling the ground in front of you with your fingertips and constantly on the alert for a noise or a smell that might give the enemy away. It was always tense down there, but the stress was worst when you were the first through a trapdoor where there might be a Vietcong lying in wait for you, ready to garrotte you or slit your throat with a knife.

'And it wasn't just the thought of running into Charlie that put a man on edge down there. Just being in a tunnel was enough to do that! The passages were hotter than hell, Rod, claustrophobic, and they smelled of stale bodies and excrement. There were bats down there, too, rats and venomous snakes, poisonous centipedes seven inches long, and spiders and fire ants that swarmed all over you and climbed into your ears and nose. And those were just the things you could see. There were tiny organisms you couldn't see – supposedly half plant and half animal – and these buggers would burrow into the tissue below the surface of your skin and cause itching that's hard to describe.

'Nobody in his right mind should have loved being a tunnel rat, Rod, but there were those of us who did, and I'm not ashamed to say that I was one of them. I felt like a warrior down there, like one of those Japanese samurai fellahs, and in my own mind I was there for the right reason: I was fighting for the cause of freedom and against communism.'

Donald admitted that his world view at this time of his life had been overly simplistic and largely influenced by *The Manchurian Candidate*, a film that had confirmed his suspicion that there was an international communist conspiracy afoot in the world that, if not confronted, would bring democracy to its knees. And in his mind, and from his understanding of American politics, there was only one politician who could stand up to this menace: Richard Milhous Nixon.

Nixon had been Eisenhower's vice-president for eight

years and had, in Donald's opinion, been robbed of the top slot in 1960 by the Kennedys. Donald had been satisfied with Lyndon Johnson as head of the American nation – a man who also seemed to understand the dangers of communism – but he was as pleased as punch when his 'bonzer' hero Richard Nixon won the presidential election of 1968. Effectively Nixon became not only commander-in-chief of the American forces, but also *his* commander-in-chief. Donald fought communism and killed communists in the name of Richard Nixon and this suited him fine.

'I'd signed up for a six-year term with the Australian Army and my time came to an end in the summer of 1971. By then the war was already unwinnable, and there was nothing more that Donald J Walker could do to prove himself. I was given the chance of re-enlisting for a further three years, but by that time I was more interested in leaving Vietnam alive than returning home in a body bag.

Fortunately for me – in that it was now growing dark and close to my dinnertime – Donald lost interest in telling me about his life after he'd returned to England, and he skipped over these years in a matter of minutes.

'After my time in the tunnels, I had difficulty adjusting to the humdrum of life in Brierley Hill and so I moved to London, which at least had an Underground. I lived off what savings I had while I figured out what to do with my life, ate my meals in Chinese restaurants, and spent most of my time below street level, riding the tube and forcing rowdy passengers from the carriages.'

The day came, however, when a member of the British Transport Police – sympathetic to Donald's aims, but unsure of the legality of his actions – took him to one side and suggested he apply for a formal job with London Underground if he was so intent on ensuring its well-being: construction of the Jubilee Line was under way and they were currently recruiting.

Donald's background in engineering and tunnels – as well as a shortage of more suitable applicants – made him an ideal hire, and for the rest of his working life Donald remained under the ground and hidden from view, one of the palest men in London to ever walk its streets.

*

'And so that's me, Rod: my life in a nutshell.'

I could only assume that Donald had been referring to the shell of a coconut, because by this time he'd been talking for almost two hours and without pause. I'd enjoyed his story, but it still didn't explain why he'd been under my house. There were no communists living down there that I knew of, and though Boiko and his men might have been communists at one time of their lives, they were now fervent nationalists who just happened to prefer living and working in any country but their own.

'I don't mean to pry, Donald,' I said, 'but what were you doing in my basement?'

'I was looking for grapefruit, Rod,' he replied matter-of-factly, as if a man searching for grapefruit in another person's cellar was nothing out of the ordinary and something I should have expected.

The word coconut again came to mind, but as he launched into another story – this time about citrus fruit and the difficulties of married life – I came to understand his reasoning.

Donald J Walker liked grapefruit. He ate two for breakfast

every morning and had done so for at least forty years. By his calculation, he'd consumed well over 29,000 and he bought them in bulk. His wife, on the other hand, hated grapefruit – not just their taste, but also their sight and particularly their smell – and she'd insisted that Donald store the fruit and eat his breakfast in the cellar. It was one of many demands that Lydia had made of him over the years and, as usual, and for the sake of keeping the peace, Donald had acquiesced.

The day came, however, when Lydia needed more space to store the dead and the dying of everyday life and she withdrew Donald's grapefruit privileges. The house became a grapefruit-free zone and the cellar a storage space for rolls of worn-out carpet and boxes of old clothes, curtains, broken appliances and out-dated technologies.

'She looks upon them as her friends, Rod, and she isn't prepared to throw them out. I've tried reasoning with her, but she won't bend and so I just work around her.'

Donald's way of working around his wife in the cellar was to quietly extend it without mentioning it to her. He'd knocked a hole in the back wall and then dug a series of exploratory tunnels in search of a band of clay that would support a larger cavity. He'd found a thin seam of suitable loam close to the party wall and discovered that it grew in size only as it ran eastwards and under my property.

He'd then knocked out another hole – this time in the party wall – and after a further four feet of tunnelling had been able to hollow out a small storage room where he could store boxes of grapefruit and eat his breakfast in peace. He'd then secured his excavations by adding side supports and roof beams made of tanalised wood, and placed strips of linoleum on the floor of the tunnel to spare his clothing. And lastly, but by no means least, considering the importance of hiding the den from his wife, he'd concealed its entrance with a large television set.

From start to finish the project had taken him five months. He'd worked during the hours of night when Lydia had been at work, and scattered the dislodged soil in the borders of Battersea Park. At the time of Boiko's men breaking through the walls of his underground storage room, Donald had been in the process of retrieving sixty-three grapefruits and was taken by surprise.

Considering the importance Donald attached to grapefruit and the hideaway he'd dug under my house, I expressed surprise that he'd given his consent to me having the basement extended.

'I didn't,' he replied. 'That was all Lydia's doing. The first I knew of it was when the drilling started.'

Fortunately for me – though less fortunate for Donald – Lydia had liked the idea of living next door to a house with a basement extension, and had been happy to sign the party-wall agreement. It was something she could brag to her work colleagues about, and it was an improvement she believed would increase the value of their own property. Having never seen the plans for the extension Lydia had approved, Donald had no idea of its size and was hoping against hope that his storage room would be unaffected.

'All this wouldn't have happened if Lydia didn't take things into her own hands,' Donald sighed. 'She forgets that marriage is a partnership and that all decisions have to be made jointly.'

Donald had met his wife at a meeting organised by the Kensington, Chelsea & Fulham branch of the Conservative Association to discuss the reintroduction of prison ships. Lydia had been on the platform and spoken forcefully for a return to the days when lawbreakers had been housed in prison hulks anchored in the mud off Woolwich.

'They didn't have televisions and they weren't allowed to play Ping-Pong!' she'd said. 'They lived in the dark and in the damp, and they shared their accommodations with rats and bumble bees and things like that – and that's the way it should be! Criminals today aren't afraid of going to prison because conditions there are better than in their own homes. Why would anyone want to be rehabilitated if it meant them missing out on the chance of going back to a holiday camp?'

Lydia had sat down to loud applause and then Donald had stood up and said that if prison ships weren't reintroduced, he knew of a place where they could get hold of lots of fire ants and seven-inch centipedes that they could release into the prisons to give the inmates a taste of their own medicine!

His contribution had also been greeted with applause, and after the meeting ended – with a vote of thirty-two to three in favour of reintroducing prison ships – Lydia had made a bumble-beeline for Donald.

'She was a good-looking woman in those days, Rod; not as stout as she is today and a lot more fun. It was unusual to meet a woman with such common sense and on the same wing of politics as I was. She was also a big fan of Barry Goldwater, and she'd cried a bucket the night he lost the election to Lyndon Johnson. Women like that are hard to find, and I knew from first meeting her that we had a future together. We've been married for thirty-two years. I'm not going to pretend it's always been easy, because it hasn't, but she's a woman I admire.'

Lydia was younger than Donald by about five years and worked in the IT department of Her Majesty's Revenue & Customs. Donald suspected that the longevity of their marriage was in large part down to her working nights and him working days, because the strains he now described had only developed after he'd retired. Lydia herself was due to retire in two years and he worried that this would be the time when the waters really got choppy.

Although he looked up to his wife, Donald never once mentioned that he loved her. Neither did he say that Lydia loved him, only that she appreciated him helping around the house and running errands.

'I don't put paste on her toothbrush, but that's about the only thing I don't do. I think she looks upon me more as a servant than the man of the house, and that's my fault because I've allowed it to happen. I take comfort in playing the trombone, but it was the grapefruit that really kept me going. I don't know what I'm going to do now that my breakfast room's gone.'

I felt sorry for Donald and said that he was welcome to eat grapefruit in my house any day of the week if he wanted to. He thanked me for my consideration, but explained that Lydia was a light sleeper and that opening and closing the front door during the day would disturb her rest.

A thought crossed my mind, but I decided to keep it to myself. I needed to know Donald better before suggesting the idea – and I was certain that Boiko wouldn't approve of it. No, it was something that would have to wait until the basement was completed – which, four months later, it was.

*

Edmundo and I had fallen into the routine of spending Thursday nights together. Nelly worked late those evenings, and Edmundo was often at a loose end for something to do.

One Tuesday morning, shortly after the night I'd entertained them to dinner, he came by my house and asked if I was free that Thursday evening. I said that I was, and asked him if he had anything special in mind.

'I have, Rod,' he smiled: 'Alcohol!'

That Thursday, shortly after 5:30 pm, Edmundo arrived at my house carrying a large plastic John Lewis bag. I thought he'd brought some new tea towels because Nelly had been telling me for some time that mine were no longer serviceable, but when I suggested this to him he simply shook his head.

'No, Señor Rod, I have brought you the makings of Peru!'

He then placed the bag on the kitchen counter and withdrew a bottle of yellowish-looking brandy, a carton of free-range eggs and some Key limes, a container of syrup and a bottle of Angostura bitters.

'Your glorious meal of Saturday night brought my homeland to life and made me long for my country of old,' he said. 'But what really brings Peru to life – and helps a man forget that he is no longer allowed within its borders – is its national drink. Tonight I will make – and we shall drink – the famous Pisco sour, and all I ask of you, my friend, is a tray of your best British ice cubes.'

Pisco sour was one of the nicest cocktails I'd ever tasted, and much preferable to the gin and tonic I usually drank. It was hard to believe that a person could get inebriated on something that tasted so wholesome, but by the end of the evening both Edmundo and I were well and truly hammered.

The next morning I woke up with one of the worst hangovers I'd ever had and stayed in bed until well after midday. Edmundo was also the worse for wear the next day, and Nelly gave him a good scolding and told him to act his age. We learned to pace ourselves after that, and on the Thursdays that followed we generally stuck to beer. And then one Thursday night, close to the basement's completion, Donald knocked on the door and I invited him to join us.

Since the day Boiko had hauled him from the cellar, Donald had become almost as regular a visitor to my house as Edmundo. He came around in the evenings, after Lydia had left for work, and we'd spend an hour or so chit-chatting and drinking the occasional glass of wine. He was a cheery man and good company, and never at a loss for something to say.

I'd wondered about introducing him to Edmundo before, but I wasn't sure if the two men would take to each other. They were, after all, from opposite ends of the political spectrum: Donald having fought communism in the bowels of Vietnam, while Edmundo had fought on its behalf in the High Andes of Peru. The only thing they had in common was the fact that they'd both killed people, and I wasn't sure if this was a sufficient reason for them to be friends.

Fortunately, and against the odds, they got on like a house on fire, and Donald became a regular member of our Thursday night get-togethers.

It helped that both men had mellowed over the years, and that Donald was less averse to communists than he had been in his youth. In fact, he now rued the day the Berlin Wall had fallen and the Cold War ended. The world, he believed, had become a more dangerous place since the demise of communism, and warfare infinitely more cowardly. Soldiers in uniform had never attacked civilians in restaurants and cafes or in supermarkets or at their places of work, and neither had they detonated rucksacks in crowded places or blown themselves up on trains or in the middle of a wedding.

Donald, who still wasn't sure what the Shining Path was or wasn't, was happy to embrace Edmundo as an old-school warrior who, like him, had put his money where his mouth was and fought for a cause he'd believed in, and not as an excuse to have sex with a group of underage girls once he was dead.

They also had other things in common – recurring nightmares, for instance, and the love of a fat woman – but what really brought them together was their love of music.

Donald had been thrilled when Edmundo told him he played the panpipes, and he'd suggested they start practising together – though preferably at Edmundo's house as Lydia didn't allow people in the house when she wasn't there, nor the sound of a trombone when she was. When Edmundo worried that the noise of a trombone might cause difficulties with his neighbours, I told them they were welcome to duet in the basement once it was completed, and they both agreed that this would be the perfect place.

It was easier to understand why Edmundo played the panpipes than it was Donald the trombone. I could imagine someone in Peru saying 'Hey, Edmundo, we're having a party tonight so bring your pipes,' but I could never envisage anyone in Brierley Hill asking Donald to take his trombone to a similar event. There was something about a trombone that made it an outsider, an awkward fit, and in this respect it was no surprise that Donald had chosen to play the instrument in the school orchestra.

What did surprise me, though, was Edmundo's enthusiasm for Donald's idea. Surprisingly – in my opinion – he thought the two instruments would complement each other beautifully, and he particularly liked Donald's idea of busking on the Underground once they had a repertoire.

'I've got the contacts and I can get us a good pitch with great acoustics,' Donald had told him. 'And it will be money in your pocket that the taxman knows nothing about!'

I cautioned Donald that Lydia – considering her position at HMRC and her interest in prison ships – might not like him doing this, but he told me that Lydia was more interested in other people paying taxes than them.

'So when can we start practising?' Edmundo asked.

I replied that this would depend on how long it took for the plaster to dry and how soon he could then start painting the walls. Donald said that he could give Edmundo a hand to speed things along, but only at night and only after Lydia had left for work, because opening and closing the front door during the daytime was out of the question.

Donald's mention of the difficulty he faced leaving and entering his house while Lydia was sleeping again brought to mind the idea that had crossed it on the day we'd first met. I'd been reluctant to express it then because I'd still been unsure of Donald as a person, but now that I considered him a friend – and as Boiko and his men would soon be leaving the premises – I felt free to share the idea.

'Donald,' I said, 'what if I allowed you to extend your tunnel into my basement again. Would this make your life easier?'

That night it was decided, and once Donald had wiped the tears from his eyes and returned Edmundo's handkerchief, we came up with a plan.

Donald would run a tunnel to the wall of the room at the rear of the basement and Edmundo would knock a hole in the wall and build a small doorway that would allow Donald to enter my property at will – though within reason. He would be able to store his grapefruit in the small room and eat his breakfast there and enter my house whenever he and Edmundo needed to practise their music.

All this, of course, would have to wait until the basement was completed.

'Beautiful! Beautiful!' Dimo said on the day of his final inspection. 'Boiko is a man of rough edges, but his walls and ceilings are as smooth as the finest silk. I hope you will feel free to recommend the workmanship of the Bulgarian Basement Company to your friends and acquaintances, Mr Pinkney.'

I told him I would be happy to do so, but wondered how long it would be before the plaster could be painted.

Dimo estimated between four and six weeks, but then plumped for seven because seven was a luckier number.

I wrote him a cheque for the balance remaining and we shook hands.

'I doubt you will encounter problems with our finished product, Mr Pinkney, but if you do, then you must call me immediately and I will send Boiko to meet with you.'

I think Dimo knew that Boiko would be the last person I'd want to see again and that the chances were good he wouldn't be hearing from me.

Donald started his excavations the next day, and by the end of the following week there was a small door measuring two feet by three in the rear basement room. Edmundo re-plastered the wall and then we waited: one week, two weeks, three weeks...

At the end of the seventh week, Donald and Edmundo got out their paintbrushes.

Although Edmundo was confident that, if given the time, he could fashion the bookshelves himself, I decided to hire a bespoke bookcase company to do the job, and its craftsmen lined the walls with shelving made of thick tulipwood that they stained ebony.

All that remained was for the books and records to

be brought down from the upstairs rooms and placed in alphabetical order on the fixed shelves. Nelly dusted the books and put them in boxes, while Edmundo and Donald carried the boxes to the basement where I unpacked and sorted them and placed them on the shelves. It was a team effort, but I suspect that I was alone in appreciating the full effect of the walls once they were lined.

I covered the floorboards in the new library with large Persian carpets, and furnished the room with leather couches, two easy chairs and a large Victorian partners desk that I'd found in an antiques shop. I placed the desk at the far end of the library, closest to the road and under the window, and from here I can look up from my writing and survey the full majesty of the room.

'You should have a grand opening, Señor Rod, and we should christen the room with the finest champagne!'

I thought Edmundo's suggestion an excellent idea, and a grand opening would give me the opportunity to thank him, Nelly and Donald for all their hard work.

'And you must bring Lydia,' I said to Donald. 'It would be nice to meet her.'

Donald agreed to invite her, but told us not to get our hopes up because no one, so far as he knew, had ever enjoyed meeting Lydia.

'She won't mean to be rude, but you can bet your bottom dollar that she will be. It's in her nature.'

Nelly said that if that was indeed Lydia's nature, then Donald should leave her at home and come by himself. I could sense Donald warming to the idea, but I told him it would be impolite not to invite her.

'Okay, I'll do it then, but with one proviso: no one mentions the tunnel!'

The library was officially opened on the second Saturday following Edmundo's suggestion. To keep the numbers even, I'd invited an old friend who was between husbands. Her name was Lorna Doom – if you can believe this – and she carried visiting cards in her purse that she handed to people whenever they got her name wrong:

My name is Lorna Doom and not Lorna Doone. Perhaps you're deaf.

If you knew Lorna, then you'd know the card was intended to be funny, but as most people she handed the card to had never met her before, they often took offence.

Lorna arrived early that evening and looked as radiant as ever. It always surprised me that a person of her standing would buy clothes at a store whose fashion sense had long since climbed out of the window, and I often teased her about this.

'There's nothing wrong with Marks & Spencer! For Christ's sake, Rod, you wear cravats but do you ever hear me complaining about the way you dress? And how many times have *you* been married? Zero times, that's how many! I've been down the aisle three times already and not once has a husband complained about the way I dress. Men are more interested in me when I'm not dressed!

'Anyway, tell me about these dullards you've invited to this basement thing? Am I likely to enjoy their company?'

I didn't really know the answer to this but I said that I thought she would, and then suggested it might be better if she slowed down on the champagne and didn't give a visiting card to a woman called Lydia.

'Jesus, Rod! You know I'm going to be drunk by the end of the evening, so why give me a piece of shit advice like this? You know damn well I'll go out of my way to offend her now!'

And this is exactly what happened.

Edmundo and Nelly were the first to arrive and Lorna took an immediate interest in Nelly.

'You're kidding me! You used to be a fucking nun? Jesus H Christ, Rod, Nelly used to be a nun! Did you know that?'

Well, of course I knew this, but there was a knock at the door and I had no time to tell her.

'Hi Rod, this is Lydia,' Donald said. 'The woman I've been telling you about.'

Lydia gave him a look of exasperation, and then took my hand as I tried to kiss her cheek.

'I'm very pleased to meet you, Rod, and I'm very much looking forward to seeing your basement,' she said. 'Now where is it?'

Donald told her it was on the next floor up, and she gave him another look.

'If you're going to be like this all evening, Donald, you may as well go home now,' she said.

Although Edmundo had suggested a 'grand' opening for the basement, I'd wanted the evening to be a casual affair and I'd asked that my guests dress informally, which Nelly, Edmundo and Lorna had done. Lydia, however, was dressed for the opera that night and had insisted on Donald wearing a suit and tie.

'I told you we'd be overdressed,' Donald said as they entered the library. 'Why the hell do you never listen to me?'

I introduced Lydia to Nelly and Edmundo, and then her and Donald to Lorna.

'Has anyone ever told you that you look like Charles Manson?' Lorna asked Donald.

'I'm sorry; who did you say you were again?' Lydia asked her.

Lorna didn't bother to reply but just handed her a card.

'Well, really!' Lydia said after reading it.

I quickly poured Lydia a glass of champagne and invited her on a tour of the basement.

It was difficult to know if Lydia liked the new basement or not. She asked questions like 'What's this?' and 'What's that?' but she never gave any feedback. The only thing she appeared to take a real interest in was the small door leading to Donald's tunnel, wondering why it was there and what it was for. Fortunately I'd taken the key from the lock and was able to tell her, without fear of any physical contradiction, that it was a narrow space for cooling wine. She'd then started to sniff the air.

'What's that smell, Rod? Is that grapefruit? Do you keep grapefruit in this room?'

I pointed to a cupboard that Donald had freshly stocked, and told her that I kept all citrus fruit there to stop the rest of the house smelling.

'I think you're very sensible to do that,' she said. 'Personally, I don't allow grapefruit in the house!'

I suggested we return to the library and rejoin the other guests and Lydia agreed.

'That woman you invited – the one who's dressed like the year's 1950. Is she always this rude?'

I laughed and said that she wasn't, that she was never purposely rude, and that once Lydia got to know her better she'd see her funny side.

I could tell that Lydia felt she knew Lorna well enough already, but she said that she was prepared to give her a second chance and allow her to apologise.

As luck would have it, Donald was talking to Lorna when we returned to the library and appeared to be enjoying her attentions.

'Thirty-two years?' Lorna exclaimed. 'The two of you have been married for thirty-two fucking years! What's your wife been doing all this time? Starving you and saving the pies for herself?'

15 July 2019

'Look, Rod, all I'm saying is that the people who take stray kittens to heart are the same people who buy guinea pigs for their children. If you want to keep the reader onside – which is something we want to do – then I suggest you take out the paragraphs on cooking guinea pigs. Edmundo and Nelly might well be Peruvian, but they're living in this country now and people here don't eat pets and aren't sympathetic to those who do. What would you have done if your friends had been from South Korea – barbecued them a dog? You have to use your common sense when…'

I interjected here and told Ric he was being too finical – a word that was new to me, and one that had been the answer to a clue in the previous week's crossword. No one in their right mind would serve a dog for dinner, I told him, and that, so far as I knew, there were no South Koreans living in Battersea. A dog might well be man's best friend, but I'd never heard the same thing said about guinea pigs, which to my way of thinking were only a hop, skip and a jump from being rabbits that were sold in butchers' shops.

'And another thing,' I added, 'if I was a rabbit, I'd rather be eaten than kept in a hutch, and I'd be surprised if a guinea pig doesn't think the same way.'

'It's not what you think and it's not what a fucking guinea pig thinks, Rod; it's what the market thinks!' Ric snapped. 'If the readership for your book was in Peru then I'd be happy for you to keep the paragraphs in, but it's not, and so I'm suggesting that you take them out. This is my professional opinion!'

'And it's nothing to do with the fact that you've just become a vegetarian?' I ventured.

Ric raised his voice when I suggested this and told me that it wasn't and that maybe I should learn to mind my own fucking business if I knew what was good for me.

I was taken aback by the vehemence of his language, and quietly relieved when the landlord came to our table and asked if everything was all right. I told him it was, and explained that Ric and I were just having literary differences.

'Well, have them in your own time then,' he said to Ric. 'Your break finished five minutes ago!'

Ric got to his feet and started to clear the glasses from a neighbouring table. It appeared our meeting was at an end, but I was reluctant to leave the Lansdowne without his permission to bring Daisy into the story. In my opinion, the four continuations had brought my life to its current circumstances and also to the occasion of our meeting. Ric was about to disappear into the kitchen and I had to raise my voice.

'Ric,' I shouted after him, 'can I start writing about Daisy now?'

He stopped and turned. 'Yes,' he said, 'but first, you need to tell the reader about your disability issues.'

I had no idea what he was talking about, and the perplexed expression on my face must have conveyed this fact to him. He then nodded – his hands were holding a tray of glasses at the time – in the direction of my mobility scooter.

My meeting with Ric hadn't gone to plan. I'd been expecting a pat on the back for the way I'd structured the stories of Edmundo and Donald, and I was more than disappointed when he chose to downplay my achievement. He described the reportage style as imitative and self-conscious and said that I'd given both men the same voice and that it was as easy to imagine Edmundo fighting in Vietnam as it was Donald in Peru. He also suggested that I'd spent too much time on their backstories, and that readers who liked love stories would be less likely to warm to two old men who'd made a practice of killing people in their day.

Ric's mood had been strange that day and his profanity more than a little jarring. It certainly wasn't the Ric of old I'd been talking to, and I could only put this down to him now being a vegetarian.

No person on earth loved meat more than Ric, and I could only suppose that it was Suzie who'd made the choice for him and that his conversion had been reluctant. By all accounts his wife was a forceful woman and, for whatever reason, had now decided that all meat, including chicken, was off the menu for all members of the family, both in- and outside the house.

Ric was obviously suffering the side effects of his new diet and taking his frustrations out on me, and, ipso facto, on the meat-related paragraphs in continuation 3. It was clear that his judgement had become skewed and that for the time being I would have to rely on my own acumen. The guinea pig paragraphs would stay, I decided – if not for literature, then for the sake of Edmundo.

Ric's mention of disability had rankled, and I suspect that this was his intention. It's true that I drive a mobility scooter and have stairlifts in the house, and also true that I favour chairs that make sitting and rising easier, but none of these should be construed as a sign of feebleness or allowed to contradict the fact that I'm an able-bodied man in the prime of life.

Ric knows this, I know this, but perhaps I should explain it to you.

Continuation 5

Miller v Lamprich

During the months that the basement was under construction, I started to watch daytime television for the first time. Usually I read during the day, but the noise and disruption caused by Boiko and his men made concentration impossible and I was forced to turn to the television for distraction.

Other than a man called Paul O'Grady loving animals more than any other person in the world, I learned little about life from watching the actual programmes and more from the advertisements, which always played at a slightly louder volume and were largely geared to people who had either been mis-sold insurance policies or been the victims of medical blunders or accidents not of their making. Life for them appeared to be difficult, especially as most of them had poor credit scores, and it was a relief to know there were lawyers and financial companies in the world willing to fight on their behalf and offer them their services free of charge.

There were other commercials, though, that catered to a more fortunate section of society, the nation's senior citizens, and it was from listening to these that I got the idea for making my own life more comfortable.

There are no two ways about it: old people in this country

have it good, and certainly better than most. Companies build special chairs and beds for them, arrange for stairlifts and walk-in showers to be installed in their homes, and design scooters that allow them to go on seventeen-mile round trips without having to use their legs.

Why, I wondered, did ease and comfort have to be the preserve of old age and not available to a wider audience? Why should the wear and tear on a younger person's body be of any less concern to society than the wear and tear on an older person's? The whole situation struck me as discriminatory and I wasn't prepared to be bound by any convention that restricted stairlifts, scooters and riser-recliners to the old and the infirm.

And so, shortly after the basement was finished, I started to make enquiries. Although the new library was my pride and joy, I found that if I ended my day there, which I often did, I now had to climb three flights of stairs to my bedroom rather than two, and as my main concern was to conserve energy for a time when I would need it more, the logical starting point was a stairlift.

After having just been through eight months of upheaval having the cellar enlarged, I was concerned that the installation of a stairlift would result in more unwanted disruption, but the company I eventually hired assured me that it would take no more than a few days. They were true to their word, and in less than two days they'd fitted two custom-designed, curved stairlifts, one that took me from the basement to the hallway and another that carried me from the hallway to the upper floors. All I had to do was to strap myself into the chair, place my feet on the collapsible footrest and press a button. It was as simple as that.

Next, I bought new chairs and a bed, all of which I'm

pleased to say were lovingly built and handcrafted in this country. I ordered two high-backed riser-recliner chairs, again custom-made and built specifically to my dimensions, and also matching sofas.

The company I approached sent a lovely young woman to the house called Fiona Nuttall. She was dressed in a navy-blue costume and looked every bit the professional – just as in the commercials I'd seen on television. Fiona fully understood my reasons for taking an interest in their furniture, and expressed surprise that more people didn't.

'People spend hours in their chairs, Mr Pinkney, and they forget how important it is to sit healthily. If a person wants true comfort and total relaxation, then the spine, neck and shoulders have to be suitably supported, and this is where our products excel.'

She explained the functions of the built-in handset she'd brought with her for demonstration purposes, pointing to the buttons that tilted the chair backwards and forwards and operated the leg rest, and then told me about the degree in media studies she had but was yet to find a use for.

I told her she was a born salesperson and that she'd go far in the furniture business if she put her mind to it. And then, as if to prove my point, she sold me an adjustable bed that raised the top half of my body and made watching television and getting up in the morning that much easier.

As Fiona was leaving the house, she asked if it would be all right if someone from their bathroom department contacted me with information of products similarly designed to make life easier and safer for a person wishing to remain active for as long as possible?

I immediately agreed to her suggestion – it was difficult to say no to Fiona – and in the weeks it took for the furniture department to build my bed and chairs, the bathroom department transformed my shower.

They made the room easy-access and fitted slip-resistant trays, and they also installed safety grab bars and a comfortable fold-up seat that I could sit and rest on if I didn't feel like standing. The best product I bought from them, though – and one that I'd recommend to anyone wishing to save energy – was an electric lift that lowered and then raised me from the tub whenever I took a bath, and again at the press of a button.

Once I'd made these changes to the house, I turned my attention to making life outdoors more effortless and purchased a mobility scooter. Although some people might say I have money to burn, I've never liked wasting it unnecessarily, and I was conscious that I was spending a considerable sum taking taxis to places I would have once walked. A scooter seemed just the answer to such profligacy.

I've driven various models over the years, both three- and four-wheeled, but the one I drive now is my favourite and it can reach speeds of 8 mph. This one has five wheels, which makes it more stable, and it can also climb kerbs. It's painted gunmetal grey and has lights at the front and rear and a basket for putting things in. The scooter is ideal for when I want to cross the bridge into Chelsea, and as long as I go no further than eight miles outward, I can return home safely before having to recharge the battery. And if, for any reason, the scooter breaks down when I'm out and about, then I have a contract with the manufacturers providing for roadside recovery, as well as for servicing and maintenance.

The only other measure I took to make life easier was to start buying ready-made frozen meals from a company that delivered to the door. I enjoyed cooking – and still entertain from time to time – but I'd become increasingly tired of preparing my own meals, which involved a lot of standing and bending, and the opportunity to buy nutritionally balanced foods that took only 8–12 minutes in a microwave or 35–40 minutes in a conventional oven, was too good to pass up.

Again, it was during the months of watching daytime television that I came across the company. Its commercials had been fronted by Ronnie Corbett, a well-liked comedian who was little more than five feet tall, and I used to wonder if he might have grown taller if he'd ordered his own meals from this company.

I'm sad to say that Ronnie is no longer with us: he died in 2016, a year that struck at the very heart of show business and left the nation reeling. Excepting for the fact that it was celebrities and not shares doing the falling, that year was like the Wall Street Crash of 1926. Every day, someone special in the world of entertainment died, and we were left to wonder who would be next, who else would be wrenched from us?

Anyway, not being a celebrity, my life went on as normal, and Edmundo, Donald and I continued to meet on a Thursday night. At first, they were puzzled by the changes I was making to the house – Donald wondering if I was going into the nursing home business and Edmundo worried that I'd been diagnosed with multiple sclerosis – and even after I'd explained the logic behind them, they were still at a loss to understand why I wanted to live like an invalid.

'I'm not trying to live like an invalid,' I told them, 'I'm trying to avoid *becoming* one.'

I think this put their minds to rest, and once they'd worked out the mechanisms of the new chairs and got into the habit of riding the stairlift to the first-floor toilet, they came to appreciate the improvements. We continued to differ on the subject of the scooter, though, which they both considered a step too far.

At first, I suspected their stance was less for the offence it might cause the outside world – which they claimed it would – and more for my refusal (for insurance purposes) to allow them to drive the scooter, but in thinking this I was being ungracious. Edmundo and Donald, I knew, were concerned for me as friends, looking out for my well-being just as I would always look out for theirs. We were, after all, the Three Musketeers of Battersea: one for all, and all for one!

We'd gather in the lounge on these evenings rather than in the basement, which I reserved for reading and working on the crossword puzzle, and later for writing my continuations. Conversation was always easy, and because it was so effortless and often as not washed down with alcohol, it was also difficult to recall.

Nelly once asked me what we talked about, and the only thing I could think to say was: well, nothing really; certainly nothing in particular.

'Hmm,' I remember her saying. 'That's what Edmundo always says.'

I wish I could have told her differently, that we spent our time pondering the big questions of life – its meaning, purpose and the reason for being – but we never did. Our conversations were just the opposite, in fact: meandering, of the moment and often trivial in nature.

Donald, for instance, who liked to think of himself as a jokesmith – and regularly submitted his homespun witticisms to a company that made Christmas crackers – once asked us the name of Norway's most famous actor.

Edmundo and I pondered the question for a time, then Edmundo hazarded a guess.

'Tom Cruise,' he said.

Donald had been drinking his beer at the time and started to splutter.

'How in God's name do you arrive at Tom Cruise?' he challenged Edmundo. 'That's about the dumbest thing you've ever said!'

After first daring him to talk like that to his wife, Edmundo replied that Tom Cruise was a scientologist and so might very well be Norwegian.

This answer made even less sense to Donald, but provoked a discussion on scientology that led to a discussion of spaceships that led to an argument about whether outer space was silent or noisy.

We then returned to Tom Cruise and agreed that the best thing about his movies was that we didn't care if he made it to the end of them alive.

And then someone mentioned Katie Holmes, an actress who'd married Tom Cruise after seeing him jump up and down on Oprah Winfrey's couch one afternoon, and this led to talk of *Dawson's Creek* – the teen drama she'd starred in as a young girl – and we started to wonder what had happened to the rest of the cast.

'Were any of *them* Norwegian?' Edmundo asked.

'No!' Donald replied. 'Look, it's going to be easier if I just tell you...

'The most famous Norwegian actor is – wait for it... Harrison Fjord! Get it?'

I groaned, as I knew I was supposed to, but Edmundo said there was no such actor and that Tom Cruise was a better answer.

'Okay, forget that one and listen to this,' Donald said, a hint of exasperation creeping into his voice.

He then told us about a girl he'd known in South Africa who'd grown up in Natal.

'She loved living there,' he said, 'and she didn't like the idea of living anywhere else. But she fell in love with a man who lived in Cape Town, and after they married she had to move to that city. She didn't like living there, though, and for the next nine months she suffered from post-natal depression.'

Donald then burst out laughing. 'Now that's a good one: *Natal*, post-*natal*. Ha!'

I could certainly appreciate Donald's play on words, but it was a joke ill-judged for a man who struggled with basic English.

'I do not get it,' Edmundo said. 'It is just as stupid as your first joke. But tell me, my friend,' he said, continuing to address Donald, 'do you find that the skin on your body is loosening these days, as if slipping from the bone? Some mornings, I feel as though I should ask Nelly to iron my arms before I leave for work…'

As I said, 'nothing in particular' was as good a summation as any for the things we talked about.

But then, the week I had a new television delivered, we started to incorporate the *Judge Judy Show* into our evenings.

The new television was the same make as my previous set – a Bang & Olufsen – but this particular model had a large flat screen and inbuilt Freeview channels. Edmundo and Donald were impressed with my purchase and asked for a demonstration. Unlike my earlier televisions that had sprung to life immediately, this one had to undergo a series of internal steps before the picture appeared and I warned them to be patient. After thirty-seven seconds – according to

Edmundo's watch – the black screen parted like curtains and Huw Edwards, one of my favourite newsreaders, came into view.

'It is like he is in the room with us!' Edmundo said.

Donald agreed, but having already watched the day's news suggested we change to another programme and recommended CBS Reality on channel 66. Within seconds we were sitting in the courtroom of Judge Judith Sheindlin, and from that day onwards, from six until seven, we joined her there every week.

Edmundo and I were unfamiliar with the show, but Donald had been a fan for years and was happy to explain the format.

Judge Judy, he told us, had been a family court judge in Manhattan, where she'd gained a reputation for toughness. She now presided over small-claims cases in a television studio and could award damages of up to $5,000. The litigants were usually estranged lovers, quarrelling neighbours or friends and family members who'd fallen out with each other; and the lawsuits mostly concerned unpaid personal loans, breaches of contract, damage to property and personal injury.

The case of the moment was one of assault, brought by a middle-aged woman against an ex-boyfriend whose head was shaped like a large pumpkin and shaved to the skull. She was suing him for pain and suffering and lost wages, and claiming damages to the tune of $4,500. The defendant denied these charges and maintained that his actions had been in self-defence, an argument that was supported by a police report indicating that the plaintiff had been as drunk and aggressive as him that evening.

Once Judge Judy had dismissed this part of her claim as a mutual argument that had got out of hand, she had little hesitation in dismissing the plaintiff's further claim for lost wages, especially when it emerged that she'd gone to Disneyland during her time of incapacitation.

The cases that followed involved a father suing a son for the balance on a truck that the son claimed to have been a gift (judgement in favour of the plaintiff); a woman suing her ex-fiancé for his share of living expenses while they'd been together and him counter-suing for the return of his property (judgement in favour of the defendant); and a more convoluted case that involved a stolen purse and an insurance claim and one that so infuriated the judge that she awarded the plaintiff the full $5,000 and wished it could have been more.

The cases in themselves didn't necessarily add up to good television, but Judge Judy certainly did! She was about the same height as Ronnie Corbett but of a very different nature, and not the person to represent a company that delivered ready-made frozen meals to the doors of old people.

Judge Judy was feisty and abrasive and appeared to enjoy dragging people over hot coals. She didn't suffer fools and she didn't like liars or people who came to court dressed inappropriately: men wearing shorts and women who revealed too much cleavage. She believed that people had to take responsibility for their own actions and do the right thing. She was no-nonsense, to the point, and not afraid to ruffle feathers: if a person looked like a duck, walked like a duck and quacked like a duck, then that person *was* a duck!

'She's quite something, isn't she?' Donald said after I'd turned off the television.

Neither Edmundo nor I could disagree with him there, but Edmundo was curious to know why anyone in their right mind would want to go on television to air their dirty laundry.

'That's an easy one,' Donald replied. 'An appearance on television is likely to be the highpoint of these peoples' lives.

You and I might be embarrassed to do this but for them, well, it's as if they've hit the big time. Besides, they get paid for being on the show and the production company pays for their flights, hotels and living expenses while they're in Los Angeles, so it's like a free holiday for them.'

'Hmm,' Edmundo said thoughtfully. 'I think we should watch it again.'

And so we became avid viewers and the *Judge Judy Show* the springboard to our Thursday nights.

At the start of each case – and based on the looks of the plaintiff and defendant – we would guess the judge's ruling and wager small bets on the number of times she'd bang her fountain pen on the bench and which of her favourite phrases she'd use.

We also grew to like the court show's other main player: a bailiff who went by the name of Byrd. His full name was Petri Hawkins-Byrd and he'd been Judge Judy's bailiff in Manhattan. He was African-American, well over six feet tall and looked to weigh about seventeen stones. He was there to guard Judge Judy and to act as a gofer between her and the litigants, couriering documents and occasionally escorting an unruly witness from the courtroom. Most of the time, though, he just stood there and worked on crossword puzzles, which I suspect were of a straightforward nature because I never once saw him consult a thesaurus.

The people who came before Judge Judy were people I'd have been reluctant to invite into my home. Most of them – both men and women – had dyed hair and were heavily tattooed, and many of them had spent time in prison. The majority of them were also overweight, and the thinner ones were always unwilling to submit to a hair follicle test.

I describe these litigants not as an act of prejudice or for any purposes of judgement, but as a necessary backdrop to the surprise I experienced when I saw Daisy Lamprich standing before the judge. Daisy Lamprich stood out from these people like a sore thumb – but a sore thumb in a good way.

By this time we'd been watching the show for almost four years. We were drinking red wine that night and, as was our tradition, we raised our glasses and toasted Judge Judy when she walked into the courtroom.

'She's wearing jeans!' Donald exclaimed.

I thought it was one of his jokes, but Edmundo had also noticed.

'They are stone-washed bellbottoms,' he said. 'I wore the same trouser in Peru.'

I stepped in here and called them to order: the programme was about to start and we still had to place our bets!

Donald wagered that Judge Judy would bang her fountain pen on the bench three times and use the phrase *God gave you two ears and one mouth for a reason*.

Edmundo said that she wouldn't bang her pen at all, but would use the phrase *I got you ten ways from Sunday*.

I plumped for five bangs of her pen and the phrase *Where did you think you were coming today – the beach?*

And then the two litigants entered the courtroom and we had to judge the likely winner. Usually we agreed on the outcomes, but this time Donald and Edmundo sided with the plaintiff and I opted for the defendant, a beautiful young girl who looked as if she'd rather be somewhere else.

Once Judge Judy was sitting in her chair and the spectators in the courtroom had taken theirs, Byrd announced the number of the case and the names of the litigants, then handed her the case file. He then picked up his clipboard and started work on the day's crossword.

The plaintiff was a man in his early thirties called Clay Miller. He was tall and broad shouldered, blue-eyed and blond, and he was dressed in a yellow polo shirt and faded jeans. He had a self-deprecating manner and an easy smile, and I could understand why Donald and Edmundo had decided in his favour.

Clay was suing his ex-girlfriend, a girl called Daisy Lamprich, for the cost of a surfboard and the return of furniture, and he'd brought his friend Brian along for company. Daisy claimed that both the surfboard and the furniture had been gifts, and she was countersuing Clay for back rent and damage to her car. She'd come to court alone, and it seemed only right that I sit with her that evening.

Daisy Lamprich was a picture of grace and quiet dignity. She had long black hair and the darkest brown eyes and a complexion that was as white and smooth as alabaster. Her lips were full and her voice was husky, and I found the slight protrusion of her front teeth endearing. She was wearing a double-breasted V-neck black dress that day, sleeveless and lapelled, and I was sure that Judge Judy would be impressed by her appearance. The screen caption described her as a twenty-five-year-old bartender, and I could imagine her being very popular with her customers and making a lot of tips. Whether she'd earn enough in gratuities to repay Clay for the surfboard I didn't know, so I crossed my fingers and hoped for the best.

Judge Judy first asked Clay about the surfboard and quickly decided that it had been a gift: he'd *given* her the board, Daisy had *thanked* him for it, and there had been no anticipation of repayment. Strike one for Daisy!

Next, she questioned him about the furniture: what was his furniture doing in Daisy's apartment? Clay explained that he'd moved in with Daisy shortly after they'd met, and because her furniture had smelled of cat urine he'd replaced it out of his own pocket and donated hers to a homeless shelter. He'd intended taking the furniture with him when he'd left the apartment, but because Daisy had thrown him out so suddenly (March 13th he rued), he'd had no place to take it. Now that he did have a place, he was constrained from taking the furniture because Daisy had a restraining order against him.

The judge turned to Daisy, who'd been rolling her eyes through much of Clay's testimony, and asked for her version of the story. She told the judge that the furniture, bought by Clay in November, had been an early Christmas present, and she had a letter from Clay stating that it was hers to keep.

Judge Judy again ruled in her favour – strike two for Daisy – but took issue with Daisy's interpretation of the phrase 'almost everything' in Clay's letter. Almost everything didn't mean *everything*, Judge Judy said, and she would have to return the property he'd brought into the relationship, namely his computer, stereo speakers and a big screen television. As the restraining order – granted to Daisy after Clay had turned up drunk at her apartment one morning – precluded him from collecting it in person, the judge arranged for Brian to retrieve it – and within five days!

So far things had gone well for Daisy, and I had no reason to believe that her countersuit for back rent ($2,100) and car damages ($2,000) would be any less successful. She told the judge that Clay had lived with her for seven months but had only paid August's rent.

'Forget it!' Judge Judy snapped. 'You should have asked for it at the time! Now move on to the car.'

Daisy tried to protest, but the judge cut her short and banged her pen on the bench: 'Car!'

I felt for Daisy at that moment, and I swallowed hard. This was a blatant denial of justice, and it was clear to me, if not to Edmundo and Donald, that Judge Judy was penalising Daisy for her height and youthful good looks.

Daisy gathered herself – heroically so, in my opinion – and proceeded to describe how Clay had keyed her car shortly after she'd thrown him out. To his credit, Clay admitted his wrongdoing, but excused his behaviour on the grounds that he'd been trashed on painkillers at the time. He then claimed to have already paid Daisy the money through intermediaries: $1,000 via her father and another $1,000 via a delivery man, whose name and telephone number he was able to provide.

Daisy said that she'd refused the money, but here Judge Judy came down on her hard, demanding to know why she was asking for the money now if she hadn't wanted it then. Far too hastily, in my view, the judge came to the decision that Daisy *had* received the money and instead of fixing her car with it she'd chosen to pay bills.

Judge Judy then excused both parties from the courtroom and stepped out for her lunch, which that day, she told everyone, was Mexican food.

At seven o'clock I turned off the television and Donald asked me the scores. It was the first time I hadn't kept track of her fountain pen and phrases, and I had to apologise for the oversight.

'I'm afraid I got distracted,' I said. 'I think we've just witnessed a miscarriage of justice.'

Donald thought I was referring to the father who'd refused to pay the balance on a motorcycle his ex-wife had bought their son, but I shook my head and told him it was more serious than that: a young woman had just been denied $2,100 of rightful back rent!

'Are you talking about that surfboard woman?' Edmundo asked.

'I am,' I said, 'but that surfboard woman has a name, Edmundo, and I'd ask you to respect that.'

Edmundo looked at Donald and then Donald looked at me:

'Since when have we been expected to remember the *names* of litigants?' Donald asked.

We spent more time discussing *Miller v Lamprich* than any previous case. Nine times out of ten we agreed with Judge Judy's rulings, but occasionally felt that she ignored the spirit of a case for the sake of its legality, which – unfortunately – was what she was obligated to do. But in this case, and in my opinion, she'd allowed her prejudices – which we usually shared – to blind her to the truth.

Judge Judy was prickly about many things but especially her height and appearance, and I'd sensed for some time that she longed to be taller and better looking. To have had Daisy standing before her, a beautiful young girl with her own apartment and a brand-new surfboard, must have been to her what a red rag is to a bull. She'd have been reminded of the life she'd never lived, a life denied her by her looks and stature, and it was envy – plain and simple envy – that had caused her to rule against Daisy that day.

'No, you have it wrong there, Rod,' Donald said. 'I'm not disagreeing with you that Daisy's a good-looking girl, but the facts speak for themselves. Clay had already paid for the damage to her car and she was wrong to try to make him pay for it again.'

I suggested to Donald that the probable reason for Daisy bringing the counterclaim was to obviate any potential losses she might have suffered if the judge had compensated Clay for the surfboard and put her in the position of having to buy new furniture.

Here Edmundo stepped in and expressed surprise that any person would spend $1,000 on a plank of wood – which was his description of a surfboard. He then criticised Daisy for her choice of pet:

'You cannot trust anyone who has a cat. Judge Judy owns a dog.'

If I didn't have enough reason already to believe that Judge Judy had been prejudiced against Daisy, then Edmundo had supplied yet another piece of evidence: Judge Judy was a dog lover and Daisy loved cats. It was surprising the two of them had managed to remain in the same courtroom for as long as they had! But I moved the conversation on.

'It's not so much the car and the surfboard that concern me – it's the back rent. Clay lived with Daisy for seven months but only paid one month's rent. He was working during this time and he bought two trucks, so why wasn't he paying her rent?'

'Daisy forgave it,' Donald said. 'She slept with him, and in Judge Judy's book that's the same thing as forgiving a debt. Daisy shouldn't have allowed him to move in as quickly as she did.

'Anyway, you have to see the case in the round, Rod. Daisy didn't lose anything, and all Clay got back were his personal belongings.'

'And if you think Judge Judy was hard on Daisy, then it is nothing as hard as she was on poor Clay,' Edmundo said. 'I felt sorry for the man.'

Edmundo had a point. Judge Judy had expressed no surprise at all that Daisy had kicked Clay out of the apartment, and had even commented that she could think of several reasons why this should have happened.

'Stop twitching, will you!' she'd shouted at him. 'Are you on some kind of medication?'

Clay had said that he wasn't and had just drunk a lot of coffee that morning, but the judge wouldn't drop the subject and towards the end of the case she shouted at him again and started to lecture him:

'You've got to stop taking whatever stuff it is you're taking because it's making you nervous and you're in danger of spinning round the room! If you harnessed your energy you could power Canada!'

'I liked Clay, too,' Donald added. 'He struck me as being a good-natured person, the kind you could go for a drink with after work and have a laugh. And Daisy must have seen some good in him at one time.'

There we agreed to disagree, but Edmundo had the last word on the subject.

'Anyway, she is too young for you,' he laughed.

*

After Donald and Edmundo had left for home that night, I set the Humax to record the following morning's episodes of the *Judge Judy Show*, which were a repeat of the ones we'd just watched. For reasons I was reluctant to admit to myself – though ones I suspected that Edmundo had already identified – I needed to see Daisy again.

I rose early the next morning and I was sitting in the kitchen when Nelly let herself into the house. Friday isn't her usual day, but the previous day – the day she should have been here – she'd had to go to a funeral.

'I'm surprised to see you up and about so early, Rod,' she said. 'Do you have plans for the day?'

I shook my head no, and asked her to join me for a coffee before she started her chores: there was something I wanted to ask her.

'Fire away, Rod,' she said, once she had a cup of coffee in her hand. 'What is it you want to know?'

'Well, it might sound an odd thing to ask, Nelly, but I was wondering if you believe in predestination.'

'Not when it comes to number nineteen buses, I don't! I got stranded on the King's Road yesterday – and not for the first time.'

It appeared that Nelly had said about as much on the subject as she was intending to say, and I had to press her a little harder.

'I wasn't specifically thinking of London Transport, Nelly, though I do share your concerns about that bus route. No, I was wondering, well, because of your background in the church I suppose, if you believed that everything in life is predetermined and that what happens to a person is decided ahead of time by God or, well, umm, something else, something like fate, perhaps.'

'You're asking the wrong person, Rod. I joined the convent because I loved Jesus and not because I liked reading books on theology. But if you're asking me if I think it was God's design for the peasants in Peru to live lives of abject misery, then the answer is no.

'Why are you asking me this, anyway?'

I told her there was no specific reason, only that the thought had occurred to me when I'd gone to the toilet that night.

Nelly gave me a strange look.

'You're not actually suggesting that it was God's plan for you to go to the toilet in the middle of the night, are you, because if you are, then He also planned for Edmundo to do the same thing.'

I smiled when she said this, but I wasn't sure if she was joking or not. I apologised for the carelessness of my words, and told her that my visit to the toilet had been only the *occasion* for the thought. I certainly didn't associate fate with the humdrum of life – only its big events.

Nelly said that if I believed in destiny then I couldn't pick and choose which events it affected – it was either all or nothing. She then said that if I was hoping to make sense of life, I would do better by focusing on the concept of free will and the relationship between cause and effect.

'No one forced wine down your throats last night: you and Edmundo drank it of your own free will. And because you drank so much, both of you had to get up in the middle of the night and go to the toilet. It's as simple as that, Rod. Don't try and complicate life.'

And with that piece of advice Nelly went to the sink and rinsed her mug under the tap and placed it in the dishwasher. I'd been hoping that Nelly, as an ex-nun, might have been more helpful on the subject of fate, and certainly taken a more Christian interest in my predicament. It was clear that I would have to decide things for myself, and there was no better place to do this than the basement. I always do my best thinking when I'm surrounded by books.

I can't remember the exact time I first wondered about fate, but it was a thought that had been with me for some time, and a concept that Avril had embraced wholeheartedly. One event in life led to a sequence of other events in life, and it was a chain reaction that was outside the control of a person and guided by an external force.

If my parents hadn't died when they did, for instance, I

would have probably remained at Pinkney Industries and never met Harriet Stowell. And if I'd never worked at the gallery, I would have never met or fallen in love with Avril. And if Harriet hadn't fallen down the stairs and died when she did, I would have remained at the gallery and never met Nelly, Edmundo and Donald.

It was the strange progression of events from the time I'd hired Nelly that exercised my mind most, though. If not for her – and the fact that I'd received an unsolicited letter from the dentist that had unwittingly led me to block the toilet with dental floss – I would have never met Edmundo. And if I hadn't met Edmundo, I would have never had the idea of transforming my cellar into a basement where Boiko unearthed Donald. And if not for Donald, and his suggestion that we watch the *Judge Judy Show* on a Thursday night, I would have never set eyes on Daisy Lamprich. It seemed as if my whole life had been a series of inexorable occurrences leading to her.

I waited until Nelly had left the house and then I went to the lounge and watched the recording of Daisy's episode – not once but countless times, and late into the evening.

Daisy Lamprich was the same exquisite girl I remembered from the previous night; the same innocent who'd stood in the courtroom alone, dragged there by a person once trusted and who now demanded a pound of her perfect flesh. But she'd fought his mercenary advances, demanded her rightful dues, and left the courtroom with her dignity intact and her head held high – even if without the back rent she'd claimed. Daisy Lamprich was an example to us all and the most beautiful woman I'd ever laid eyes on!

That night I fell in love for what I believed would be the last time in my life. Daisy, I decided, was my destined soulmate.

As much as I owed our meeting to CBS Reality and the worldwide syndication of its shows, I believed that it had been fate, rather than serendipity, that had brought the two of us together. Daisy and I lived on different continents, were divided by geography and time zones and distanced by some 5,437 miles and, if anything, should have been destined *not* to meet. And yet, against all odds, we had met.

And, in that her particular episode of the *Judge Judy Show* had been recorded in 2006, we'd also met thirteen years after the event – which certainly put paid to Edmundo's comment that Daisy was too young for me. And even if Daisy had remained twenty-five and not become the thirty-eight-year-old woman she is today, I still wouldn't have been dissuaded from pursuing her.

It's a cliché to say that age is just a number, but it's a cliché that rings true and one that would have occurred to me even if it hadn't occurred to some other person first. And it's not as if Edmundo, Donald and *I* are of the same generation: Edmundo is in his sixties and Donald turned seventy this year. No, where love and friendships are concerned, age gaps are an irrelevance. And besides, the age difference between Daisy and me was the least of my problems.

I was very much aware that I'd lost my heart to a televisual image of Daisy – however clear the picture on a Bang & Olufsen is – and not Daisy in the flesh. I was also conscious of the fact that I was in danger of breaking my own golden rule and falling in love with a person on the grounds of appearance rather than character. But in respect to these points, and regardless of how odd this might sound, I intuitively knew that I *had* met the inner Daisy and knew her as well as I knew myself. I was in love with Daisy Lamprich for the *right* reasons!

The biggest fly in the ointment, though, was that although I'd met her – however virtually – Daisy had no idea who I was or that I even existed. Similarly, I had no idea of her present-day circumstances: where she lived, if she was single or married, alive or – God forbid – dead. Needless to say, these were things I would have to uncover before I bought a plane ticket and went searching for her in a country that I'd sworn never to set foot in again.

And, if it turned out that Daisy was alive and unattached and we did meet – what then? Well, if things went as well as I imagined they would, Daisy and I would marry and live together happily ever after. If, however, such an outcome proved impossible – for reasons I would undoubtedly respect – then I would simply hand Daisy a sealed envelope with a short note inside:

This is the money Clay Miller owed you for back rent: $2,100.

Continuation 6

The Parable of the Winnebago and the Intercession of Mr Stenger

The firm of solicitors I use is called Grant, Burdett and Hargrave, and the company is known colloquially as GBH. In my opinion, the acronym doesn't suit an establishment that serves to better the lives of others, but the partners don't seem to mind. They probably think the abbreviation makes them stand out from the crowd, and doubtless Ric would agree with them. Their offices are in Clerkenwell, and I was first introduced to them by Harriet Stowell after I'd complained to her about my own solicitors.

I say my *own* solicitors but they were in fact my father's, and I had the impression they viewed me more as an unrightful heir than a valued new client. Whenever I went to their offices, the man who looked after my affairs – and the one to have looked after my father's – would stare at me from behind his desk and shake his head from side to side.

'You're not your father, are you, Herod?' he'd say, obviously disappointed by this fact.

He'd then regale me with stories about my father, the lunches they'd had together and the bars they'd drunk dry on an evening and then let out a deep sigh, as if saddened by the fact that my father was no longer alive and I was all that remained of him.

I never warmed to Mr Jeffries and I always felt uncomfortable when we met. I'm not saying that he was a bad person – I didn't know him well enough to make this judgement – but if I'd learned he was wanted for war crimes in another country, it also wouldn't have surprised me.

My present solicitor, Graham Simpson, is fortunately nothing like Mr Jeffries, and I was looking forward to discussing the matter of Daisy with him once he returned from his holiday. If anyone could point me in the right direction, it would be Graham.

The offices of Grant, Burdett and Hargrave – I refuse to refer to them by their acronym – are situated in St John's Lane, and though the surrounding area has been taken over by the modish – the old industrial buildings converted into luxury flats, designer offices and trendy restaurants – the company remains reassuringly stolid. Graham, I'm pleased to say, is without a trace of charisma and has a comfortingly grey personality. He also has an office on the ground floor, which again suits me.

It had been three weeks since I'd seen Daisy on the television, and my feelings for her were as strong now – in Graham's office – as they had been then.

'I hope you don't mind me asking this, Rod, but is this the first time you've fallen in love with someone on television? I mean, it's not something you're in the habit of doing, is it?'

I assured Graham that this was the first and only time it had happened, but for the sake of full disclosure mentioned that I had once developed a crush on a late-night presenter of Sky News.

'But that's all it was, Graham – a crush. I never once considered introducing myself to her.'

'But you want to introduce yourself to Daisy,' Graham said.

'I do. I know it sounds strange, but I feel as if there's a connection between us – even though Daisy isn't aware of this. The problem, though, is that I don't know her circumstances, or even her whereabouts for that matter, and I don't want to act hastily and make a fool of myself. If Daisy is married, and happy in that marriage, then my interest in her will end immediately. I'm an honourable man, Graham, and you know this.'

Graham said that he did know this and had, on occasion, even singled me out as a person worthy of imitation.

'What I suggest we do then, Rod, is hire a private investigator licensed to work in the United States. I'm not sure if the operatives we use in this country are allowed to practise there, but I can soon find out. It should take no more than an hour.'

Rather than wait in the vestibule and sit on a hard leather chair that was easier to slip out of than remain comfortably in, I popped over the road and whiled away the time in a small cafe. I ordered a large black Americano and a blueberry muffin, and took the tray to a window table. Although I'd have preferred to have been served, I was relieved, after my only other experience of dining in Clerkenwell, that I hadn't been asked to grind the coffee beans and bake the muffin myself.

I'd been with Lorna at the time, and she'd invited me to meet her new husband-to-be – and also the sister of her new husband-to-be – in a Mongolian restaurant, where customers were expected to cook their own meat on a large open grill rather than remain seated and have it served to them. It was a passing fad that quickly lost vogue, but on the night, and in its favour, it gave me an excuse to periodically leave the table and escape her and her companions' company. Although I have a soft spot for Lorna, I've never been able to understand her taste in men or, for that matter, her friends. She's a bright woman, but when it comes to people, she has very little quality control.

Although younger than me, Lorna had already been divorced twice at this time of her life, and the man sitting next to her, evidently three times. His name was Colin and he flew planes that carried machinery and engineering parts to places in Africa and the Middle East. He had an easy manner, but he was overly friendly for a first meeting and his laugh was too ready. He struck me as a person who spoke from a script and one that he'd used a thousand times before. His repertoire was one of set pieces and old jokes, and he peppered his speech with worn phrases like: *quickly moving on, follow that* and *don't go there*. And he would never answer a question with a simple yes, but with: *I am indeed, I certainly am* or *absolutely*. For Lorna's sake I wanted to like Colin, but as the evening progressed it became increasingly difficult.

And Colin's sister, Diana, was no better company, even though her conversation was more off the cuff. She never mentioned if she'd been married herself, but I suspected from her manner that she hadn't. She was, I'm sorry to say, a mean-spirited woman with nothing good to say about anyone or anything, and her favourite word was phallic: Big Ben was phallic, Nelson's Column was phallic, and Battersea Power Station was big-time phallic.

Every time she said this word, Colin would laugh like a horse.

'For a midget she's quite something, isn't she?' he said.

I think Colin was joking when he described his sister

as a midget, but there was no doubting that she was small. She was, in fact, the smallest woman I'd ever met and it was difficult to believe that she'd reached her intended height. Even if she hadn't been sitting on a cushion to bring her body to the height of the table, her feet still wouldn't have touched the floor, and from a distance it must have looked as if we were dining with a precocious child.

And because she was such a small woman, she also had small features and struggled to fit the large amounts of food she heaped on her fork into her tight, lipless mouth. Sensing her difficulty, and wondering if the precarious nature of the cushion was somehow affecting her cutlery skills, I offered to cut her food into smaller pieces. The gesture was well intended – as much for the tablecloth as for her – but she gave me a look of such malice that for one awful moment – and from the way she gripped the handle of her knife – I thought she was going to stab me.

'Just fuck off and mind your own business, will you,' she said.

Fortunately, in this restaurant, I could do this without drawing attention to myself.

Colin, I'm glad to say, was the one that got away, and he and Lorna never did marry. Just like his sister, he too turned out to be 'quite something'.

Although Lorna and Colin fixed a date for their wedding, the ceremony had to be called off at the last moment when Colin's third divorce hadn't finalised in time. The honeymoon, however, which had already been paid for, went ahead, and they spent two romantic weeks holidaying in the Seychelles. It was on their return to England that things went sour.

Lorna moved into Colin's loft conversion, not far from the Mongolian restaurant, and this new proximity appeared to abate Colin's feelings for her. I can't remember the exact time it happened – if it was weeks or months after they'd moved in together – only that Colin phoned her from Addis Ababa one night and told her that their relationship was over and that she had two weeks to vacate the apartment.

Lorna, disbelieving that Colin could have expressed such sentiments at a distance and not to her face, wondered if she'd somehow misunderstood his words over such a crackling line and for the next three days did nothing and waited for him to return. And then, on the morning of the fourth day, there was a knock on the door. When Lorna looked through the peephole and saw no one there she became hopeful and wondered if a bouquet of flowers had been left on the doormat with an accompanying note of apology from Colin. Consequently, when she opened the door and found Diana standing there, she was more than disappointed.

'Colin wants his key back,' Diana had said.

And so that, as the saying goes, was that.

It's funny the things you remember when you're drinking coffee and eating a blueberry muffin.

I was about to order another coffee when my phone rang, and for a split second I thought it was Colin calling me.

'Whenever you're ready, Rod,' Graham said.

I left the cafe and returned to his office.

'Everyone I've spoken to recommends the Turnipseed Agency. It has offices in all the major cities, but it's headquartered in New York and I think we should start there.'

Graham was staring at his computer screen while he told me this, scrolling down the main page of the company's website and clicking on relevant links.

'Hmm, this is proving more difficult than I thought. I

can find the company's history and address, but not a list of contacts.'

'Don't worry about that, Graham,' I said. 'Just give me the address and I'll write to Mr Turnipseed himself. It's always best to deal with the top man.'

'I'm afraid that's impossible, Rod. It says here that Mr Turnipseed died in 1910, but it doesn't say anything about who runs the company now. Hang on a minute, here it is – it's been staring me in the face the whole time.

'The person you need to contact is John Stenger and his email address is…'

I made a note of the address, but I told Graham that I'd prefer to contact Mr Stenger by letter in the first instance. It would give my enquiry a greater air of formality and allow me to use my headed notepaper.

*

Although Graham had offered to initiate proceedings with the Turnipseed Agency, assuring me that Mr Stenger would be more interested in the health of my bank balance than any motives I might have for finding Daisy, it was something I preferred to do for myself. Irrespective of Graham's judgement, I wanted Mr Stenger to invest in me as a person rather than just another faceless client – which, at this distance, I certainly was – and for him to know that my motives for finding Daisy were pure and my intentions honourable. It wasn't an easy letter to write and it took me the best part of two days, but I was happy with the final draft.

Dear Mr Stenger:

My full name is Herod S Pinkney and I live in a mortgage-free, four-storey house in the city of London. I am 48 years of age, independently wealthy and a citizen of good standing. I am also a non-smoker. I have, in the past, contributed to the Conservative Party, and I recently donated a large sum to Sightsavers.

I am trying to locate the whereabouts of a woman called Daisy Lamprich, who appeared on the Judge Judy Show in 2006 (case #242 Miller v Lamprich). She owned a surfboard at the time and so I suspect she was living close to the ocean. She is now 38, and this, I'm afraid, is all I know.

A situation has arisen recently that will likely benefit Ms Lamprich, and it is of paramount importance that I locate her whereabouts and learn of her circumstances. Your services have been recommended to me by Graham Simpson, a senior partner at Grant, Burdett and Hargrave, who also commends me to others.

I am familiar with The Rockford Files and therefore appreciate that a private investigator is paid a daily rate plus expenses. The character in the above series – played by James Garner, I believe – asked for $200 a day. Is this still the going rate? If not, then please be assured that I can afford your services whatever the cost.

I am happy for you to correspond by email, and I hope you will address me as Rod, which is my given name.

I look forward to hearing from you.

I hope you are having a nice day.

Yours sincerely,
Rod

Rather than ask Nelly to post the letter, I went to the Post Office myself and arranged for it to be sent by special delivery. It was too important a communication to be placed in the hands of the ordinary mail, especially if the carriers in the United States were as unreliable as the man who delivered to my own door. Although I was on speaking terms with the postman and found him polite, he was always on his mobile phone or listening to music through earphones when I met him, and he was forever posting letters through the wrong box and dropping rubber bands on the road. He was from Newcastle, I think, and whatever the weather, he would wear short trousers and no more than a thin shirt.

When I returned to the house, I was surprised to find a small film crew milling around on the pavement, and I was obliged to warn them of my approach by beeping the horn. All eyes turned to me, and then a man called to me by name.

'Mr Pinkney, it's Ding-Dong. Is it okay if I do an interview with Channel 4 in your garden and explain the construction of the living walls?'

Ding-Dong was the man who'd originally built the walls, and I was happy to give him my permission. He apologised for turning up without an appointment, and could only surmise that the letter sent by Channel 4 had got lost in the post. In light of my existing misgivings, I could readily believe this.

Ding-Dong wasn't his real name, of course, but a moniker. I'd always assumed it had something to do with his last name being Bell, but I was told by one of the men who'd planted the walls that it was a play on the carol *Ding Dong Merrily on High*, because Ding-Dong – whose real name was Francis – was anything but merry when he was at the top of a ladder.

While the film crew was setting up the equipment, I tried to engage Ding-Dong in conversation, and remembering that he'd moved to Sweden since we'd last met, I asked him what it was like living there.

'It's no different from living in Scotland, Mr Pinkney. It's fucking cold for six months of the year and it's populated by bastards.'

He didn't elaborate on this statement, and nor did he seem interested in answering any further questions. He seemed on edge – seemingly the same edge he'd been on when first working at my house – and he no doubt wanted to save his voice for the interview and avoid the possibility of a panic attack.

I waited by the gate while the interview took place, and I was surprised by how relaxed he was in front of the camera and how often he smiled. He told the woman holding the microphone that he'd first attached a frame to the wall and then screwed a plastic backing board to it. Next, he'd added a layer of felt made from recycled clothes and inserted horizontal drip lines at intervals of two metres. He'd then added another layer of felt, and into this layer cut pockets – forty per square metre – and tucked and stapled small plants into them. Apparently he'd used thirty different types of plant, but the only ones I remember him mentioning were fuchsias, lavenders, elder flowers, junipers and agapanthus. What the other twenty-five are I have no idea, but I'm sure that Edmundo does: he's the one who trims and weeds the walls and replaces the plants that die.

Both Ding-Dong and the crew were very professional and the interview was over in less than an hour. Once the cameras had stopped rolling, Ding-Dong's smile disappeared and he returned to his old cheerless self. I offered to raise his spirits with a cup of the finest Peruvian coffee, but he declined my overture and said that he was expected at the Athenaeum Hotel. We then shook hands and he climbed into a waiting car and buckled his seatbelt. From the expression on his face, he might just as well have been strapping himself into an electric chair.

That moment, I was reminded of the day I'd first met Edmundo and told him to cheer up and that it might never happen and him replying that it already had. Ding-Dong's work brought beauty to the world, yet he appeared to see no beauty in his own. Maybe he, like Edmundo, was also the survivor of a Shining Path – however different its circumstances – and I felt sorry for him.

If only everyone in the world could be happy.

I pottered for the rest of the morning, and in the afternoon watched an episode of *Matlock*. The main character of the show is a defence attorney who practises law in Atlanta and he always wears the same white suit and eats a lot of hot dogs. I can't tell you what happened in this particular episode because I fell asleep before it ended, but you can be certain that his client was found not guilty because his clients always are. If I ever got into trouble in the United States, he'd be the kind of person I'd want defending me.

The following Thursday, Donald and Edmundo arrived shortly before six and, as usual, we watched the *Judge Judy Show* for an hour. If I'm honest, my heart was no longer in the programme – how could it have been after Judge Judy had ruled against Daisy? – and Edmundo sensed this:

'What is wrong, Señor Rod? You do not seem your old self tonight.'

I hadn't intended telling them of my decision to track Daisy down until I'd heard back from Mr Stenger, but in light of Edmundo's comment – and because it seemed churlish to keep such news from my closest friends – I decided that this was as good a time as any.

'Do you remember the episode of the *Judge Judy Show* when she ruled against a woman called Daisy Lamprich? It was about four weeks ago, and on the night you both took the side of the plaintiff – a man called Clay Miller.'

'You mean that woman with the plank?' Edmundo asked.

'It was a *surfboard*, you numbskull,' Donald said. 'Who in their right mind would litigate over a piece of wood?'

'I can think of several...'

'Gentlemen,' I said, calling them to order. 'Now that we've established who Daisy is, would you please allow me to continue? What I have to say isn't easy, and when you hear my words you might well think that I've lost my mind.'

That got their attention.

I started by confessing my feelings for Daisy, and told them about my meeting with Graham and said to them the same things I'd said to him. I then read them a duplicate of the letter I'd posted to Mr Stenger that morning and asked for their thoughts. They glanced at each other, as if silently agreeing that I *had* lost my mind, but proved remarkably supportive. I should never have doubted them.

'There is nothing wrong in what you are doing, Señor,' Edmundo said. 'The quest for love is a noble quest, and one that has led me to the door of my beloved Nelly. Donald's search, I am sad to say, was less successful, and he ended up with Lydia.'

Donald, never one to stand up for his wife, burst out laughing but then became thoughtful.

'It's all down to Daisy's circumstances, then,' he said. 'If she's single, you'll travel to America and meet her, and if not... well, that will be the end of it.'

I agreed that this was indeed the situation, and that until I heard from Mr Stenger my hands were tied.

'In that case, you'd better pray to God that Daisy isn't married, then,' he added.

'Or dead,' Edmundo said, a little too brightly. 'She might have been eaten by a shark. You need to pray to God that she is *alive!*'

Regrettably, though I didn't say it, such an avenue was no longer open to me.

*

I mentioned earlier – towards the end of continuation 2, I think – that I lost my religious faith in the same place the Bulgarian workers found Donald. Then it had been a crude basement, but by the time of my disillusionment it had become a library and a room for reflection.

Although Bishop Williams had put his arm around me on several occasions, I'd never once been tapped on the shoulder by Jesus and was without religious experience. I'd continued to watch *Songs of Praise* on a Sunday after leaving the Assembly of Christ, but I was ready to accept that any programme presented by Aled Jones was unlikely to lead me to an understanding of something that supposedly surpassed all understanding, and that if I ever wanted my faith to grow into something more than one of groundless assertion, I would have to take matters into my own hands. And so reluctantly, considering my previous experience, I returned to the source of God's wisdom and determined to read the Bible from cover to cover.

It took me four months and left me even more confused.

The Bible was held to be the word of God – written by others, but inspired by Him – and it was natural to assume that its message would be coherent. But it wasn't: some stories appeared twice, there were different versions of the same event and even the teachings were contradictory. It was also difficult to understand why God had chosen Israel to be His special people, because He was forever falling out with them and they did some really bad things – things that would have landed them in prison today or at least prompted a visit from the Social Services. What struck me most about the Bible, though, was that there was no laughter in it – not even a smile. I wanted to read about Jesus sharing a joke with people or playing a prank on His disciples, but He did neither and, if anything, He came across as a bit snippy and not the nice man I'd known in Sunday school.

Although I was pleased with myself for having read the Bible – an achievement I placed on a par with the first time I completed the *Daily Telegraph*'s cryptic crossword puzzle – I was no nearer to knowing God for having done so. Rather than doubt the effectiveness of His teaching methods, I questioned my own intellect and went in search of an explanation to the King's Road branch of Waterstones. I described the books I was looking for to an assistant there, and she was kind enough to drop what she was doing and lead me to the relevant section. I spent an hour browsing the shelves and eventually selected five books – commentaries on the Bible, Jesus and religion in general. I bought them in the hope of drawing closer to God but, in the event, they only served to drive a wedge between us.

It wasn't so much the things I learned about the Old Testament that troubled me as the circumstances of the New – I was, after all, trying to become a better Christian and not a more observant Jew – and most troubling was the suggestion that Jesus wasn't the man I'd supposed Him to be. And neither, for that matter, was Jesus the man that *He*'d supposed

Himself to be. The Jesus of the New Testament was the man *the Church* considered Him to be.

The real Jesus, I read, had never claimed to be the Messiah or the Son of God while He'd been alive, and neither had His contemporaries made these claims for Him. Similarly, there had been no mention of His miraculous birth at the time. He was, in fact, portrayed as just another itinerant preacher who travelled the country healing people and casting out demons, and was only unusual in that He didn't charge for these services. He was, however, a fierce nationalist and a vocal enemy of the status quo, and it was for this that the Romans executed Him.

In all likelihood, Jesus would have gone down in history as just another failed prophet but for one thing: He came back from the dead and started to pester people. And though people had been raised from the dead before – by Elijah and Elisha, for example – not once had anyone raised *themselves* from the dead, and it was this that puzzled people and made Jesus stand out from the resurrected crowd. For the disciples, however, the matter was more straightforward and proof positive that Jesus was the promised Messiah: Jesus had been raised from the dead by God.

And so His followers formed a club called The Way and elected James, the younger brother of Jesus, to the position of chairman and appointed Peter treasurer. They set up shop in an old Winnebago they'd purchased in Galilee and parked it close to the temple in Jerusalem and preached that Jesus was the Son of God and that He would return and the world would end in their lifetimes. The disciples had passion on their side but little knowledge of the Scriptures, and it wasn't always easy for them to convince people that the long-awaited Messiah was the man who'd just been crucified. Consequently, membership of The Way – which had been open only to Jewish people – grew slowly.

But then, one day, while the disciples were out having their hair cut and the keys had been left in the ignition, a man called Paul – who'd never known Jesus, yet still thought himself a better apostle than either James or Peter – hijacked the Winnebago and set off in the direction of the Gentiles, even though Jesus had repeatedly said that His message wasn't for them. And then, to cap it all, he unloaded all the Jewish baggage he found in the vehicle and dumped it by the wayside and started to preach his own brand of Christianity that had little to do with either Judaism or Jesus. He taught that Jesus had existed before time and that He'd died on the cross to redeem mankind of its sins and that all who accepted Him as their Saviour would enter an afterlife that was both eternal and joyful. And, if anyone told them differently – like Peter or James, for instance – then they should ignore them, because Peter and James were stupid people who talked codswallop.

Paul's brand of Christianity took off like a rocket, and as more and more people converted to Christianity, the new owners of the Winnebago gave it a full service and added tailfins, spotlights and a large spoiler. Most notable of the refinements were the four Gospels that connected Jesus to the prophecies of the Old Testament, and were intended to appeal to the same Gentile audience that Paul had targeted. And just as Paul had never known Jesus, neither did the people who continued His story, and in the absence of any records to the contrary they were free to make up any story that served their purposes.

To allow for the birth of Jesus to take place in Bethlehem, for example, and not in Galilee, which was more like Doncaster and full of slow people and not a fit place for a future king to be born, they invented a census that required Joseph and Mary to travel to the City of David, even though such a census, had it been called, would have brought the economy to its knees. And because they were appealing to a Roman audience, the writers of the Gospels put all the blame for Jesus' death on the Jews and even depicted Pilate, one of history's more unpleasant characters, as a kindly man! But however they conjured their stories for the New Testament, they were unable to escape the fact that there was no mention in the Old Testament of the promised Messiah being crucified and then rising from the dead.

No one considered this to be a problem, though, and the Winnebago rolled on and came to an eventual halt in Rome, a place as distanced from Galilee as it was possible to be. And here the Church established itself and started to invent even stranger doctrines than the ones Paul had come up with.

I couldn't envisage Jesus going along with any of this or having anything in common with the likes of the Pope or the Archbishop of Canterbury. I couldn't see Him admiring their clothes and palaces and telling them that He'd seen His career going the same way if only He'd lived long enough to find a decent tailor and save enough money for a deposit on a nice house. And He'd have talked to them in plain English and told them off for complicating His message and channelling it through a language that was unintelligible to any person without a degree in theology.

I admired Jesus, but I came to view Him as a remarkable man of history rather than the Son of God. It was a change that happened gradually rather than with the suddenness of a Damascene conversion, which, incidentally, was something that Paul never talked about when he was alive and a story that only came into vogue after his death – and written by the *same* man who'd invented the story of the census at the time of Jesus' birth!

And so, one morning, I simply woke up a non-believer, though more in the way of a shy agnostic than a bold atheist. God existed for others but not for me, and I was content to leave it at that. I don't know why, but I never felt comfortable telling Edmundo and Nelly about my loss of faith. I suppose it was because I was worried they'd think less of me and I didn't want things between us to change. I would have had no qualms telling Donald of my change of heart – a man who appeared to have difficulty differentiating Jesus from Richard Nixon – but the subject never arose and so I made no mention of it.

And so, in light of their ignorance, I'm sure that both Donald and Edmundo left for home that Thursday evening in the certain knowledge that I would be kneeling by my bed that night and praying to God for Daisy to be alive and unmarried.

Given the circumstances, it seemed wiser to rely on the intercession of Mr Stenger.

*

From the time I left the gallery and decided against employment, my days have always passed easily and often slipped by unnoticed. I've never been at a loss for something to do, and not once felt lonely. Lorna tells me that I've been blessed with an empty mind and perhaps she's right. Although I read most days and listen to music, I can also sit contentedly for hours and do nothing.

My life, however, had now entered a period of flux and I was finding it hard to settle. I couldn't stop thinking about

Daisy or wondering if Mr Stenger – who still hadn't replied to my letter – would agree to represent me. And, if Mr Stenger did accept me as a client and find Daisy, would his report be the news I was hoping to hear? It was the not knowing and the waiting that were hard to bear. Once I knew the answers to these questions I could come to terms with the situation, but in the meantime my life was in a state of limbo.

'For heaven's sake, Rod, you're like a cat on hot bricks today,' Nelly said. 'Why don't you go for a walk or something? Drive to the King's Road and treat yourself to lunch at the Bluebird.'

I didn't know if Edmundo had told Nelly about Daisy or if she was just tired of me getting under her feet that morning, but I took her advice and left the house. I had, however, no intention of patronising the Bluebird after my last visit there.

Occasionally I ate in the cafe's upstairs restaurant, but mostly I sat in the outside area and drank coffee or ordered a small snack. On the day in question I'd arrived there late morning, a time of day when most tables are open, and I was surprised to find a large area cordoned off and the few remaining tables taken. There was no obvious reason for this division, and certainly no hint of activity within the restricted zone, so I unclipped the rope and made myself comfortable at a table closest to the ones occupied. I saw no harm in doing this, and it wasn't as if I was unknown at the establishment. I was, in fact, on first name terms with several of the waiters.

Quicker than anyone had ever rushed to serve me before, however, a young man I didn't recognise came to the table and explained, without apology, that the tables in the roped-off area were reserved for the stars of *Made in Chelsea* and that filming would be starting shortly.

Made in Chelsea is a television series about a group of rich, young people who wander the streets of London bumping into each other. They ask each other about their relationships – who they're dating, who they're cheating on and suchlike – and arrange to go to parties in the country or for drinks at exclusive bars and clubs.

I was no particular fan of the programme, but I knew for a fact that there were only a handful of people in the show. Even if the whole cast climbed out of bed in time for lunch that day – which was something I doubted – there would still be tables available for bona fide customers like myself, and I made this point to the waiter.

He answered somewhat testily, as if under no obligation to provide me with further details, that the tables had been set aside for paid extras and suggested I try the restaurant. I told him that my preference was to remain outside and that I would be happy to play the role of an extra and settle for a small espresso and a croissant by way of compensation.

He smiled when I said this – or at least I think it was a smile – and said that this wouldn't be possible because I was too old for the show, and that it wouldn't help the image of *Made in Chelsea* if my mobility scooter came into shot.

I didn't like the young man's attitude and I took offence at his ageist comments.

'Do you know who I am?' I asked.

He said that he didn't, and in that moment I realised that I didn't know who I was either, because I've always squirmed when I've heard other people ask that same question.

There was a slight pause in the conversation, and then he threatened to call the manager if I didn't leave.

It seemed pointless to waste more breath on the man, and so I rose from the table and climbed back on my scooter. I told him, in parting, that the Bluebird had just lost one of its best customers and that I would be writing a letter of complaint to the owner. He then gave me a card with the name and address of the restaurant on it and made a point of telling me that his name was Marc with a 'c', should I wish to mention him in my communiqué. He then added insult to injury by wishing me a nice day.

And so, rather than take Nelly's advice and journey to the King's Road that morning, I decided instead to drive along the Embankment in the direction of the Tate Modern and view the progress being made in transforming Battersea Power Station into a complex of luxury apartments, shops and restaurants. I've always respected creative people and none more so than the architects and engineers who transform skylines and build edifices of monumental proportion. If I had their job I wouldn't know where to start or how to finish, but I derive enjoyment from watching their projects take shape.

Although people have always referred to Battersea Power Station as if it were a single entity, it is in fact two: one power station being completed in the 1930s and the second in the 1950s. I know this only because my father told me. We'd been on one of our forced walks together – on the north side of the river, where the view of the station was unimpeded – and he'd boasted that Battersea Power Station was the largest brick building in Europe and large enough to shelter both St Paul's Cathedral and Trafalgar Square if they ever decided to go into hiding. It was now the biggest building site in Europe, and the highlight of a mile-long development that stretched from Vauxhall to Chelsea Bridge. It was, in the words of the developer, London's Newest Neighbourhood.

It was a warm day and I was wearing a light seersucker jacket that I'd recently bought at Harvey Nichols after failing to find a pair of socks, and a pair of dark linen trousers that

I'd had for some time. I was also sporting one of my favourite cravats made from plain red cotton.

Rather than drive down the adjacent mews, which is cobbled and not easy to negotiate on a scooter, I'd stuck to the pavements and entered Battersea Park through Sun Gate. I followed the pathway down to the river and drove along the Embankment as far as Chelsea Bridge, where I crossed the road, and then continued on the Embankment to the construction site.

From a vantage point, I could see a deep excavation and unwanted rubble being tipped into a waiting barge, but little of the actual construction further afield. In the hope of getting a closer look, I followed a passageway running along the fenced-off site, away from the river and adjacent to a high-end grocery store and completed office building. I was about to go further when I was approached by a security guard wearing a yellow hi-vis vest. He asked me my business, but before I could answer him he was joined by another guard who explained that I was Mr Pinkney and probably looking for a job.

'You had your lunch yet, Rod?' Clarence asked.

'I haven't,' I said, more than a little surprised to see him here.

'Okay, give me ten minutes and I'll join you.'

I'd known that Clarence worked in security, but I'd wrongly assumed that he was a bouncer who stood at the doors of clubs and kept people out. He was a big man, well over six feet tall, and his appearance lent itself to such a position. He lived in the same block of flats as Edmundo, and Nelly sat for his children when he and his wife went out for an evening. He also played a steel pan drum and occasionally joined Edmundo and Donald in my basement when they rehearsed.

'Do you know how weird it is to walk alongside a man riding a mobility scooter when you know that man has a functioning pair of legs? People are going to be thinking I'm your carer or doing community service or something. Man, if my grandparents could see this, they'd be turning.'

Clarence was of Jamaican descent, and he was as proud of the fact that his grandparents had sailed to England on the *Windrush* as any descendant of the *Mayflower* living in America. He joked that they'd immigrated to Britain 'to scare the shit out of whiteys and send them spinning like tops', but after careful consideration had decided to give them a break and make do with the menial jobs no one else wanted.

'Not me, though, man. I got a job pushing people around. Ha!'

Clarence, who had left his helmet and yellow vest at the site, led me back in the direction of Chelsea Bridge to a restaurant that was situated below a railway arch. It was a large vaulted space and at this time of the day almost empty. The restaurant described itself as an Italian pizzeria without the nonsense, and was owned by a Danish company that had originated in the meatpacking district of Copenhagen. Its pizzas, the menu said – seemingly contradicting the earlier statement – were made from organic sourdough and Italian seawater.

'It's one of these new-fangled artisan joints and pretentious as hell, Rod, but the food's good,' Clarence said, scanning the menu. 'I'd recommend the porcella.'

'Well, if the porcella's good enough for a man your size, then it's certainly good enough for me,' I said. 'Would you like to share a small bottle of wine?'

'I'd love to, man, but it's the wrong time of day for me. I work for a living, remember, and you're driving, in case you've forgotten.'

Clarence attended the Assembly of Christ on a Sunday and was prone to moralising. He remembered me from my own attendance there, the time Edmundo introduced us, and I was embarrassed that I didn't recall him.

'No reason why you should, Mr Pinkney,' he'd said at the time. 'I only recognise you because you were the only white man there. *Everyone* knew who you were, and there's still some who ask after you. You should pay us a visit one Sunday and let people know you're alive.'

I mentioned the hardness of the pews and *Songs of Praise*, and then told him about a similar invitation I'd had from a dentist that had led me to meeting Edmundo.

A waiter came to the table and introduced himself. He asked if we'd like still or sparkling water and Clarence told him that we'd stick to tap water and spend our hard-earned money on the food. The waiter, whose name was Nick, laughed when Clarence said this. He then took our order for porcella pizzas and Diet Cokes and left with a nice smile on his face.

I told Clarence about my experience at the Bluebird and commented that the waiter there could take lessons from Nick. Clarence agreed that there was no substitution for politeness, and he considered this quality the greatest weapon in his arsenal when he was dealing with unruly people.

'You treat them well and they'll treat you well. And if they don't, well, that's another story, and one that usually takes them to the hospital.'

I asked him then about his wife and children, whose names I couldn't remember, and he replied that Tyanna, who I presumed to be his wife, had just started a new job in a department store on Oxford Street and that Glenmore and Alyssa, by default his children, were doing well in school.

'It's the boy who's got the real smarts,' Clarence said,

tapping a finger against the side of his head. 'Reads something and just stores it away, comes to him easy. Alyssa, she has to work hard to understand things, but it's her that deserves the praise. A father shouldn't take sides when it comes to his kids, but it's her I'm rooting for. Glenmore can stand on his own two feet and don't need any encouragement from his dad, and I sure as hell don't want him following in my footsteps. Security's a good job for a man with no qualifications, but I want more for him, Alyssa too.'

Clarence was easy company and did most of the talking, which I liked. I'm more of a listener than a conversationalist and I usually have little to say. I couldn't talk to Clarence about my family or what I did for a living, because I didn't have a family or need a living. But one thing I did have was money, and when the waiter came to the table with the bill I immediately picked it up.

'This is on me, Clarence,' I said, 'and I don't want to hear any argument. I've enjoyed our lunch together and it's my treat.'

I signalled to Nick that I was ready to settle the bill, and he came back to the table holding one of those machines that reads credit cards.

I always make a point of asking waiters if the gratuity goes to them or to the restaurant before adding it to the total on a credit card, and when Nick said that it would go to him but thanked me for asking, I took the machine and punched in a generous tip.

I noticed Nick looking a bit concerned when he read the amount, but I told him not to worry because I was good for the money and that he deserved every penny.

'All five of them?' he asked. 'I haven't upset you in some way, have I?'

I had no idea what he meant by this. The meal had come to just short of £30 and I'd given him a tip of £5. Clarence glanced at the receipt on the tray and burst out laughing.

'What century you living in, man? You gave the poor guy 5p! Ha!'

I took the receipt and looked at it carefully, but it was a few seconds before the penny – or rather the five pennies – dropped. To say the least I was embarrassed by such a stupid mistake and I quickly placed a ten pound note on the tray and apologised to Nick.

Outside the restaurant Clarence was still laughing.

'Wait till I tell Edmundo about this, man. I'm going to dine out on this story. I just hope to God you'll be more generous when you hear us play Battersea Square. Ha!'

I returned home in a much better frame of mind than when I'd left. Lunch with Clarence had been a welcome distraction and the restaurant, I decided, was a perfect substitute for the Bluebird. After the mix-up over the tip had been settled to Nick's advantage, I knew I would be welcome to return there anytime, and Nick had assured me that there would be little chance of the restaurant closing its doors to honest customers for the sake of a television programme that aired on a small channel like E4.

Nelly was gone by the time I returned home, but had left a note to say that the Danters, who had recently moved into the house opposite, had invited me to an informal drinks party. I made a note of the date in my diary and then went to the basement and turned on the computer.

I had three new messages: one from Bang & Olufsen informing me about a new sound system I might be interested in; another from Amazon suggesting that because I'd previously bought a book from them I might like to buy another; and finally – and the one I'd been hoping for – an email from Mr Stenger to say that he'd be happy to represent me and that he *would* find Daisy Lamprich!

I was cock-a-hoop when I read his message, and that evening I went to the Lansdowne for a celebratory drink and to share the news with Ric.

'I told you there was a book in this, Rod, and a book that could well capture the nation's imagination,' he'd said. 'I used to be a literary agent and I know these things. I have the instincts...'

Continuation 7

Keeping Busy in the Time of an Interregnum

I've had to rewrite the last paragraph of continuation 6, because when I reviewed it this morning I discovered a mistake. Originally I'd written: *I was cock-a-hoop when I read his message and doubted the day would get better. In thinking this I was correct, because when I turned on the local news that evening it took a complete nosedive.*

I liked the paragraph's cliff-hanging nature, but it suddenly struck me that the cliff didn't yet exist and that I'd forgotten that your present is my past, and my present your future. I'd fallen into the trap that Ric had warned me about, of rushing a story rather than allowing it to unfold naturally, and described an event that, had it happened at this particular juncture, would have entailed me having written all six continuations in a single night. I'm a fast writer, and I can finish a continuation in a week if I put my mind to it, but I'm not that fast, and it's fortunate I caught the mistake.

It's funny, although as a rule I don't like talking about myself, I've had no problem writing about myself. In fact, I've found it surprisingly easy, and in an odd way cathartic. It's interesting to review your life from a distance, to dredge up the past and perhaps understand it better. I've written about events and people I haven't thought about in years, and though I'd have preferred some of the events not to have happened and for some of the people still to be in my life, I don't look back on the past and think it a better place.

I had to break off here and go to the opticians for an eye examination. I wear glasses for reading and working on the computer, but not for everyday activities. I was, however, having problems with my left eye, which had been bloodshot for the past two weeks and felt as if it had a piece of grit in it. At first, I'd thought it was a simple eye infection that antibacterial drops would cure, but the doctor said that it wasn't and that I should consult an optician whose equipment would allow him a better look.

Donald had volunteered to drive me to the opticians on King's Road, but when he arrived at the house he was without his car keys.

'Lydia's hidden them,' he said. 'And there's no point asking me why because I don't know why, and I doubt God does, either. I'm sorry, Rod, but we'll have to take a taxi.'

In view of the changed circumstances, I told Donald that I'd be happy to make my own way to the opticians, but he insisted on accompanying me. It would, he said, give him an excuse not to return home.

'She'll be as right as rain by the time I get back, but between now and then… well, I'm steering clear.'

Donald was quiet in the taxi, no doubt brooding over Lydia, and we passed the time looking out of the window. He offered to pay the fare when we arrived, but I waved his money away. The receptionist asked us to take a seat when we entered the opticians, and after a short wait, Mr Procter, the optician I'd made the appointment with, led me to a small room at the back of the premises.

The examination took about twenty minutes and then Mr Procter sat down on a swivel chair and turned to face me.

'You have what we call a pterygium in your left eye, Mr Pinkney. It's nothing to worry about, but it's this that's causing the irritation and something we need to keep an eye on – no pun intended.'

The closest word to pterygium I knew was pterodactyl, and I wondered if the two were related. When I mentioned this to Mr Procter, he smiled at me wonderingly, as if impressed by my vocabulary, but assured me that they weren't and that he hadn't seen a single reptile flying around in either my left or right eye.

A pterygium, he explained, was a growth of fleshy tissue on the conjunctiva – the clear tissue that covered the eyeball – and the condition was often referred to as surfer's eye and likely caused by lengthy exposure to ultraviolet light.

When he said this, my mind immediately turned to the surfboard that Clay had given to Daisy as a present, and I wondered if she too had a pterygium in her left eye. What a coincidence that would have been!

The optician asked me if I wore sunglasses and I said that I didn't because my father had drummed it into my head from an early age that only pretentious people wore sunglasses – an assertion later lent weight by some of the people who turned up to evening events at the gallery wearing dark glasses.

'And was your father an optician?' Mr Procter enquired, confident of the answer.

'No, he wasn't. He was many things, Mr Procter, but he wasn't an optician. I take it I should start wearing them.'

He said that I should – not only when the sun shone, but also when the light was bright.

'We have a selection of quality sunglasses in the shop, all

with polarised lenses, and Jess will show you the range. In the meantime, use these drops to alleviate the symptoms. They're non-prescription and you can buy them over the counter at the chemist's.'

When I returned to the display area, Donald was trying on different frames and looking in the mirror.

'I didn't know you wore glasses,' I said.

'I don't,' he replied. 'I was just wondering what I'd look like if I did. I think they suit me. Make me look intellectual. What do you think, Jess?'

Jess, evidently Donald's new friend, agreed with him, but asked him to be careful with the pair he was handling because they retailed for £400. Donald replaced the frames on their stand and then tidied his hair in the mirror with the metal comb he always carried.

I spent the next fifteen minutes trying on different pairs of sunglasses and left with the two that Donald and Jess agreed suited me best – one made by Ray-Ban and the other by Maui Jim. At Donald's suggestion we then went for a coffee.

'There's no point in me going home just yet, Rod. Once Lydia gets a bee in her bonnet, it takes time.'

'Does she get like this often?' I asked.

'She's always had the tendency, but it's got worse since she retired. I don't think retirement suits her and she resents me for enjoying it. If she's miserable, then I have to be miserable. It's the way her mind works.'

'I'm very sorry to hear this,' I said. 'Doesn't Lydia have any hobbies, or friends she could spend time with?'

'A woman like Lydia doesn't have friends, Rod, and as for hobbies, well, that's making my life miserable. She hit me last week, and a woman her size packs a punch. I know... hard to believe. She was full of remorse afterwards, but it wouldn't surprise me if it happens again. She knows I'm not going to hit her back.'

'It was Lydia who gave you the black eye! I thought you said you'd walked into a cupboard door.'

'I said that at the time, Rod, because Lydia was standing right behind me, if you remember, and it wouldn't have been gentlemanly if I'd told you the truth while she was there.'

I was shocked by Donald's news and didn't know how to respond. You hear about these things, but you never expect them to happen to people you know. I said something like, I'm here for you, Donald, all you have to do is ask, my door is always open, but every phrase I used sounded tired and so I stopped talking. I'm not very good in situations like this.

I was expecting the conversation to stall at this point and for the two of us to stare at the table or the cakes in the display unit for a long time, but Donald dispelled the unease – quite cheerfully given the circumstances – and said that that was enough about him and wanted to know what the optician had said. I followed his cue and pretended that the previous conversation had never happened.

'I have a pterygium in my left eye,' I said, fully expecting to have to explain the condition.

'I know all about them, Rod. A fellah in Nam had one, and the tunnels came as a blessed relief to him: got him out of the sun and away from the light. Mind you, the pterygium was the least of his worries. Poor fellah lost his mind.'

The man's name was Harry Grimes and he came from a small town in rural Minnesota. He was one of the best rats the company had, fearless but mean as a rattlesnake; always wanting to be the lead man and happy to take risks. Donald had lost count of the tunnels Harry had explored, but vividly remembered the last one.

'I don't know what went on down there, Rod, but something bad must have happened because he emerged a different person – as if the circuits in his mind had blown. His eyes were dead as nails when he hauled himself out, and he had this blank expression on his face. He just stared at us, one of those hollow stares that creeps the hell out of you, and for the longest time said nothing. The damndest thing, though, was that when he did open his mouth and start talking, he was speaking French!

'Grimes had barely made it through high school and never even studied the language. He didn't know anyone who had – not his family, not his friends, and no other soldier in his company. It just came out of nowhere, and it turned out he was more fluent and grammatical in French than he had been when he'd spoken English. And an even odder thing was that he couldn't speak or understand English anymore. It was as if he'd been reincarnated backwards or something.

'He was taken back to base and everyone figured he'd sleep it off, wake up the next morning and be his old self again. But he didn't, and when he went to shave the next day and saw his reflection in the mirror, he started screaming. Claimed there was a strange man looking back at him and he wanted to know who it was. It was him, of course, but he wouldn't accept this and he figured he was having an encounter with the devil. Next I heard he was back in the States and in a sanatorium, and for all I know he's still there. The tunnels took their toll, Rod, and no one suffered more than Harry. Like I said, the pterygium was the least of his worries.'

It was interesting to hear of Harry's pterygium, but I was more interested in returning to the subject of my own.

'The optician said that a person with a pterygium suffers from a condition called surfer's eye, and when he said this

I immediately thought of Daisy because she's a surfer, or at least she used to be. It's odd how the compass always points to her these days. It makes you think, doesn't it?'

'About what?'

'Well, about the serendipity of life, I suppose, or if something's meant to be... I've heard back from Mr Stenger, by the way, and he's agreed to represent me. I really do believe I'm meant to find her.'

'That's good to hear, Rod. Did this Stenger fellah give you an idea of how long it's going to take?'

'I got the impression it wouldn't be a problem locating her, but it would take longer to learn about her circumstances and probably involve a period of surveillance. But the wheels are in motion, and that's the main thing. It's the waiting that's hard.'

'Well, remember I'm here for you Rod, all you have to do is ask, my door is always open...'

He'd then burst out laughing.

'I'm not making fun of you, fellah, but men shouldn't tie themselves up in knots saying things that don't come natural to them. We're no good at it and it embarrasses the hell out of us. But we know, don't we? I know you're in my corner and you know I'm in yours. We don't have to say it.'

In a gruff kind of way it was a touching moment and I smiled my agreement. But touching moments between men can also be uncomfortable, and so I changed the subject.

'Did you get an invite from the new neighbours – the Danters? They're having a drinks party.'

'We did,' Donald said. 'I can't see Lydia wanting to go, but I will. She's already decided they're common people, mainly on account of Mr Danter not wearing a tie when he leaves for work on a morning, and I'm sure it won't be long before she finds some fault with his wife. She doesn't have to try too hard when it comes to finding fault in people.'

'Why does Lydia judge people she's never met? If she met them, she might well find that she likes them and has something in common with them – just like she did when she came to the opening of my basement.'

'I doubt it,' Donald said. 'Lydia doesn't like you, either.'

*

I was surprised when Donald let slip that Lydia disliked me. It's true that I find her a difficult woman, but I would never have gone so far as to say that I didn't like her. There have, in fact, been very few people in life I've disliked, and apart from my parents and Aunt Thelma and Uncle Horace and the policeman who accused me of murder and Bob Fawcett the Australian sheep farmer who ran off with Avril and the landlord of the Lansdowne and the owners of the pet store where I tried to buy the guinea pigs and my first solicitor Mr Jeffries and Lorna's friends Colin and Diana and Helen Mirren, I can't think of any. People are different and it's important we respect this.

When I pressed Donald for Lydia's reason, he seemed spoilt for choice.

'Well, you're unmarried and you live alone for a start, and that's more than enough to set the alarm bells ringing in Lydia's head. You're also a friend of mine – which goes against you without saying – and also a friend of Edmundo, who's a foreigner and can't speak English properly. But what really sank your boat was Lorna. She hates that woman with a passion and it was you that introduced them. If you think about it, you're lucky she only dislikes you.

'By far the biggest reason, though – and why you shouldn't care one way or another about what she thinks – is that Lydia's crazy in the coconut and doesn't know it. If I die first and she dies in the house alone, it will be years before anyone misses her. She's an alienator, Rod, and there's only me prepared to put up with her nonsense. Count your blessings that you only live next door to her and not in the same house.'

It was the first of Lydia's reasons that touched a nerve – and one I believed to reflect a wider bias: she disliked me because I was unmarried.

In a society increasingly inclusive of minorities, it appeared to me that it was still open season on the single person. Single people were discriminated against and judged inferior to married couples, and it was a given that there was something odd or suspicious about them, as if they'd purposely remained on the shelf to throw rocks at those who'd escaped its confines. Consequently, married couples preferred the company of other married couples and kept single people at a social length.

I was a presentable man, but I was ready to admit that it was my wealth rather than my marital status that validated me in the eyes of married couples and allowed me entrée to their world. I was appreciative of the fact, however, that those who didn't enjoy such advantage – people like Miss Wimpole, for instance – fared less well in life, and were often penalised just for *being* single. They were charged supplements for inferior hotel rooms, seated at the worst tables in a restaurant and disallowed the financial allowances and discounts given to a married couple. And, if this wasn't enough, they also had to do their own ironing.

Single people lived alone, ate alone and often holidayed alone, and – unless it was Christmas and the single person as old as the hills – they were shown little consideration. If I had more about me, I would try to do something about this state of affairs – create a foundation or start a newsletter or something – but I'm afraid that I don't.

I'm hoping instead that the government will intervene, though more likely it will be someone like Richard Branson, a philanthropist who cares deeply about people and has UK plug adaptors for visitors to his private island in the Caribbean. I've never been to Necker Island myself, but I understand from friends who have that Richard is very respectful of the local community and is also sympathetic to the flamingos. Thinking about it now, Richard would be the ideal person to champion the cause of single people, and I should write and suggest this to him.

Both Richard and I have more money than most, but unlike him, I prefer not to flaunt mine and risk alienating the ordinary people I identify with. Edmundo and Donald are aware that I have money, but I doubt they comprehend its immensity, which sometimes surprises me. Money has a habit of taking care of itself, and my own financial adviser appears to have a Midas touch. Indeed, I have more money today than I did when I inherited Pinkney Industries.

My father continually told me that I'd have to get off my fat backside if I ever wanted to amount to anything, but he was wrong: I've been sedentary for most of my life and still done well. I came to the conclusion long ago that it was wiser to pay others to take care of my affairs and make the complicated decisions for me, though the one time I did decide something for myself, I still came up smelling of roses.

I can't remember the exact amount I paid to have the basement extended, but the additional value it generated has already paid for the cost several times over. Although I can take some credit for this outcome, my providence has been at the expense of others, I'm sad to say, and largely the result of a broken housing market. I suppose it's the way of the world these days, especially in London, but it makes you wonder about things – though, in my case, not enough to do anything about them. My attentions are more small-scale, and the most pressing of these is to meet Lorna's godson at the Tate Modern tomorrow afternoon.

Lorna loves her godson but prefers not to spend time with him – especially if there's an unexpected opening at a top hairstylist's – and she farms her responsibilities out to others. She sends him cards and presents during the year and joins the family for landmark celebrations, but to date these have been few and largely restricted to birthdays. Apart from their son's longevity, it appears the Hudsons have little to commemorate.

'He's a nice boy,' Lorna said when she'd phoned to ask if I'd meet Henry at the Tate, 'but he's aimless and he needs direction and I'm not sure I'm the person to give it. He's thinking about a career in the art world and he's looking for some pointers. You're my last resort, Rod!'

I wasn't sure how to take this comment. Was I a 'last resort' from a standpoint of consideration, or had all the competent people Lorna knew turned her down? Usually, I would have declined such a request and found a reason not to go, but in the circumstances of her desperation and my own desire to keep busy while I waited for Mr Stenger's report, I reluctantly agreed. And who knew, I might even enjoy Henry's company – even if we were meeting at the Tate Modern.

I told Lorna I'd be happy to help her out, but wondered how I'd recognise Henry.

'It's impossible to miss him,' she said. 'He's got pink hair and it's braided in cornrows. It's a leftover from one of his modelling jobs. Oh, and one more thing, Rod... He'll be late!'

I've been to the Tate Modern only once, and never felt the need to return. I went with the impression that I liked modern art and left knowing that I didn't. I found several of the paintings interesting, but the installations left me cold and I had difficulty differentiating them from the planks and ladders left behind by a firm of contractors. The building itself is impressive, though – another converted power station – and if you like concrete, then you'll certainly like the Tate Modern.

When I arrange to meet someone I always like to arrive early: I hate the idea of keeping another person waiting. If cleanliness wasn't already next to godliness, then in my book it would be punctuality, and this was the first pointer I gave Henry when he eventually arrived half an hour late.

'Yes, I know all about punctuality, Mr Pinkney – it's just that I'm not very good at it. Didn't Lorna mention this to you?'

'She said you'd be late, Henry, but I was thinking in terms of five and not thirty minutes. I've been waiting here for at least forty.'

'Forty! You arrived early? Why would you do that?'

We were sitting at a table in the cafe next to the Turbine Hall entrance, drinking coffee that had been roasted in a WWII Nissen Hut and tasting none the better for it. Henry, as Lorna had indicated, was easy to recognise with his pink hair, but it had been him who had approached me. He spoke to me by name, then pointed to my cravat.

'Lorna said you'd be the only person wearing one. Sweet!'

Henry himself was dressed in what appeared to be a pair of green ballet tights, tan work boots and a long, shapeless white sweater that was torn at the neck. He was a handsome young man and had a winning smile, but his attributes were genetic rather than hard won. Life for him would be easy, but I suspected it would be a life funded by others: if not his parents then a benefactor or rich girlfriends.

He was intelligent but lazy, he told me, and qualified this statement by listing a string of expensive schools he'd been asked to leave and the university he'd left of his own accord. For the last five years he'd been modelling the clothes of well-known fashion houses, but was now, according to his agent, nearing his sell-by date and in need of a new challenge.

'I was thinking about getting into the art world, and Lorna said she knew someone who could advise me on that – that's you, by the way, Mr Pinkney. I'm not interested in the old stuff: the religious crap and those bowls of fruit and dead fish and portraits of ugly people. It's contemporary art that I like.'

I told Henry that if his godmother was happy to be called Lorna, then I was happy for him to call me Rod.

'Okay, Rod, but do you mind addressing me as Mr Hudson?'

For a split-second I thought he was being serious, but then he started to smile.

'I had you going then, didn't I? Ha!'

I told Henry that although I'd worked in a gallery for several years, I had little idea about the art world and didn't even understand the paintings in my own house. And, as to his suggestion of touring the Tate Modern together and me explaining the different mediums, I told him there'd be little purpose as I knew even less about the paintings here. (It would also have involved a lot of walking and climbing stairs and I preferred not to do this.) I did, however, agree to buy him a piece of cake and share with him some observations that had served me well over the years. This, after all, was what Lorna had asked me to do. Or so I thought.

'Jesus Christ, Rod!' Lorna said when I answered the phone

that night. 'Henry's not intending to time-travel back to the nineteenth century! You were supposed to advise him about the art world and tour the Tate Modern with him and not share a load of bullshit about carrying a handkerchief in his pocket and making sure his shirt was tucked into his trousers. How do you think this made me look? His parents think I palmed him off for the afternoon, and now, thanks to you, I have to take him to that stupid concert in Battersea Square!'

'Well, you should have been more explicit then,' I said. 'All I remember you asking me to do is give him pointers. I also told him to wear clean underwear and not to cut lines and to read books, if you're interested in knowing. I thought I was doing him a favour – and you too, if you haven't forgotten. And all I did was mention that I'd be seeing you at the concert in Battersea Square. It was Henry who decided to join you.'

'I know I said I was going to the concert, but I had no intention of actually making an appearance! Why in God's name would I want to waste a Saturday afternoon listening to your stupid friends play their instruments. Jesus, Rod, I'll have to turn up and talk to Henry for a whole afternoon now. Thanks a million!'

Lorna calmed down a little when I told her there'd be alcohol there, but I could tell by the way she slammed the phone down that she was still unhappy. I didn't even get a chance to ask her about her hair.

*

I've mentioned the upcoming concert in Battersea Square twice now, and I should probably say something here about Donald and Edmundo's band.

At first it was just the two of them, Donald on trombone

and Edmundo on panpipes, busking on the Underground and occasionally playing in the street. Donald's connections at Transport for London had secured them a licence to play at twenty-five stations, but they'd struggled to find a good pitch. The times of day that suited Donald weren't always the times that suited Edmundo, and it was difficult for them to commit to a schedule. And, as the pitches were allocated on a first-come, first-served basis and quickly snapped up, they often found themselves playing their assigned two hours in the least popular locations.

Their repertoire, although eclectic, was also limited, and restricted to three pieces: *The Flight of the Bumblebee* (Rimsky-Korsakov), *Sweet Caroline* (Neil Diamond) and *Carry on Wayward Son* by Kansas. As the trade was passing and unlikely to dawdle, Donald was happy with the short playlist, but others – mostly rival buskers who'd gone to the trouble of learning at least twenty songs – were less happy and complained to the licensing authority. Donald's licence, despite his connections, was subsequently suspended until a time when he and Edmundo could present a more comprehensive set.

Increasingly, they played their three tunes on pitches above the ground, in places that either didn't require a licence or where the law was so grey that simple politeness would allow them to escape without a fine. Edmundo preferred this arrangement. He'd never enjoyed the ambience of the Underground, and he much preferred to have the wind in his hair and the sun warming his face when he played the pipes. And, as these above-ground pitches didn't have to be reserved ahead of time, it was easier to fit the busking around his work schedule.

They went, at first, by the handle of Donald and Edmundo,

but once Nelly joined them on tambourine they changed their name to the NEDs (**N**elly, **E**dmundo and **D**onald), and only became the Donald Walker Experience after Clarence came on board with his steel pan drum and they started playing church halls and community centres. No one but Donald could have thought of combining such a strange mix of instruments, but somehow it worked – or at least, the music they played was so different from the norm that it was impossible to know if it was or wasn't working. It was through me, however, that they became a Brian Jonestown Massacre cover band, and I'm happy to take credit for this.

I have an extensive record collection, both on vinyl and CD, but the music isn't a chronological reflection of my life. I tend to stumble on artists after their day rather than at the time, and this was certainly true of people like Captain Beefheart and Gruppo Sportivo. I've never been a trailblazer, just a person who happens along after the dust has settled, and this is how I discovered the Brian Jonestown Massacre.

I'd long been a fan of an American group called the Dandy Warhols and, unusually for me, had been so from the very start of their career when I'd heard a song played on the radio called *Not if You Were the Last Junkie on Earth*. I was driving at the time and was so impressed by the song that I pulled over to the kerb and made a note of the artist. They were good for about three albums and then they got less good, but I always hoped for a return to form and continued to take an interest in them.

I was trawling through Amazon one day and found that a film had been made about them, so I added it to my basket and placed an order. It was called *Dig!*, but the film was more about their relationship with a band called the Brian Jonestown Massacre than a straightforward recording of their appearances. And it turned out that the song *Not if You Were the Last Junkie on Earth* was intended as a tip of the hat to the BJM, whose career appeared to be going nowhere.

Watching the scenes that featured the BJM was like watching a car crash in slow motion: they brawled with each other on stage, fought with their audiences and kept getting arrested. Despite there being no evidence of this on film, everyone interviewed by the director spoke highly of their music and so I made an exploratory purchase – and then a further fifteen. To say the least, I was smitten with their music, though not to the extent of ever wanting to invite them into my house. Music is one thing, but breakages are another matter entirely.

The songs Donald and Edmundo played were a hotchpotch, and increasingly so after Clarence joined the band. Although the four of them played well together, they had difficulty agreeing on a set list, and after tiring of their bickering one night I asked if I might make a suggestion. As it was my basement they were practising in, it was hard for them to say no, and so I went ahead and played them a song by John Prine that had the prettiest of tunes. I'd thought that the title alone – *Donald and Lydia* – would have sold the song to Donald, but as the story was about an overweight woman and a young soldier, Donald thought that it would be too close to home to play the song in public, especially after Clarence had suggested that the lyrics were about masturbation.

It was then I played them *Anemone* by the BJM and this one they jumped on. Donald substituted his trombone for the looping guitar while Edmundo played the vocal melody and Clarence extemporised around them. Nelly liked the song because it gave prominence to the tambourine – as did most

BJM songs – and she and Donald asked to hear more of their music. I was happy to oblige them, but careful not to show them the film.

And so, in this way, the Donald Walker Experience found their sound, and – as few, if any, people had heard of the BJM – it became known locally as the Battersea Sound and earned them an invitation to play in the Square.

I was about to close the computer for the day when an email arrived from Mr Stenger. I took a deep breath before opening it, fearing the worst but hoping for the best. It was like going on a blind date.

The news, however, was positive: Mr Stenger was pleased to report that he'd found Daisy. Ms Lamprich, he continued, was living in a rental property in Huntington Beach, a coastal town in Southern California not far from Los Angeles. She was divorced, currently single, and raising an eight-year-old daughter called Amelia. At this stage of the investigation it was impossible to know if Daisy was in a relationship or not, but this would be ascertained after a period of surveillance. Consequently, Mr Stenger was passing my file to the Los Angeles field office and the case would be handled in future by an agent called Phil Seymer. Mr Stenger, who signed himself Johnny, then wished me a pleasant day and asked that I settle the attached remittance within thirty days.

I typed Huntington Beach into the search engine and learned that the city was known locally as HB. It was named after a railroad magnate called Henry Huntington, but had previously been known as Shell Beach, Smeltzer, Gospel Swamp, Fairview and Pacific City. It was famous for its long beaches and surfing waves – which explained Clay's gift of a surfboard – and was nicknamed Surf City USA. No one of any real importance appeared to have been born there, but it was a slight worry that so many adult film actresses had. Daisy's name, I'm glad to say, wasn't one of them.

Until I heard from Mr Seymer I was back to playing the waiting game and I was unsure of how best to fill the time. I wondered about calling in at the Lansdowne to share the news with Ric, but decided against it. He'd been missing the last few times I'd visited the pub, and when I'd asked the landlord where he was he'd replied that this was something he'd like to know too and wondered if I'd like to earn some extra pocket money by clearing the tables.

I hummed and hawed for a time, and then decided to incorporate a stack of new and recently read books into the alphabetically ordered bookshelves. They were piled on the basement floor and Nelly was forever complaining about their untidiness and threatening a lawsuit if she ever tripped over them.

I organise my books by author, and the addition of one displaces another. If, say, I add an author to the 'A' section, it has a ripple effect that disturbs the order of all the shelves, and reorganising them can take time. The end result is always satisfying, but the task is a thankless one and easy to defer. It was, however, now the ideal project to keep my mind occupied.

I'd got as far as the 'Gs' when I noticed that the position of the Imperial spike helmet had changed. It sits on a shelf of its own and usually looks outward, as if staring you in the face. It was now placed sideways, and I suspected that Clarence, despite me asking him not to, had again worn the helmet during the band's last rehearsal. It wasn't a toy, I'd told him, but an object of sentimental value, and I was now annoyed that he'd chosen to ignore my words.

The helmet had belonged to One-Take Malone, the tailor Harriet had introduced me to. He'd been one of the mourners at her funeral, and after the service had ended he'd taken me by the arm and asked if he could rely on my continued custom. I'd assured him that he could, and he'd then moved on to other mourners and asked them the same question or handed cards to prospective customers.

One-Take's tailoring was second to none and over time, and as we got to know each other, he became less taciturn, though never to the point of explaining why he wore the helmet. Although his fingers remained nimble to the end, his eyes failed him and the day came when he had to close up shop. He was well past retirement age by this time, but he was short on hobbies and seemed despondent about the future.

'Well, if there's anything I can do, Mr Malone, you must let me know,' I'd said, never expecting to hear from him again.

But, five years later and out of the blue, he'd phoned and asked me if I could take him to the hospital for an appointment. He wasn't averse to taking taxis, he explained, but he was now so blind that it was hard for him to see where he was going and he was in need of a second pair of eyes. I was still driving at the time and so I was happy to oblige him. After all, if we can't help others, then how can we expect others to help us?

I arrived at his house and found him standing on the pavement. If it hadn't been for his helmet, however, I wouldn't have recognised the man. He was wearing a dark blue pinstriped suit, a white shirt and a red silk tie, and a gleaming pair of patent leather shoes. I'd never seen him looking so presentable.

'You're dressed more for a night on the town than for the hospital, Mr Malone,' I said. 'Why so smart?'

'I'm going for an MRI scan,' he replied. 'It's best to look your best for one of those.'

I didn't quite understand his logic, and neither did the

hospital staff when he asked if he could keep his helmet on during the scan.

'It's the one thing that's been keeping me alive,' he told them.

'If you wear it during the scan, Mr Malone, it will be the one thing that kills you,' a nurse said. 'Now be a dear and give it to your son, will you? He'll look after it for you.'

I took One-Take to the hospital one further time and this for the results of the scan. It was terminal cancer. I didn't know what to say.

'So much for the damn helmet!' he'd said.

For the first and only time, he then told me its story.

'My dad spared the life of a young German soldier during WWI. A corporal, he thought. My dad was about to bayonet him when the soldier begged for mercy. Told him he was a promising artist or some such. Anyway, he conned my dad into taking his helmet in return for his freedom. Said it had magical powers and staved off cancer and that anyone wearing it would live to be a hundred. My dad took it and asked the man how he was going to survive the war without a helmet. He said he didn't know, but that once the war was over he was going home to Austria and forming a political party. I don't know if he did or didn't, but my dad wore the helmet for the rest of his life and lived to be a hundred! Anyway, the helmet passed to me after his death, and I've worn it ever since. It didn't save my eyes, but I was convinced it was going to save me from cancer. I reckon that soldier duped my dad, and if he fooled him then he probably fooled others.'

One-Take was dead within three months and there were few of us at his funeral, mostly old customers like myself. His wife was already departed and his only son estranged and living in New Zealand. I'll say one thing for the funeral though: the mourners there were the best-dressed I've ever seen, even if we were all wearing the same suit.

A month later, I received a registered parcel in the mail and a short note from Mr Malone's solicitor bequeathing the helmet to me. I was touched that One-Take had thought of me, and when the bookshelves were completed I gave the helmet pride of place.

I then started on the 'Hs'.

*

'I'm telling you, they either ply the audience with drink or they drug them! There's no other way to explain the laughter. Do you really think that anyone in their right mind would laugh at his jokes? The fellah's not funny, and most other comedians on television aren't funny, either! Hell, if they weren't introduced as comedians, you'd never know they were comedians! And what's more, I have to pay a licence fee for all this bull dust. Do you think that's right, because I don't?'

Edmundo pooh-poohed Donald's theory, and said that Michael McIntyre was a lot funnier than he was and that his jokes were stupid. Donald disagreed, and countered that Edmundo was either too dumb or too Peruvian to understand the nuances of his humour. Edmundo objected to this and said that just because he couldn't speak English fluently didn't mean that he didn't understand the trickeries of the language, and he asked me for my thoughts on the subject.

'I think you speak English perfectly well, Edmundo, and you should stop selling yourself short,' I said

'No, Señor Rod. I am asking you what you think of Michael McIntyre!'

As a rule I don't like to speak ill of people, but I had to agree with Donald here. I added that I also had reservations about Graham Norton and thought that his show was more a format for product placement than for genuine entertainment.

'I know exactly what you mean there, Rod,' Donald said. 'Those bigwig film actors stick in my craw! All that lovey-dovey stuff, and them pretending they find each other funny. He'd do better having us on his show: Edmundo and I could play him a tune and you could tell him about your cravats. Ha!'

In case you haven't gathered, this is an account of one of our Thursday nights together, and at this stage of the evening we were on our second bottle of wine. Considerate of my sensitivities, Donald and Edmundo had forgone the *Judge Judy Show* this evening, and had been happy for me when I told them that Mr Stenger had found Daisy.

'Does her having a child bother you?' Edmundo asked.

'Not in the least,' I said. 'I like children, and I think I'd make a good father. I could provide them both with a good life.'

'And you think they'll be happy moving to this country?'

'Hmm, now that's something I *don't* know, Donald. I'm hoping they will, but I have to consider the possibility that I might have to move there. It's not something I'd want to do, but... well, let's cross that bridge when we get to it.'

'I bet it will not be as nice as the Albert Bridge,' Edmundo said. 'Clarence says that the Albert Bridge is the happiest bridge in the world!'

'Talking of Clarence,' I said, 'has he been wearing the German helmet again? I've asked him not to.'

'No,' Donald said. 'It was Nelly who moved it. She keeps imagining there's a dead head inside it and she says it puts her off her stride when she's trying to keep time.'

'I wonder if the head had a nice send-off,' Edmundo said to Donald, and the two of them started to snicker.

It was a running gag between them, and one that stemmed from a commercial shown on television advertising a funeral protection plan. The advert usually featured two friends talking in a garden centre and commiserating about the death of someone they'd both known. 'I miss Jane,' one would say, 'but at least she had a good send-off. I doubt I'll be able to afford anything like that when my time comes.' Fortunately for her, the person she was talking to was an expert on funeral plans and had just signed up for one with a lifetime payback guarantee. The monthly instalments cost less than a weekly cup of coffee, she explained to her friend, and by acting now she was sparing her children the expense of having to pay for her funeral. There appeared to be no happier person in the world.

For Donald and Edmundo the joke was in the send-off – as if the send-off alone made a person's life worthwhile. No one actually recalled the person in these adverts or alluded to their life, only their departure. It mattered little if Jane had suffered during her years on earth, because any misfortune or misery she might have endured had been trumped by a pre-paid funeral plan that allowed others to have a party at her expense. In other words, a person's life was judged not on the life lived but on the quality of the funeral spread and the lack of inconvenience their death posed to others.

I didn't tell them the story of One-Take's helmet because it was a confidence he'd shared with me. I did, however, say that no person had ever died wearing it and that Edmundo should tell Nelly this.

By the end of the evening – as with all Thursday evenings – we were all a bit worse for wear, and I insisted on calling Edmundo a taxi.

'You can call me anything you like, Señor Rod, but please do not call me a taxi. I am a simple man but I am not a machine, and I shall walk the short distance to my beloved Nelly's doorstep and hopefully fall into her arms a little less drunk than I am now. The air of the night, I believe, is known for its restorative powers.'

'Well, just make sure you don't fall in the river,' Donald laughed.

'If I decide to fall in the river, I will fall in the river,' Edmundo replied. 'I am a free man and unbeholden to others.'

Donald decided that it would be in the interests of the Donald Walker Experience if he accompanied his valued panpiper to the end of the street and saw him safely across the road, and when he returned, and in no hurry to fall into the arms of his own beloved wife, he accepted my offer of a nightcap.

'Do you think he'll manage to find his way home all right?' I asked.

'Sure he will. The fellah found his way here from Peru, didn't he?'

We then relaxed into companionable silence and drifted off into our own worlds: mine, a long sandy beach in California and Donald's, no doubt, a claustrophobic tunnel in Vietnam. I was about to pour him another measure of the single malt when he placed his hand over the glass to signal he'd had enough.

'I hope you don't go and live in California, Rod. I like living next door to you and I enjoy these evenings together. It wouldn't be the same if you left. And I know Edmundo feels the same way. Make sure that Daisy comes here, will you?'

He then pressed the chair's button and tipped to his feet. It was while he was trying to put his arms through his jacket sleeves that he remembered something he'd been intending to mention earlier in the evening.

'You know that fellah at the Lansdowne who's helping you with your book?'

'You mean Ric?'

'Yes, that's the fellah. Well, I was in the Lansdowne last night, leaving some flyers for the concert, and I heard from one of the servers that he's been fired and barred from returning to the premises. The landlord reckons he's lost his rocker.'

2 August 2019

The news of Ric's dismissal unsettled me and it was a while before I fell asleep that night. Although his recent behaviour had caused my eyebrows to rise occasionally, I hadn't once considered that he might be losing his mind. It was true that his manner had become more strident, but I'd considered this to be a temporary aberration, and one that would be settled once his body adapted to its new regimen of lentils and celery sticks. And his stridency, after all, had always been of a professional nature, focused on the world of books rather than the world at large.

Ric had previously vented his anger on literary agents and publishers, but had now taken to cudgelling the literati and the writers they championed.

'They're a bunch of smug bastards, Rod, and they can't tell the difference between a pile of shit and a pudding! And you know the writer they love the most, the one they want to curl up in bed with at night? Fucking Hilary Mantel, that's who! The woman's no better than Barbara Cartland and neither is her dress sense! And you can bet your shirt on her winning a third Booker because it's already been decided. Thomas fucking Cromwell! Who in their right mind wants to read about him?'

Strangely, considering he'd always stressed the importance of me keeping the reader onside, Ric had also started to fire bullets in their direction. Ultimately, he'd argued, it was they who turned shit books into shit bestsellers.

'Few people hunt for books these days or develop their own tastes in literature,' he'd commented on one such occasion. 'Rather than spend time figuring things out for themselves, they'll rely on the opinions of others and the filters that tell them what they should or shouldn't be reading. They're sheep, Rod, fucking sheep, and they follow the leader. They buy books that win prizes, books reviewed in newspapers and magazines, and the books endorsed by the likes of Richard and Judy. They don't have a mind of their own, they're a collective; and if you could count its fucking brain cells you wouldn't need more than the fingers of one hand.'

Although I was uncomfortable with Ric's language – which I appreciate is inconsistent with my acceptance of Lorna's – I continued to admire his passion. I was also flattered by his faith in me as a writer and his belief that my book, under his guidance, would blow the existing publishing paradigm to smithereens and allow for a better world. The two of us, he'd told me, would go down in history as the saviours of literature and our names would be fêted for generations to come. In these circumstances, and shouldering such responsibility, it was imperative that I remained in contact with Ric, but his dismissal from the Lansdowne now made this difficult.

Ric was an analogue person and had failed to embrace the digital age. He considered Steve Jobs to be a man with blood on his hands, and he'd commented on more than one occasion that if the inventor ever came back to life, he would personally stand him against a wall and shoot the hell out of him. Ric had an email address and a mobile phone but refused to use either, and he insisted on me printing the continuations and handing them to him in person. If it was true that the landlord had barred him from the premises, then this would no longer be possible and, as he didn't know where I lived, it was essential that I learned his whereabouts.

The next day, shortly after it opened its doors for business, and at a time when I'd normally have been eating lunch, I went to the Lansdowne and asked one of the bar staff if I might have a quiet word with the landlord. The girl said that she'd go and find him, but suggested I didn't make the conversation too quiet as the batteries in his hearing aid were running low that day. She left the bar, and on her return told me the landlord was on his way. How far he had to travel I have no idea, but he kept me waiting for a good twenty minutes and I had to fortify myself with a bag of dry-roasted peanuts and a small orange juice.

'Well, what is it?' the landlord asked when he finally made an appearance.

I couldn't address him by name because I didn't know his name, but wishing to show the man some respect, I decided to call him by his profession.

'It's about Ric, landlord,' I said in a loud voice. 'He's a friend of mine and I understand from another friend that he's been fired from his job. I was just wondering why, and if you could give me his address.'

Considering the number of times I'd gone to the pub and found Ric missing, my guess would have been that he'd been dismissed on the grounds of reliability, or possibly for his use of bad language, and I certainly wasn't expecting the answer I got.

'He's a thief is why I fired him,' the landlord said, and then looked at the empty bag of peanuts on the table. 'Did you pay for those?'

'Well, of course I paid for them! I wouldn't have eaten them if I hadn't paid for them. I'm surprised you asked.'

'I asked the question because by your own admission you're a friend of that thief, and in my book there's a good chance that a friend of a thief is also a thief.'

In another century I would have slapped the man across the face with a glove and challenged him to a duel in Battersea Park which, when it was known as Battersea Fields, had been a popular venue for such affairs of honour. I was, however, in need of the landlord's help and at a consequent disadvantage, so I could do little but assure him of my honesty. But then, after I'd had a chance to calm down and think things through, I asked him if Ric had been dismissed for stealing dry-roasted peanuts.

'No, he's been stealing meat from the fridge and eating it raw, if you must know. I caught him red-handed last week with a piece of liver in his mouth and blood down the front of his shirt. He looked like a damned cannibal! No one in their right mind eats raw liver – and God knows how many uncooked sausages he's wolfed. I'm going to have to put up my prices because of him – unless, of course, you, as his friend, would like to make good the shortfall.'

I thought about this for a moment and came up with an idea.

'I will if you give me his address,' I said.

'Okay,' the landlord agreed. 'You owe me £62.'

Fortunately I had the money on me and I handed it over. He held every note to the light and checked the watermark and the thin metal strip before putting it in his pocket. He then made to leave and I had to remind him of our bargain.

'London,' he said. 'He lives in London,' and he then started to walk off again.

'I know he lives in London, but where? What's the address of his house?'

'I can't tell you that because the law doesn't allow it. You've just been had, whoever you are, but your friend had me and so I consider us even.'

He'd then thrown me a bag of peanuts and told me they were on the house.

I left the Lansdowne with an even lower opinion of the landlord, and felt justified in having added his name to the small list of people I'd met in life and disliked. My higher concern, though, was for Ric's mental well-being. If he'd been caught eating raw beef I might have understood his behaviour better, but stealing and ingesting a piece of uncooked liver was a far cry from savouring a dish of steak tartare, and hardly the actions of a level-headed person.

There was, however, little I could do in the circumstances. I emailed and texted him, left a message on his mobile phone offering my help and reminding him of our mission, but I had no expectation that he would reply. It was obvious that Ric needed time, and probably the help of a professional to work through his issues, and that for the immediate future I would have to respect his privacy and leave him to recuperate. And, if push did come to shove, and I managed to remember how he spelled his last name, I could always ask Graham to hire an investigator to locate him. No, the best thing I could do to help Ric in his time of need was to continue writing and present him with a finished manuscript once he'd recovered.

Continuation 8

The Battersea Square Concert

Donald and I were the first and only neighbours to arrive at the Danters' house that Saturday night, all others having politely declined their invitations or simply ignored them.

'I told Jez it would have been better to have the housewarming on a weeknight, but he wouldn't agree to it, would you Jez?' Edie Danter smiled once the four of us were settled in the lounge and it was clear that no one else was coming.

'No, weeknights are school nights, Edie, and Roy needs to focus. St Paul's isn't cheap and it's important he makes the most of his time there. Being a gay couple,' he said, turning to Donald and me, 'you won't have these concerns. Did you ever consider adopting?'

I looked at Donald and he looked at me, and I noticed him bristle. Even though we weren't a couple, I thought it best if I replied for us both.

'Donald and I aren't gay, Jez: we're neighbours. We live next door to each other and Donald's married. We're friends.'

'I also play the trombone,' Donald added.

I was puzzled by Jez's misreading of our relationship. Donald and I had arrived at the house together, but there was nothing in our bearing, so far as I knew, that might suggest we were gay. I had once been mistaken for a lesbian when I'd worked at the gallery, but never for a gay man, and I asked Jez why he'd thought this.

'The cravat,' he replied. 'You're wearing a cravat.'

I was trying to make sense of his reply when Edie changed the subject, but to one that would as likely upset Donald as the accusation that he was gay.

'Jez and I have just joined the Labour Party,' she said.

'St Paul's is an independent fee-paying school, isn't it?' Donald queried. 'How do you square that with being members of the Labour Party?'

'Well, we weren't members when we enrolled Roy,' Edie replied. 'Politics is very much in the timing.'

'In my day it used to be about the principle,' Donald said.

'Let me refresh your glass, Donald,' Edie promptly suggested. 'It's Fairtrade wine.'

Donald said that he would have expected no less from members of the Labour Party and held out his glass for a refill. I sensed then that the evening was either going to be very long, very short or possibly both, and I did what I could to retrieve the situation.

'How did the two of you meet?' I asked.

'We met at the BBC,' Jez said.

'We both worked in the current affairs department and so we thought it would be appropriate if we had one of our own,' Edie laughed. 'We were both married at the time but to the wrong people. We realised we were soulmates the first time we were alone together.'

'Where was that?' I asked, wondering if they'd been assigned to one of the world's more troubled areas and been beguiled by its danger.

'In the stationery room,' Edie replied.

Edie's answer was more matter of fact than I'd anticipated and caused me to pause. I pretended to savour the wine for a moment, and then asked a suitable follow-up question: did she and Jez still work for the BBC?

'No, Jez works for Channel 5 now and I'm a freelancer,' Edie replied.

'Why would a person move from the BBC to Channel 5?' Donald asked, draining the last of his wine. 'I thought that would have been a backwards step, a bit like a columnist at *The Times* moving to the *Daily Sport*.'

'It's more cutting-edge and it pays better,' Jez replied without elaborating.

'Do many people wear cravats at Channel 5?' Donald asked.

'No. Why would you ask that?' Jez replied.

'Just curious,' Donald said.

Starting a dialogue with Jez was like getting an old car engine to turn and the conversation repeatedly stalled. I suspect that the evening's gathering was more intimate than any of us had bargained for, and we were all having difficulty thinking of things to say to each other.

The only subject Jez had shown any interest in was his son, and so I asked where Roy was that evening.

'He's out with a friend.'

'We're trying to raise Roy gender-neutral,' Edie said.

'Okay, that's it!' Donald said, banging his glass on the table. 'You'll have to excuse me, but it's time I made a move. It's close to Lydia's bedtime and I have to get her hot-water bottles ready. Are you coming, Rod?'

I glanced at my watch and noticed that the time was only 8:30. It seemed a little rude to leave so early, especially as Edie had just put a tray of sausage rolls in the oven, and so I reluctantly told Donald that I'd stay a while longer.

'How long will you be staying?' Jez asked, looking at his own watch. 'I have to pick Roy up in half an hour.'

'Fifteen minutes,' I suggested. 'I'll just have a sausage roll and then I'll be on my way.'

Donald left, and for the next fifteen minutes I tried to think of something that might lead to a meeting of the minds and divert my attention from their hands, which appeared to be attached to the wrong bodies. Jez's hands were small and delicate, like those of a Victorian doll's, while Edie's were noticeably manlier and ideally suited for shovelling coal. It was as if a rogue surgeon had entered their house in the middle of the night and transposed their hands without them knowing.

Although Edie had a particularly warm smile, she was, at heart, as humourless as Jez, and the only topic she wanted to discuss was Lydia's hot-water bottles. Why, on a warm August evening when most of the houses in the street had their bedroom windows open, would Donald's wife need hot-water bottles? And, if she did suffer from poor circulation – as she suspected – then why, in this modern day and age, didn't she have an electric blanket? I didn't know the answers to these questions, and nor did I know for a fact that Lydia did require hot-water bottles or if this was just an excuse Donald had invented to allow him an early exit.

The sausage rolls, once served, proved to be vegetarian and, like the evening itself, a bit of a disappointment. It was a relief when Jez made ready to collect Roy and I could take my own leave. I thanked the Danters for a wonderful evening and told them how much I'd enjoyed their company and then left for my house and opened a bottle of brandy, which was still sitting on the kitchen counter when Donald arrived the next morning.

'It's a bit early, isn't it?' he said, nodding at the brandy.

'That's from last night,' I said, knowing him to be joking. 'I needed a stiff drink after meeting our new neighbours.'

'You did, too, eh? I went straight to the Lansdowne! And if I hadn't left when I did, I'd have probably punched that fellah in the gob. And if I ever hear that he's been going around telling people I'm a shirtlifter that's exactly what I *am* going to do. I still can't believe he said it.'

'And purely on the grounds of me wearing a cravat,' I said. 'If Jez knew his history as well as he claims to know his current affairs, then he'd know that the cravat is of military origin and has nothing to do with a man's proclivities.'

'And all that guff about Fairtrade wine and bringing their son up gender-neutral. The neighbourhood's taken a hit, Rod, and what riles me most is that Lydia was right about them. I hate it when Lydia's right about something – right about *anything*! That's why I went to the Lansdowne after I left. I couldn't bear to go home and see that smug look on her face when I told her she'd been right all along about the Danters.

'And another thing: do you think anyone in that house owns an iron? I've never seen so many creases in a shirt – and God knows what Edie was wearing. The two of them looked driven from home, and I doubt either one of them had bothered to wash their hair that day. If they ever put a Labour poster in their window I'm going to throw a brick through it – and that's a promise!'

Donald eyed the brandy again and asked if it was okay if he poured himself a small measure.

'Medicinal purposes,' he smiled. 'I'm suffering from Danteritis.'

I brought him a glass and pushed the bottle towards him.

'Did they talk about me after I'd gone? Make any remarks I should know about?'

'No, but Edie's concerned that Lydia has poor circulation after you mentioned the hot-water bottles. You might have come up with a better excuse.'

'Excuses are in the timing, Rod – just like Edie's politics. I just tweaked the time frame.'

'You mean Lydia *does* go to bed with a hot-water bottle – even in August?'

'Sure she does. She has three of them. She's cold-blooded by nature, Rod, and she always has been. I like my sheets cold when I climb into bed, but as long as she keeps the bottles on her side then I don't mind. It's just one of the many ways in which we're incompatible. We should have probably discussed sleeping arrangements before we got married, but when you're in love with a person you don't necessarily think to ask about hot-water bottles.'

It was difficult to picture Donald and Lydia being in love, though at one time of their lives I'm sure that they were. Now they were two people with things in uncommon, who stayed together for the sake of marriage rather than for themselves. As a concerned friend I thought Donald would be better off divorcing Lydia, but it wasn't my place to say so. And for all I knew the dynamic they enjoyed might well suit them both. One thing I've learned in life is that it's difficult enough to make sense of your own relationships without interfering in another's.

'Do you remember the first time you got drunk?' Donald asked, pouring himself another measure of brandy.

Worryingly, I didn't, but Donald's question was rhetorical and didn't require an answer.

'My first time was in Australia, the night before we set sail for Nam. I wasn't much of a drinker in those days and the alcohol hit me harder than it did my mates. We were in a club in Townsville and there was this fellah on stage singing – one of those paid amateurs who'd have done better sticking to his day job. The man had a face like a dropped pie and a knack of crucifying any song he sang. We tried to heckle him off the stage, but he just kept on singing like he was doing us all a big favour and throwing us V-signs.

'But then he started singing *Land of a Thousand Dances* and, for me, that was a step too far. I jumped on stage at that point – as much for Wilson Pickett's sake as my own – grabbed the microphone from him and started to sing the song myself. I'd just made it through the first verse when a couple of bouncers grabbed hold of me and rough-housed me out of the club and into the street.

'I was lying on the pavement for a while – quite contented with life in the circumstances – and the next thing I knew the bouncers who'd thrown me out were lying right there next to me. It turned out my mates had taken umbrage at what they'd done and decided to see how they liked being turfed out of a place. The fellahs then carried me back in on their shoulders, put me back on the stage, and I finished the song in triumph.

'Ha! That was a night to remember, all right.'

I think I'd have remembered a night like that, especially if I'd been shipping out to fight in a war the next day, and so I wasn't unduly concerned that I couldn't remember the first time I'd been the worse for wear. I suspect it would have been around the time when Avril broke up with me, but I doubt I'd have been singing a song at the time.

The talk about songs reminded me of Donald's upcoming performance in Battersea Square and I asked him how rehearsals were going. The concert was four weeks away, but the last time I'd talked to him he'd given me the impression that they still hadn't decided on a set list.

'They're coming along, Rod, but we need more practice. Finding a time when everyone's available is the biggest problem. Take today, for instance. I'm free all day and Edmundo's okay for this afternoon, but Clarence is tied up at church – he goes to three services, if you can believe this – and Nelly, because she was a nun I suppose, considers Sunday a day of rest. It's a pity you can't play the tambourine.'

'It's far too energetic for me, Donald. I don't know how Nelly manages it.'

'Ha! That's a good one, Rod. That's funny.'

'It wasn't a joke, Donald. I'm being serious.'

'Sure it was, and do you want to hear some of mine? I've had a productive week.'

I told him I'd be happy to listen to them, and he then told me about a man who'd gone into the wilderness to find himself and got lost; about a man who'd eaten so many square meals he'd become round; and then asked me if I knew the difference between the Inuit and Intuits. I didn't – and, as yet, neither did Donald – but he believed there was a joke in there somewhere and it was only a matter of time before he found it.

He ended with an adage: the world's your oyster, Rod, but don't try opening it with your teeth!

I liked that one, and I decided to join Donald in a brandy. It was always difficult to know what to do with a Sunday.

*

The following two weeks passed without event, though during this time, and for the first time ever, I started to suffer from dyssomnia. I've always slept well – my head hitting the pillow and the next thing I know it's mid-morning and time to get up – but my sleep now fell into a strange doughnut pattern, where I'd fall asleep as easily but wake up three hours later and remain awake until it was time to get up, which was usually the time I'd fall back to sleep again.

It was obvious, even to me, that the source of this restlessness was the matter of Daisy weighing on my mind, and for distraction at such times, and in the hope of falling back to sleep, I would tune into a talk radio station and listen to callers voice matters that concerned them, even though it was unlikely they would concern others. There was one presenter, though, who didn't accept calls, and he just talked about himself for three hours and read out texts and emails from people who liked him and thought he was the funniest man in the world. Reluctantly, I became a part of what he called the 'Four o'clock Spike', which was the time of day he started broadcasting and when the ratings jumped – or so he claimed. I can't remember a morning when he didn't mention this.

But then, seemingly out of nowhere, everything happened at once and my sleep pattern returned to normal. I received a definitive report from Phil Seymer clarifying Daisy's relationship status; Ric made an unexpected appearance on *London News*; and Edmundo and Nelly moved into my house and took up residence on the top floor.

I'd exchanged several emails with Mr Seymer since he'd become my point of contact at the Turnipseed Agency, him telling me of the progress he was making and me thanking him for his efforts, but his final communiqué arrived sooner than expected. He advised me that the report was factual rather than interpretive and without judgement. It was also staccato in style, as if the words were being delivered by a machine gun and each word cost money.

Subject born Huntington Beach, August 16 1981. Only child of Jack and Clara Lamprich. Father, engineer (McDonnell Douglas / Boeing), mother, registered nurse. Parents retired, Newport Beach, keen sailors.

High school diploma, HB High School. One year Golden West Community College, dropped course. Moved to Sunset Beach (location at time of Judge Judy Show). Tended bar / waitressed 7 years. Married (2008–14) to Dwight Mayberry, local hairdresser. Daughter, Amelia, born 2011. Police called to residence twice (spouse threatened subject with pair of scissors; spouse punched fist through door and got arm stuck). Spouse moved to Salt Lake City, remarried.

Surveillance period, five weeks, 24/7. Weekdays: subject takes daughter to school, works on checkout at Albertsons Grocers, collects daughter from school. No callers. Weekends: subject and daughter go to beach, visit parents in Newport Beach. Subject went out two evenings alone: dinner with a girlfriend; drinks with girlfriends. No evidence of relationship.

Advise as to proposed travel date.

It was the news I'd been hoping for, and within the hour I'd emailed Mr Seymer and promised him a travel date by the following week. It was, after all, a time I would first have to discuss with Donald and Edmundo if they were to accompany me to Huntington Beach, as I hoped they would.

Donald's band had upped their rehearsals and now practised in the basement on Monday and Wednesday nights. Clarence and Nelly would usually go straight home after these run-throughs, but Donald and Edmundo would always stay behind and discuss what was working and where there was room for improvement. Ordinarily, they'd stop by the lounge on their way out, but for no more than a few minutes. On this occasion, however – the day of Mr Seymer's report – I opened a bottle of wine and asked them to remain a while longer: there was, I said, something important I wished to ask them.

'Are we making too much noise,' Edmundo enquired, 'because if we are, then it is the fault of Donald. He blows too hard. Just say the word and I will throw him out of the band.'

'How can you throw me out of my own band?'

'Because we live in a democracy, my friend, and I have the numbers. Nelly and Clarence will side with me and you will be thrown to the wolves. We will change our name to the Edmundo de la Puente Rhythm Kings and you will die a pauper.'

Usually I enjoy their banter, but on this occasion I brought it to a swift halt and asked them to take a seat. I told them then about the report from Mr Seymer and his judgement that Daisy was single and unattached and of my intentions to travel to Huntington Beach.

'I'm thinking of flying out there in early September and I'd very much like the two of you to come with me. It would be my treat and I'd pay for everything. It would be a holiday for you, and you'd be doing me a favour. I don't like travelling alone, especially to new places, and I'd welcome your support. And you'd get to meet Daisy, too.

'I appreciate that this is something you'll have to discuss with your wives before committing to the trip, but it would be helpful – for the purposes of booking flights and hotel rooms – if you could give me an answer by tomorrow evening. What do you think to the idea? Are you up for it – at least in principle?'

'I can give you my answer now, Señor Rod,' Edmundo said. 'In principle I am up for it, but in practice I am at the bottom of a deep well. Donald J Walker may well be my friend in this country, but his namesake who leads America is not. The

Shining Path is still classified as a terrorist organisation by the United States, and though I am no longer a member, and ashamed that I once was, my name is on a list of names that would result in my arrest and extradition to Peru if I ever entered that country. It is a chance I cannot afford to take. My beloved wife and the plants that cover your walls depend on my freedom, and I would be unable to attend to either if I was incarcerated in a cell thousands of miles distant. I am afraid that I must decline your kind offer, my friend, but I wish you well and I hope that one day I will meet Daisy in this very room.'

I was saddened by Edmundo's explanation, but I understood it. And I was glad that he was more acquainted with his situation than I was, because if we had travelled to California and he'd been arrested, it would have certainly soured the trip and left me in a poor frame of mind for my meeting with Daisy which, after all, was the sole reason for making the journey.

'There's a distinct possibility that I'll be able to go with you,' Donald said when I looked to him for an answer. 'After we play Battersea Square, the band doesn't have a gig until October, and a break from Lydia would do me good. And from memory, Yorba Linda isn't far from Huntington Beach and that's a place I *would* like to visit. I'll check my passport and make sure it's current and I'll give you a definite answer tomorrow.'

Donald was true to his word, and the next day he told me I could count him in!

Edmundo, however, was missing this evening. He'd phoned and said there was a plumbing emergency at a neighbour's flat and that we shouldn't expect him until late, or if at all. In his absence, Donald and I planned our upcoming trip. We decided to fly from Heathrow to Los Angeles and take a taxi to Huntington Beach. Hiring a car would have been a better option, but as I no longer drove and Donald was reluctant to drive in another country, it seemed the right decision, especially as the journey from LAX to Huntington Beach was less than an hour.

I suggested we travel on Tuesday 3 September and Donald thought that this was as good a day as any. Conscious that Daisy might be reluctant to move to Battersea and insist upon me moving there, I wanted to spend a few days acclimatising and getting a feel for the city before meeting her, and Donald thought this sensible. He then suggested we use one of the days to visit Yorba Linda, a small town twenty-five miles from Huntington Beach where the Richard Nixon Presidential Library and Museum was located. For him it would be a pilgrimage, just as meeting Daisy would be mine.

When Donald left that night, I emailed Mr Seymer and advised him of our travel plans and suggested he arrange a meeting with Daisy for the evening of Monday 9 September. I then went online and booked two seats in BA's business class – leaving on the 3rd and returning on the 16th – and reserved two rooms in one of Huntington Beach's more prestigious hotels – or so the room rate suggested.

Mr Seymer wasn't one to waste time, and the following afternoon I received an email from him confirming that Daisy was available on the night suggested and looking forward to hearing my news, which, I presumed, referred to the sentence in my letter to Mr Stenger *a situation has arisen recently that will likely benefit Ms Lamprich*. Mr Seymer said that he'd travel from Los Angeles on the day and meet me for a drink at the Lemonade restaurant in the Pacific City complex and then introduce me to Daisy at a place called Dukes.

I was cock-a-hoop when I read his message and doubted the day would get better. In thinking this I was correct, because when I turned on the local news that evening it took a complete nosedive. (You might remember these sentences from the opening paragraph of continuation 7, which I'd originally used to bring continuation 6 to an end. Rather than leave you cliffhanging, as I'd intended to do at the time, I'll explain the situation directly.)

The odd thing about me watching the local news that evening is that I don't usually watch the local news, and so it was purely by chance that I saw Ric being arrested. I prefer to get my news in bullet form from the BBC's red button service, and I only tune in to the actual news if I've seen something of interest – a terrorist attack, for instance, or news of a royal wedding. I'd been about to press the red button when I recognised Ric on the screen, seemingly having a barbecue on Charing Cross Road, and I immediately turned up the volume. I was, however, too late to the story to make sense of it. It appeared there'd been some kind of fracas and, as Ric was waving a large pair of tongs in the air and shouting at the people entering and exiting Foyles Bookshop, I could only assume that he'd been the cause of it, especially when the last few frames showed him being led away by the police and bundled into a van.

The next day I scanned the pages of the *Evening Standard* and found a short caption under a photograph of the incident on page 12.

Ric Leszcynski, a former employee of the literary agency Perry, Strauss & Mann, was arrested outside Foyles Bookshop yesterday after barbecuing 26 sausages and 3 copies of Wolf Hall *by the award winning author Hilary Mantel. Mr Leszcynski is currently undergoing psychiatric tests and was unavailable for comment.*

Well, this news was certainly unwelcome, and I immediately phoned Charing Cross Police Station for an update. After it became clear that I was neither a relative of Ric's nor a person who could pronounce his last name – and despite my assurances that I was a close friend and business partner – the policeman who'd answered the phone politely brought our conversation to an end. I then called Graham and asked if there was anything he could do, and when he phoned back, two hours later, he said that there wasn't.

The only information he'd been able to gain – and this from a detective at the station who occasionally did 'odd jobs' for Grant, Burdett and Hargrave – was that Ric was claiming to have been protesting the moribund nature of books at the time of his arrest, and that by barbecuing copies of *Wolf Hall* alongside two-dozen sausages he had been doing little more than highlighting an embarrassing truth – that present-day publishing was dead meat.

Rather than the act itself, however, it had been the rambling nature of Ric's answers and his attempt to grab an officer's whistle that had caused them most concern. It appeared to the psychiatrist on call that Ric was suffering from a form of nervous breakdown and had, for Ric's own safety, arranged for him to be sectioned.

It appeared that our mission to blow the existing publishing paradigm to smithereens was on hold – certainly Ric was.

And the bad news just kept on coming. I'd no sooner put the phone down when Edmundo rang and told me that he and Nelly, at least for the time being, were homeless.

Edmundo and Nelly lived on the eleventh floor of a mid-rise block of flats overlooking the Sacred Heart Church. Nelly had joked once that they were spoilt for choice when they rose on a morning: they could look up to God or down on the church. Either way, it was a winning situation, especially as Edmundo had use of one of the lock-up garages in its grounds.

Clarence and his family lived in the same building, and it was with them they'd stayed the previous night after a part of their neighbour's floor – and their ceiling – had come crashing down. It was something to do with broken water pipes, but more than that I can't say. I don't really understand these things.

When Edmundo said that the council had yet to find them alternative accommodation for the time it would take to restore their apartment, I immediately told him that he and Nelly would stay with me.

'That's the end of the subject, Edmundo,' I said when he tried to protest my kindness. 'Mi casa es tu casa,' I added, which was about the only Spanish I knew and a phrase I'd never expected to use.

It took Edmundo three trips to bring what was salvageable of their belongings: clothes and bedding mostly, but also boxes of photographs and precious keepsakes like Nelly. They had contents insurance to cover their losses, and once they'd settled into the top floor, which had its own bathroom, their spirits started to rise. I insisted they make the house their own. We would eat together and watch television together, and if I ever felt like being alone, either to write my journal or to read, then I would leave them in situ and go to the basement.

Donald came by for a short visit that evening and, as always, greeted Nelly by giving her a kiss on both cheeks, something that Edmundo and I would have never dared do to Lydia, and probably something that Donald shied away from, too.

'You managed to save your pipes, didn't you – and the tambourine?'

Edmundo and Nelly said that they had.

'Well thank God for small mercies, then!' Donald said. 'We'd have looked well if it had just been me and Clarence playing next week. The spotlight would have gone to the fellah's head.'

It was easy living with Edmundo and Nelly, and I grew to like the arrangement. And it was comforting to know that there'd be someone looking after the house while I was in California. It's a safe neighbourhood, but, well, you never can tell, can you? And I have an electric toothbrush these days, and I wouldn't have wanted it used by some ne'er-do-well who broke into the house and decided to clean his teeth while he was there.

The full band practised their set four times in the days leading to the concert, and on the Thursday night Nelly joined us for the evening, though not for long. After listening to our gibber-jabber, as she called it, for no more than twenty minutes, she decided that her time would be better spent ironing clothes, and so this is what she did. She did, however, take the bottle of bourbon with her and, by the number of times the back door opened, she must have smoked at least four cigarettes.

'Nelly doesn't smoke when she's playing, does she?' I asked, wondering if she modelled her stage persona on Keith Richards.

'There's no drinking or smoking allowed when we perform,' Donald said. 'We're role models for a younger generation, Rod, and we have to set an example.'

I think Donald was probably overstating the sway of the band when he said this, but it was good to know that Nelly wouldn't be puffing away on stage.

'No one but us knows that Nelly smokes,' Edmundo added. 'From everyone else she hides it, and she would never allow herself to be seen smoking in public. Take this as a compliment, my friends. She relaxes in your company, though why is a mystery to all but God, who, no doubt, will confiscate her cigarettes and give her a good talking-to when she goes to heaven many years from now.'

*

Because parking on the street and in surrounding streets was for residents only, Edmundo had been forced to leave his car at the flat, and we drove to the square in Donald's small Fiat. The car only had two doors, and it was difficult for a grown person to enter and exit the backseat. It would have been more practical for Nelly to sit in the front, but once I'd reminded her whose roof it was she was sleeping under that night, she was kind enough to offer the passenger seat to me.

'It's lucky for us that Lydia has a headache,' I said. 'Otherwise one of us would have been walking to the concert.'

'And who do you think that person would have been, Rod?' Nelly asked. 'You or me?'

I think Nelly was teasing me when she said this, but I noted a slight edge to her voice.

'Lydia doesn't have a headache,' Donald said. 'She might have told you she did, but she doesn't. She's staying home because she thinks we're demeaning ourselves by playing in public and she wants no part of it. Good riddance is what I say.'

'Me, too,' Edmundo said. 'I say good riddance, too. I like the word and I will add it to my vocabulary.'

'Well, I think she's missing out,' I said. 'And it's not as if you're busking without a licence, is it? You've been *asked* to perform. Who did ask you?'

'Some friends,' Edmundo replied.

'Do I know them?'

'They're not that type of friends, Rod,' Donald explained. 'It's a civic society: Friends of Battersea or Battersea Square or something. They arrange events to bring residents and local businesses together. They're the ones who organised the carol service we went to.'

All I knew about the history of Battersea was what I'd read on a paper placemat in a local restaurant. It had, according to the mat, been named after a small island during the Saxon period, but before I'd had a chance to read any further the soup arrived. Because it was 1 September, though, I presumed the day held some importance for Battersea and I asked Donald if something of significance had happened on this day.

'The only event I know of is Germany's invasion of Poland, which would make today – give me a minute – the *eightieth* anniversary of the outbreak of World War II. I doubt we're celebrating this, though.'

'A friend of mine was born on 1 September,' Edmundo said. 'His name was Mateo.'

'I was thinking more along the lines of something that happened in Battersea,' I said. 'Do you know of anything, Nelly?'

'No. I'm just sitting here thankful that Jesus' disciples had more about them than you three. And I'm going to need some help getting out of here when we get to Clarence's!'

Clarence was standing with his wife and children in the parking area of the flats when we arrived. He gave Donald a visitor's sticker to put in his windscreen and then lent me a hand getting Nelly out of the car when he saw me struggling.

It was the first time I'd met his family and Clarence had good reason to be proud of them. Tyanna was a beautiful young woman and the children, Glenmore and Alyssa, were no less charming. I complimented them on their appearance and told them how much I admired their father's ability to play the steel drum with two pan sticks in each hand. At this point, Donald looked at his watch and suggested we make a move to the square, even though it was only a short distance and the band wasn't expected for another hour.

'You okay to walk, Rod, or would you like me to carry you?' Nelly asked.

Everybody thought this was funny and so I smiled along with them, even though I was getting a little tired of Nelly's ribbing. Maybe I'd been wrong to sit in the passenger seat, but it was out of respect for Nelly that I'd allowed her to sit in the back. We do, after all, live in an age of equality, and no one is more sensitive to this than me. To have allowed Nelly to sit in the front simply because she was a woman and overweight would have been discriminatory.

Although Battersea Square is known as a square, it is in fact more of a triangle; a two-way road running the length of its base and an open apex leading to Battersea High Street. The buildings in the square are occupied by small restaurants, offices, hairdressers and estate agents, but the central area is open and designed for sitting. There'd been a farmers' market in the morning and the stalls were being cleared when we arrived. I don't know why, but I was surprised by the number of people there, and I started to worry that we wouldn't find a seat. It was then I heard Henry's voice:

'Rod, Rod – we're over here, Rod!'

Henry was wearing a pair of long chequered shorts and a T-shirt depicting a man shaving his face with a weasel. Thankfully, he and Lorna had managed to secure a table close to the stage and, judging by the number of empty glasses, had been there for some time. It was one of those wooden picnic tables with attached benches and could seat eight at a pinch. Henry stood and gave his seat to Tyanna, and Nelly squeezed in next to Lorna. I made the necessary introductions before kissing Lorna, and then Henry put his arms around me and gave me a big hug.

'Good to see you again, dude. Cool sunglasses.'

I'd obviously made an impression on Henry, because the next thing he did was pull a large tartan handkerchief from his trouser pocket.

'What do you think of this, Rod: sweet or what? I can tie it around my head, too.'

Lorna was looking at Henry as if she'd like to tie the bandana around his neck, and when he turned his head to talk to Clarence she mouthed the words 'two fucking hours!' which I presumed was the length of time she'd already been in his company. It struck me that Lorna was in need of a drink and I gestured to a man wearing a large apron who proved to be the local cheesemonger.

'It's self-service,' Lorna said. 'That's why my glass is empty. Give Henry some money and he'll get them. Henry! Help Rod with the drinks, will you?'

Henry returned to the table and made a note of the orders on his phone. I then pressed some notes into his hand and told him to keep the change.

'Thank you, sir,' he replied in an overly theatrical voice, 'I don't mind if I do.'

'Do you ever get nervous before you play?' I asked Clarence.

'Only for the others,' he smiled. 'I'm the background guy, and so no one notices my mistakes.'

'Donald is the only one who makes mistakes,' Edmundo said. 'Is that not right, Donald?'

'I suppose it is,' Donald said. 'I mean, I made the mistake of befriending a fellah like you, didn't I, and if I was dumb enough to do that then there's a good chance I've made others. But they're the mistakes of a well-meaning man and not the faults of a trombone player.'

'What do you know about nothing?' Edmundo said by way of reply. 'Nothing! That is what you know about nothing. Good riddance!'

'Do you people actually like each other?' Lorna asked.

'I wouldn't go so far as to say that,' Donald laughed, 'but we're *alike*, and that's the main thing. It's a lot easier spending time with these fellahs than it is my wife.'

'It would be easier spending time with a gynaecologist than it would your wife, Donald. It's hardly a commendation. Where is she, anyway?'

'She's got a headache,' Donald replied.

'Well, better her than me,' Lorna said.

No sooner had Henry returned with the drinks than a man, who I presumed to be one of the organisers, approached Donald and took him to one side. After a short conversation, Donald came back to the table and asked the other band members to gather their instruments and follow him to the green room, which was a small makeshift space above the bakery.

Now it was just me, Lorna, Henry, Tyanna, Glenmore and Alyssa, and we were able to spread out more. The two children gravitated towards Henry, no doubt drawn by the colour of his hair, and Lorna and Tyanna chatted easily. I was left to my thoughts and I was content to be so. It was a warm day without a cloud in the sky, and I wondered if it was a day like this when the Germans invaded Poland. What a poor use they put to that day!

'I've just been telling Tyanna that Henry wants to be an actor,' Lorna said.

'An actor? I thought you said he was looking for a career in the art world.'

'That was last month. I don't suppose you know any actors, do you?'

I didn't, and nor did I have any ambition to meet one. And nor, for that fact, did I have any desire to meet the Danters that day, yet there they were, heading to our table with Roy in tow wearing a sparkly pashmina with a large Momentum button pinned to it.

'I told Jez it was you, didn't I, Jez?' Edie said by way of introducing herself to the table. 'I said that's Rod sitting over there, and you said it wasn't, didn't you?'

'I did,' Jez said. 'Hello, Rod.'

'Hello, Jez.'

'We can't stay long,' Edie said after taking a seat. 'We just wanted to give Roy a taste of some live music before he goes for his dance lesson. Do you know anything about the Donald Walker Experience?'

'Well, yes, as a matter of fact I do,' I said. 'They practise in my basement, and the man who came to your house the other night *is* Donald Walker. The Donald Walker Experience is his band.'

'Christ!' Jez said.

'You must be Donald's wife, then,' Edie said, turning to Lorna. 'How's your circulation?'

'I have no idea what you're talking about, Edith, but if you think that I'm married to Donald Walker then you must be out of your fucking head!'

Lorna then turned to Tyanna and apologised for her language.

I was surprised by how easily Edie collected herself after such a comment, but she barely skipped a beat before telling us that Roy had stunned them both that morning by pointing out that Jeremy Corbyn and Jesus Christ had the same initials.

'You know how people say that kids say the funniest things?' Lorna said.

Edie immediately nodded her head in agreement.

'Well they don't! And it's not the first time I've heard that said about Jeremy Corbyn. I don't want to worry you, but I think your son might be a plagiarist.'

Even I couldn't rescue the situation from this assault, and it was no surprise when the Danters chose to leave. In some ways this was a pity, because even if they hadn't enjoyed Donald's music, they would have certainly appreciated the politically correct mix of his band members.

'Ladies and Gentlemen,' a man's voice boomed over the speaker. 'It gives me great pleasure to introduce Battersea's very own – the Donald Walker Experience!'

The band climbed to the stage – located at the top of the square and away from the traffic – wearing black T-shirts emblazoned with the initials DWE in red, and Donald waved to the crowd as if he'd known them his whole life. They paused for a moment, waited for the noise to die down and then launched into *Anemone*.

Although tending to stay in the same area, Donald, Edmundo and Clarence were never stationary when they played their instruments, but Nelly remained stock-still and stared at the audience like one of those living statues you see in Covent Garden. It was her favoured pose when she performed, and if I hadn't known this already I would have worried that she was still annoyed about the seating arrangements in the Fiat.

Henry, Glenmore and Alyssa joined the people dancing at the front of the stage, while Tyanna, Lorna and I remained seated. I was proud of my friends that day. Their practising had paid off and they were giving the performance of their lives.

'I take it all back, Rod,' Lorna shouted into my ear. 'Your friends aren't stupid, they're fucking fantastic!'

I couldn't have agreed more.

The last song they played was my favourite Brian Jonestown Massacre song. It was called *Nevertheless* and I vocalised the words until Lorna told me to shut up. And then the last note played and the band stepped from the stage to loud and prolonged applause.

'Not bad, eh?' Donald said when he reached the table.

'No, not bad at all, Donald,' I said. 'Not bad at all!'

I offered to pay for another round of drinks, but because he was driving Donald suggested we take the party back to my house. I was happy to agree to this, but disappointed that Clarence and Tyanna were unable to join us and that Lorna and Henry also had other plans.

'Look, Rod,' Lorna said as she was about to leave, 'I've been invited to a dinner party next Saturday and it's couples only. Can you pick me up at seven?'

'I'm afraid I can't, Lorna,' I apologised. 'I'm flying to Los Angeles on Tuesday.'

'Los Angeles?' she repeated, surprised by the news. 'What the hell are you flying there for?'

'I have to meet someone in Huntington Beach,' I said.

Continuation 9

Huntington Beach

The day before the flight, and while Lydia was out of the house, Donald came round with his suitcase and left it in the hallway. Ever considerate of his wife's well-being – or so I thought at the time – he'd decided to enter my house through the tunnel on our day of departure, rather than disturb Lydia at an hour of day she was unfamiliar with by opening and closing the front door. Edmundo had once volunteered to plane the swollen wood, but Donald had declined his offer on the grounds that Lydia wouldn't allow it. His wife, he explained, was averse to change – even change for the better.

Early the next morning, just as Edmundo, Nelly and I were finishing breakfast, Donald arrived with his hand luggage and wearing a boiler suit.

'You're not travelling to America dressed like that, are you?' Nelly asked. 'You look like a mechanic.'

'Of course I'm not. I've got my best bib and tucker on underneath these dungarees. Maybe your husband would crawl through a tunnel wearing a suit, but I've got more sense than him.'

He then took off the overalls and revealed the suit he'd worn on the night we'd christened the basement, and when

Lydia had arrived dressed for the opera.

'It wouldn't surprise me if they bump me up to first class when they see me dressed like this,' he said. 'I'm surprised you're not wearing a suit, Rod.'

In all likelihood, Donald would be the only person in business class dressed so formally, but I chose not to mention this. The taxi would be arriving shortly and there was no time for him to change into something more comfortable. Besides, the combination of a suit and his long hair gave him a distinguished air, and one that served him well.

'Are you going to miss me?' Donald asked, standing over Edmundo and resting his hands on his shoulders.

'Probably not,' Edmundo smiled, 'but I will miss Señor Rod. Take good care of him, my friend, and bring him home safely.'

'And don't drink too much!' Nelly advised us.

'We're not schoolboys, Nelly, we're grown men,' I said.

'That's what worries me. Schoolboys have more sense.'

At this point I received an alert from the taxi company advising me that the car would arrive in ten minutes. I made a final check of my travel documents and asked Donald to do the same, and then went to the bathroom to brush my teeth.

When I walked back into the kitchen, I could have sworn I heard Nelly saying that I was making a fool of myself.

'Why would you think that, Nelly?' I asked.

Surprised by my sudden reappearance – I'd used a regular toothbrush that morning rather than the electric one that takes longer – she appeared startled.

'Think what?' she said after a moment's pause.

'That I'm making a fool of myself.'

'I was talking about Edmundo,' she said.

'Me? What have I done?' Edmundo asked.

'Well, for one thing...'

'The taxi's here,' Donald announced.

While Edmundo carried my case to the car still wondering what he'd done to upset Nelly, the person he was thinking of gave me a hug and told me to take good care of myself and to say hello to Daisy for her.

'Tell her I'm looking forward to meeting her, Rod, but remember – if it doesn't work out the way you want it to, there are plenty more fish in the sea.'

'You mean the ones you haven't eaten?' Donald said.

We arrived at Heathrow in good time. The flight wasn't due to leave until 11:00 but we had to be there three hours early. Everything ran smoothly until we entered the security gate and had to take off our shoes, belts and jackets and place them in a plastic tray for screening. I walked through the body scanner without problem, but when Donald followed me the machine beeped and he was taken to one side and patted down by a security guard, who found his metal comb in a back trouser pocket.

'I'm going to have to confiscate this,' the guard said. 'It's a dangerous weapon.'

'I've got dangerous hair,' Donald said, thinking the guard was joking.

When the guard made it clear to him that he wasn't joking and was, in fact, being deadly serious, Donald started to protest. He told the man that he'd had the comb for over thirty years and not once considered attacking another person with it, and that, when he'd fought in Vietnam, neither the Australian nor American armies had seen fit to arm him with a metal comb before sending him into battle. And then, after these common-sense arguments had failed to convince the guard, Donald became further agitated and questioning of life's fairness when another passenger, carrying a black titanium charge card, was allowed to continue his journey with the metal card still in his possession – and this after Donald had pointed out that the card could be sharpened into a razor blade.

'And that man wasn't even wearing a suit!' he added for good measure.

I approached the guard and asked if it was possible to send the comb to Donald's home address if we paid the expense. He said it was, and he was happy to accept the £20 note I gave him. In exchange, he gave me his name and promised to take care of the matter. Although Donald wasn't happy with the situation he agreed to the compromise, but insisted on the comb being sent to my home address.

In truth, it was a relief for me when Donald's comb was taken from him, because the one thing that annoys me about Donald is the frequency with which he combs his hair, and often in public. Already that day he'd combed his hair at my house, twice in the taxi, once during check-in and another time after we'd gone through passport control, and on most of these occasions it had been unnecessary.

After we'd put our shoes back on and re-threaded our belts, Donald went off in search of a plastic comb and I arranged to meet him in Pret a Manger. Although the tickets allowed us use of the executive lounge, I preferred to remain in the concourse and rub shoulders with ordinary people. I don't like segregation, and if it wasn't for the comfort afforded by business class, I would happily fly economy. I ordered coffee and bacon sandwiches for us both, and took the tray to a small table close to a large television screen.

I was halfway through my sandwich before Donald joined

me. After buying his comb, he'd taken a detour through the duty-free shop and been annoyed to discover that the whisky he'd been hoping to buy was more expensive there than at Waitrose.

'It's a con is what it is, Rod. False representation! And I've probably paid over the odds for this comb, too.'

He showed me the comb he'd bought. It was large and pink and fortunately, in so far as I was concerned, too big to carry on his person.

'The colour's a bit loud, isn't it? Don't they sell black combs?'

'Only small ones – and the teeth would just break off if I tried combing my hair with one. I've got strong hair, Rod, and this is the strongest comb they had. It's a woman's comb.'

He then started to eat his sandwich and occasionally glanced at the television.

'That friend of yours hasn't been on again, has he? That barbecue fellah.'

'No, Ric's still in hospital. If I knew which one, I'd send him a card from California.'

I bought two more coffees and we stayed at the same table until it was time to board the flight. Our seats on the plane were adjacent, but separated by an opaque plastic screen that could be lowered and raised at the press of a button. We were served glasses of champagne while the crew readied the plane for take-off, drinks of our choice once the plane was airborne and a luncheon worthy of The Ivy.

'This is the life, eh, Rod? Real glasses, real plates and proper knives and forks; better than all that plastic stuff they give you in economy. A man could get used to this, especially these seats. But tell me, what happened to all those good-looking women who used to be air stewardesses? The dolly who served me when I flew back from Vietnam was a real stunner, but the one on this flight could give Diane Abbott a run for her money. Did I ever tell you about getting back from Vietnam?

'Well, rather than return to Australia after my tour of duty ended, I thought it would be quicker and cheaper if I just hitched a ride home with the British Air Force and go through the discharge process at Australia House. The New Zealand Air Force flew me to Singapore where the RAF was stationed, but when I got there the buggers refused to fly me because they said the Vietnam War was nothing to do with them, and I ended up having to pay for a commercial flight. It cost me £220 and just about wiped out my savings. And that was economy class, too!'

I warned Donald to keep his voice down because the stewardess he'd been referring to was now heading our way. I also told him I was about to take a nap and that I'd be shortly raising the screen.

'No worries, Rod. I was thinking of watching a film, anyway.'

Despite his admiration for the United States, this was Donald's first trip to the country. I'd been there only once, and my stay had been so miserable that I'd vowed never to return. I'd been working for Pinkney Industries at the time, and my father had offered me a position in a towboat company operating out of Greenville, Mississippi.

Because my father looked upon me as an employee rather than a blood relative, he'd insisted on me flying there economy – first to New York and then to Memphis – and travelling by bus from Memphis to Greenville and rooming in a cheap boarding house close to the river. My understanding was that I was there to help manage the company, but when I was met by Mr Martin, the man who oversaw my father's operation, he told me I was to be a deckhand on a boat currently moored in Savage, Minnesota. And so, two days later, and courtesy of my father, the worst six months of my life began.

The *Sarah Drew* was triple-decked and painted white, and the newest of the company's fleet. It was 150 feet long and 35 feet wide and powered by a large diesel engine. It had a shallow draft and a square bow mounted with large metal plates and could push as many as eighteen barges. The barges each measured 200 by 35 feet and were lashed together with thick steel wire into tows 1,200 feet long and 105 feet wide. The boat delivered cargoes of chemicals, coal and petroleum to points along the river, occasionally picking up and transferring other barges en route, and operated on a twenty-four-hour cycle.

There were eleven crew members: a captain and relief captain, two engineers, a cook, a mate and five deckhands. As the most recent and least experienced of the crew, I was given one of the two square watches, working six hours on and six hours off. My basic duties were to clean the cabins and the galley, the toilets and showers, make coffee and wake other members of the crew when it was time for them to go on duty.

If these had been my only responsibilities, I might have enjoyed my time on the boat, but they weren't. I also had to help with the tow, and for this particular task I was ill-suited. Every part of moving a tow involved lifting something heavy – either ratchets, coils of wire or rolls of thick rope – and moving the occasional desk at my father's offices had done little to prepare my muscles for such work.

I learned quickly that the commodities of sympathy and understanding were as scarce on a towboat as they were in my father's house, and for the time I worked on the river I became a lightning rod – called Rod – for blame and ridicule: if anything went wrong during a manoeuvre, then I was the one at fault – and this, I'll accept, was invariably true. But, to my way of thinking, the responsibility lay as much with them as with me. Why, for instance, would they expect me to be capable of throwing a rope when I could barely lift one? And why, of all people, would they send me back to the boat for two ratchets urgently needed at the head of the tow when I struggled to carry one?

'The only thing you're good for, limey, is changing beds!' the captain once yelled over the loudspeaker when the barge I was standing on came loose from the tow and started to drift downriver.

And that wasn't the only thing to drift downriver: I did, too!

With the help of another deckhand, I'd been trying to secure a front barge to the boat when it happened. A sudden swell caused the wire we were struggling with to tighten, and when the man on the barge let go of his end I was dragged overboard. I was wearing a life vest at the time and in no danger of drowning, but there was a distinct possibility of me being sucked underwater and killed by the turbine propellers at the rear of the boat. My luck, however, was in that day, and the wash pushed me away from the boat and out of harm's way. I don't know how long the captain and crew debated my rescue, but I'd drifted a good three miles by the time the launch arrived.

It was usual for a member of crew to work for thirty days straight and then take the next thirty days off, but my father had insisted on Mr Martin keeping me active. Consequently, I spent no more than ten days on dry land during my stay in America, and these in Greenville, a town with little to offer anyone not born there. I became stronger and leaner in those months but no more proficient in my duties, and though I grew accustomed to the crews I made few, if any, friends.

I know I didn't experience the real America when I worked on the river, but it was an episode that coloured my view of the country and I never intended to return. And yet, for the sake of a young woman I'd seen on television, I was now doing this very thing – and, if the captain were to be believed, I would be treading its soil in less than thirty minutes.

'It was easier getting in than it was leaving,' Donald commented when we were standing in line for a taxi. 'I'll admit that no one seemed particularly pleased to see us, but I was expecting more of a grilling, weren't you?'

There were now only three people in front of us, and when they all climbed into the same taxi Donald and I were free to take the next cab. The traffic was heavy but flowing that evening, and we arrived at the hotel in under fifty minutes. The fare was $120 and I gave the driver an extra twenty when he took the suitcases from the trunk and left them at the door to the hotel.

From the kerb, and in the half-light, the Huntington Beach Inn looked just as nice as it had on Expedia, and I was surprised when no bellboy came for our luggage. The doors, which I'd expected to open automatically, remained shut when we approached them and we had to push our way into the lobby. The young man behind the reception desk was dressed in jeans and a T-shirt and eating a sandwich.

'Messrs Pinkney and Walker,' I announced. 'We have pre-paid rooms.'

The man wiped his mouth with the back of his hand and checked the computer.

'Where you guys from?' he asked.

'England,' Donald said, 'and we've been travelling for a considerable time!'

The night clerk took the hint and focused on his work. He handed us two key cards for rooms on the third floor and wished us a pleasant stay. Donald asked where the bar was and the man replied there wasn't one. And neither did the hotel have a restaurant, only a small breakfast room. And if this wasn't bad enough, it turned out that there was someone already sleeping in Donald's room, and because the hotel was full that night we had to share not only the same room but also the same bed.

'I'm sorry about this, Donald,' I said. 'I thought the hotel would have been better. It was certainly in demand when I made the booking because three other people were trying to reserve rooms at the same time and the hotel only had two left. At least, that's what Expedia said. I think now that I might have been panicked into buying them, but at £200 a room I was expecting something a bit more luxurious.'

'£200 for two weeks isn't bad,' Donald said. 'And the room's clean enough. I've stayed in a lot worse places.'

'No, it's £200 per room *per day*,' I said. 'That's why I'm surprised the hotel isn't better.'

Donald gasped when he heard this and wondered if Expedia was owned by the same people who ran the duty-free shops at Heathrow Airport. He asked me which side of the bed I preferred to sleep on and I told him the right. This pleased him because he always slept on the left. I changed into my pyjamas and Donald changed into a pair of boxer shorts and a T-shirt and we climbed into bed.

'It's a good job that Danter fellah can't see us now,' he laughed. 'If he thought we were gay just because you were wearing a cravat, there'd be no explaining this... I should warn you I snore, Rod, so if I wake you up in the night just give me a poke in the ribs. That's what Lydia does.'

'What did Lydia say when you told her you were going to California? I never thought to ask.'

'Nothing – I didn't tell her.'

*

Although Huntington Beach is a city of some 200,000 residents and stretches for many miles inland, it is defined by its beach culture and the small locale close to the pier. The one advantage of our hotel was its proximity to this neighbourhood, and the next morning, shortly after breakfast and once Donald had been assigned a new room, we set off on foot.

The Inn was located on 8th Street, four blocks north of the historic centre, and it was a walk of less than ten minutes to Main. The street was crowded with restaurants, bars and shops selling surfboards, surfing clothes and wetsuits, and once we'd walked its length, we stopped at a cafe called The Coffee Bean and Tea Leaf and sat at an outdoor table close to the fountain and watched a man mop the sidewalk.

'The coffee's a lot better here than at the hotel,' Donald said. 'If that's a Best Western then I'd hate to stay at one of their worse ones. You ought to write that Expedia fellah and give him a piece of your mind when you get home, Rod. £200! It annoys me just to think about it – and it's not even my money! And I'd be surprised if those people in the breakfast room were paying that rate. They looked too cash-strapped.'

I suspected Donald was right. The guests we'd seen over breakfast – both men and women – looked to have been low-budget tourists or construction workers, and all had been heavily tattooed. And the breakfast itself had been a disappointment: self-service, and the choice limited to orange juice, cereals, cold pastries and what passed for scrambled eggs. The coffee cups had been cardboard, the glasses and cutlery plastic and the plates, polystyrene. All in all, it had been a step down from eating a meal in the economy class of an airplane.

The previous night, after telling me that Lydia had known nothing of the trip, Donald had fallen asleep almost immediately and I was left to wonder why, and if this was the reason he'd left his mobile phone at home. The tables in the breakfast room had been set too close together for intimate conversation and so I asked him about it now.

'Because she'd have just said no and we'd have ended up fighting about it. And knowing her, she'd have probably tried to hide my passport. No, it's easier having the argument when I get home and after the fact. I left her a note, though, so it's not as if she's going to report me missing. I told Edmundo to act dumb if she asked him about it, and that's a role he was born to play. Ha!'

I hadn't wanted to cause problems for Donald by inviting him on the trip, but he seemed untroubled by his situation. I worried, though, that he'd left Edmundo to face the music and I hoped that Nelly, a woman who gives as good as she gets, would be there to defend him if Lydia ever decided to confront him.

'It's a pity Edmundo can't be with us,' I said. 'I think he'd like it here.'

'I'm sure he would, but I doubt there'd have been room for him in the bed last night. It was a squeeze with just the two of us.'

We finished our coffees and walked to the pier at the intersection of Main and the Pacific Coast Highway, a road that runs the length of the shoreline and divides the city from the beach. While we were standing at the crossing area, waiting for the lights to change, Donald pointed out Dukes Restaurant where Mr Seymer had arranged the meeting with Daisy.

The pier, according to Donald, who'd picked up an information sheet at the hotel and was acting as tour guide, was one of the longest on the West Coast. It was 1,850 feet long and built to withstand 31-foot waves and earthquakes of 7.0 magnitudes. Unlike the original pier, which had been constructed in 1904 from uncreosoted timber, the current structure was made of concrete and dated from 1992. It had three octagonal platforms, a diamond at the end, and offered panoramic views of Catalina Island, Newport Beach, Long Beach and San Pedro.

The temperature that day – indeed, for the duration of our stay – was in the high seventies and the sky was cloudless. We walked at a leisurely pace, occasionally stopping to allow Donald to jot down the various rules and regulations that took his interest, and for a longer time, after buying ice creams, on a concrete bench dedicated to Viola Hartunian whose *love lived on,* and presumably in the concrete. There was a diner at the end of the pier called Ruby's and we decided to eat breakfast there the next day.

Most of the people strolling on the pier were tourists like us, but those fishing appeared to be locals, many of them of Asian origin, and Donald wondered if they were Vietnamese. Most of the fish they caught were mackerel, but one man landed a stingray. He hauled it from the ocean with a grappling hook and put it in an ice chest.

'All these fish are making me hungry,' Donald said. 'Where do you fancy eating lunch?'

I suggested the restaurant we were supposed to meet Mr

Seymer in the following week, but I didn't know where it was. We stopped to ask directions at the information kiosk in the small plaza at the foot of the pier, and then continued south until we came to Pacific City, an upscale development of oceanfront shopping, dining and entertainment.

Lemonade was a cafeteria-style restaurant close to the entryway, where you ordered your food at the counter and had it delivered to a table. There was a wide choice of salads, braised meats and sandwiches, and it took time to make sense of the combinations. Eventually, I ordered pineapple chicken and green beans and Donald plumped for a bowl of mango chicken. Unsurprisingly, for a restaurant calling itself Lemonade, it also sold lemonade, and we ordered two large glasses of the old-fashioned variety.

While we were sitting at a table waiting for the food to arrive, Donald scanned the notes he'd made that morning and asked me how many regulations I thought applied to the pier. I had no idea, but I guessed at six. He told me I wasn't even close, and then, supposing I'd be interested, gave a full enumeration.

'You can't fish for white sharks and you can't cut bait or clean fish on the benches or on the pier's deck. There's no overhead casting and no dogs allowed. And you're not permitted to smoke on the pier, leave litter or feed birds and other wildlife – though what they mean by that beats me. I can't see a deer or a bear finding its way to the pier, can you?

'And no one's allowed to jump off it or climb on the railings or tamper with the life-saving equipment. There's no roller-skating, skateboarding or cycling allowed, and any authorised vehicle is limited to a speed of 5 mph. To my calculation, that's fourteen.'

Donald thought that rules and regulations were important,

and the bedrock of any civilised society. And as he viewed the United States as the greatest civilisation on earth, he thought that fourteen was a fitting number for one of its piers and one that put the by-laws of Battersea Park to shame, which, so far as he could remember, only prohibited planes from landing and taking off and people from shaking carpets and abandoning dead animals.

As the day progressed, Donald was further comforted by the rules and regulations applying to the beach (nine), swimming in the ocean (four), and the paved boardwalk that ran its length (six). If, indeed, the United States was the land of the free, it also appeared there were a lot of things a person living there was prevented from doing.

The restaurant was busy, but the food arrived in good time and we enjoyed both our meal and the lemonade. We left the cafeteria and wandered the various floors of the galleria, noting the restaurants and deciding which ones to visit.

By now, I was feeling tired, and I suggested to Donald that we return to the hotel for a siesta. It wasn't so much the jetlag affecting me as the distance I'd walked that day, which was well beyond anything I was used to. I didn't tell Donald this because it would have only vindicated his opinion, often expressed, that unnecessary use of a mobility scooter would weaken rather than save a man's legs. No doubt he had a point, but I was too set in my ways to take heed of such counsel, and I certainly had no intentions of joining the Ramblers' Association when I returned to England.

We crossed the Highway and walked back to the hotel on the boardwalk. There were lifeguard huts along the beach positioned at 200-yard intervals and set on stilts, and volleyball courts at either side of the pier. People were out walking, exercising or riding bicycles rented by the hour, and Donald recalled the days he'd spent cycling the streets of Brierley Hill and wondered if he should give it another try.

We left the boardwalk close to the hotel and climbed the steps to the Highway. I waited while the desk clerk punched Donald a new keycard and we rode the lift together, arranging to meet in the lobby at seven. Donald got out at the second floor, which in England would be the first, and I continued to the third and top floor of the two-storey hotel.

I hadn't intended falling into such a deep sleep, but the next thing I knew the phone was ringing and Donald was on the line. I quickly washed my face and changed into a clean shirt, and then went down to the lobby where Donald had been waiting for fifteen minutes. He asked me where to, and I suggested somewhere close. The last thing I wanted was another long walk.

We went to Main Street, thinking we'd have a quiet drink before eating in one of its restaurants, but it was so crowded and noisy when we got there that we decided to find somewhere quieter. Donald suggested a pizza place he'd seen on 5th Street, one block nearer to the hotel, and so we went there.

The Pizza Press was a newspaper-themed pizzeria that gave its customers the option of creating their own pizzas or ordering one of its specialities. Neither of us was interested in making our own food and so we ordered two of the specialities and a bottle of red wine, once it was clear there was only microbrewery beer on tap.

Donald and I weren't beer drinkers and we'd been looking forward to drinking traditional American lagers like Budweiser and Michelob, and in this respect Huntington Beach was a disappointment. The fad there was for craft beers with unusual names like Hoppentrice, Alpha Galactic,

Amalgamator and Grandma's Pecan Style Brown, and this type of beer suited neither of us.

'So, what do you think of Huntington Beach, Rod? If push came to shove and Daisy refused to move to England, could you live here?'

'I don't know. We've only been here a day. I like it that it's flat and suitable for a mobility scooter and that the climate's warm, but it's difficult to get a feel for a place without knowing the people. I was a bit concerned by all the smartphones and not seeing anyone with a book in their hand or reading a newspaper, but it's getting like that at home now. And the number of tattoos surprised me, especially the ones on the legs of women. I hope to goodness Daisy doesn't have any. I don't know how I'd feel about that.'

'It's the dogs that got my attention,' Donald said. 'I've seen more dogs today than in all my years in Battersea. And if they weren't pit bulls, they were those small, yappy types no bigger than a cat. Come to think of it, I didn't see a cat all day. I wonder why that is?'

'I think cats are probably less of a fashion statement in California, and it would be difficult tying one to a leash. I saw one woman with a dog in her handbag and I can't see a cat standing for that. Still, it's too soon to make generalisations without having actually talked to anyone. Starting tomorrow, I think we should make a point of talking to the locals and trying to get to know them.'

*

When we walked to Ruby's Diner the next morning there were even more people fishing from the pier, and on this occasion they were exclusively Asian and almost all elderly. The men caught the fish and the women washed and cleaned them in the basins provided. They chatted in their native language and, again, Donald wondered if they were Vietnamese.

There were also more surfers in the ocean at this time of day, and they were all wearing wetsuits. Most of them idled in rows just beyond the waveline, waiting for a swell that would carry them to shore, while others duck-dived and paddled their boards through the impact zone to join them.

The diner sat in the middle of the diamond at the very end of the pier. It had a red roof, white walls and blue windows and was designed to look like a diner of the big band era. The manager seated us at a window table and handed us menus, and shortly a waitress came to take our order. She was dressed in a red and white striped uniform and wore a hat and told us her name was Kaley. Donald ordered hotcakes with a side of bacon and I ordered the scrambled eggs with sausage.

Halfway through the meal, the manager came to our table and asked if the food was to our liking. We told him it was, and then Donald asked him a question.

'What do you know about these fellahs fishing on the pier? We saw them yesterday and I told Rod – he's the gentleman sitting with me – that they reminded me of my time in Vietnam. They're not from there, are they?'

'They are,' the manager smiled, 'but these days they live in Westminster. They arrive at five every morning and wait for the pier to open. You can set your watch by them.'

'What do they do with all the fish they catch?'

'They'll keep some for themselves, but most they'll sell,' the manager said. 'Westminster's got the largest Little Saigon in the country and they'll peddle them to the shops and restaurants there. Apart from the money they spend on gas getting to the pier, it's all profit. I wish my margins were as good.'

Donald laughed, and the manager moved to the next table.

I asked Donald if he'd like to visit Westminster but he said no, adding that if the South Vietnamese had put as much effort into fighting the war as they did now to catching fish, then they'd still be living in the real Saigon and not in some enclave in Orange County.

After a full day in Huntington Beach that was, after all, a beach resort, it was understandable we were running out of things to do. At some point I wanted to see the house Daisy lived in and the grocers where she worked and accompany Donald to Richard Nixon's Presidential Library and Museum in Yorba Linda, but after the previous day's exertions we'd decided to take things easy and limit the day to a tour of the International Surfing Museum.

When I think of a museum, I always imagine a large building with an imposing facade, but the one on Olive Avenue was nothing like this. It was, in fact, more like a bar on Main Street: small in area, one-storey high and coated in pink render. Having said that, Donald and I were given a warmer welcome here than at any other museum I'd visited, and the small woman sitting behind the reception desk even apologised for having to charge us the $2 entrance fee. She introduced herself as Ruth, and told us she'd be happy to answer any of our questions.

'In the meantime, I'm going to sit right here and let you enjoy your visit in peace,' she said. 'There's nothing worse than a person getting in your hair when there's no need.'

I couldn't have agreed with her more. Ruth was a person after my own heart.

The museum had been founded by a woman who didn't surf to commemorate the history and culture of those who did, and it was dedicated to a man called Duke Kahanamoku.

Over two rooms, the museum told the story of surfing through a mixture of historic objects and memorabilia – old surfboards, posters of classic surfer films, illustrated biographies of legendary surfers and a guitar that had once belonged to Dick Dale. We also watched a short film about 66 people riding a surfboard measuring 42 feet by 11 feet by 16 inches and breaking the Guinness Record for most people riding the world's largest surfboard. The event had taken place in Huntington Beach and the surfboard was now affixed to a pole in the parking lot.

It was a nice museum but without too much to it and no one but us in it, and Donald suggested we spend some time talking to Ruth before we went for lunch.

'So, how did you find the museum?' Ruth asked.

'We had a map,' Donald said, misunderstanding the question. 'You can't get a laundry bag at the hotel, but you can take as many leaflets as you want.'

'Where are you staying in town – the Hyatt?'

'No, we have rooms in the Huntington Beach Inn,' I said. 'It's closer to the centre than the Hyatt, but otherwise... well, I was expecting something a bit better, to tell you the truth.'

'I'm sorry to hear that,' Ruth said with genuine concern. 'I know it's not much of a consolation, but if you'd checked into the hotel a hundred years ago you *would* have got something better. It was called the Huntington Inn in those days, and it was known as one of the finest hotels on the coast. It was sold to the Elks Club in the 1950s and then, in 1969, the building was torn down. The Best Western group bought the site and kept the name, but their standards are probably different...

'Anyway, what did you think of the museum? Have you enjoyed your time here?'

'It was an education,' Donald said, 'but I have a question.'

'Then you ask it,' Ruth smiled.

'The museum's dedicated to Duke Kahanamoku, but I thought George Freeth was the father of modern surfing. At least, that's what I read in one of the hotel's leaflets.'

'That's a very good question. What's your name, by the way? It's always nicer to address a person by name when you're having a conversation.'

Donald introduced himself and I introduced myself, and for the purposes of full disclosure Ruth told us that her last name was Muntz.

'Well, Donald,' Ruth continued, 'George gets the credit for introducing surfing to California – and he gave a demonstration here at the pier in 1914 – but he died of the flu in the epidemic of 1919 and it was Duke who really popularised the sport. He was a resident of Newport Beach for a time, just down the coast from here, and he used to play the ukulele for his neighbours, though that's a bit by the by.

'You could argue that both men deserve the title, because if it wasn't for them – and for others like them – it's doubtful that surfing would have survived long enough in Hawaii to have ever made it to California. The missionaries who went there in the nineteenth century tried to stamp it out, believe it or not. They were Calvinists from New England and they were uncomfortable with nudity, and even more discomfited by the Hawaiian belief that there were spirits living in the waves. It was Christianity versus surfing in those days, but today they live happily together and every year we have a Blessing of the Waves ceremony down at the pier plaza. It's on Sunday, if you're interested in going, and they'll be selling souvenir T-shirts you could take back to England with you. Am I right in thinking that's where you're from?'

'We are,' I said, 'Donald and I live in London.'

'What a wonderful city,' Ruth said. 'I went there once with a girlfriend and we toured all the sights on a red bus. It was one of the best holidays I had.'

Donald had veered into the concessions area and was looking at the postcards.

'What's this one of?' he asked.

Ruth got out of her chair and shuffled to where he was standing. Her gait was awkward and her body appeared stuck in its sitting position. The natural vista for her eyes was now the floor, and she had to swivel her head to look at the postcard.

'It's a frigate bird in the Galapagos Islands,' she said. 'I don't know why we're stocking it really, because most visitors to Huntington Beach want to send postcards *of* Huntington Beach and not of a place they're not visiting. We've got ten miles of uninterrupted coastline here, beaches to die for and the most consistent swells on the West Coast, but there's no evidence of this in the postcards we sell. I've told the owner we should be celebrating our own backyard rather than someone else's, but she doesn't listen. You'll find much nicer cards at the CVS, Donald, and you should buy them there.'

'I'll take three,' Donald said.

'Well, you're the customer,' Ruth said, slipping the cards into a small paper bag, 'but if you're interested in any of those old advertising boards, then buy them at the pier. They're a third of the price there and they all come from the same place.'

Ruth's sales technique, if indeed it was a technique, was a confusing one, and when Donald started to look through the advertising boards I was half-expecting him to buy three of those as well.

'Were you born in Huntington Beach or did you move here for the sea air?' I asked.

'I've lived here all my life, Rod, and in precisely seven minutes,' she said, looking at her watch, 'I'll have been here sixty years.'

'You're sixty today!' I said.

'Yes,' she beamed, 'and I've confounded all the doctors.'

'Well, congratulations!' Donald chimed in. 'How are you celebrating your big day?'

'Oh, I'll probably order a pizza and then catch up on my shows,' Ruth answered. 'I'm not one to get carried away.'

'Nonsense,' Donald said. 'You can't let a birthday like this pass unnoticed. No, Ruth, you'll come out to dinner with us tonight, and it will be Rod's treat. Now where would you like to eat?'

It was a pleasure to see Ruth's face light up when Donald asked her this, and once she'd made a phone call to the restaurant and secured a reservation, we agreed to meet her at Dukes at seven-thirty.

I offered to send a taxi for her, but she said there was no need because the restaurant was only a short distance from where she lived and she'd be able to get there on her mobility scooter.

There was certainly no denying now that Ruth Muntz was a person after my own heart, though her reasons for riding a scooter were probably more legitimate than my own.

Donald and I ate lunch, simple sandwiches and soft drinks, at a small deli on the Highway between 5th and Main, and then decided to stroll northwards in the direction of Long Beach.

'What do you suppose is wrong with Ruth?' Donald asked.

'I don't know. I thought it better not to ask.'

'That's what I thought,' Donald said. 'I'm going to pretend she's normal tonight. That's what I do when I watch the

Paralympics. I just pretend they're normal people.'

'Well, they are normal people,' I said. 'They just have different issues. It wouldn't surprise me if Ruth hasn't suffered at the hands of children, though, because children say what comes to mind too easily. I was visiting a friend's house during the last Paralympics and she had relatives staying with her who had a small child. We were watching television at the time and the youngster kept calling the wheelchairs wheelbarrows and the athletes, dwarves. The boy didn't mean anything by it, but if an adult made these comments, it would be offensive.'

'I take your point, Rod. I should choose my words more carefully. What about a present, though? Do you think we should buy Ruth something?'

'I don't think there's any need for that. We only met her this morning and we're buying her dinner. I think that should be enough.'

We walked along the Highway for several blocks and then found ourselves walking alongside an oil field, which neither of us had expected. We crossed over to the boardwalk at this point and started to retrace our steps, large tankers visible in the distance moored close to Long Beach, and two offshore oil platforms closer to the waterfront.

'We should ask Ruth about this when we see her tonight,' Donald said. 'If she knows the history of the hotel we're staying in, then it's likely she'll know about these oil wells.'

And, as president of the local historical society – now down to eleven members – Ruth Muntz did.

'It's what put Huntington Beach on the map,' she said over dinner that evening. 'They struck oil in 1920, and in a matter of three months the population rose from 1,500 to 7,500. They had to erect tent cities to accommodate all the people, and some of the newcomers ordered houses from the Sears, Roebuck Catalogue. You could buy a five-room house kit for as little as $672 in those days, and all you had to do was pick it up at the railway station and either assemble it yourself or pay someone to do it.

'And the pumpjacks and nodding donkeys you saw this afternoon are the same pumping units that created Huntington Beach. They're real workhorses. They can pump oil twenty-four hours a day and last for fifty years.'

'Ah, so *that's* what I'm seeing when I look down from my balcony,' I said. 'It's an old pump and storage tank! I'd been thinking it had something to do with the hotel's air-conditioning system and wondering why they didn't look after it better.'

Ruth had dressed in a short-sleeved floral print dress that evening, and I'd been surprised to see that she too had a tattoo on her arm. And the inscription, I believed, provided a clue as to her disability. It was a delicate matter and so I approached it in a circuitous manner.

'Donald was in the army, too,' I said. 'He fought alongside the Australians in Vietnam.'

'Well, that's surprising,' Ruth said. 'I didn't even know the Australians fought in that war. But what do you mean by "too"? Were you in the army as well?'

'Umm, no, I was thinking you were. I couldn't help noticing that the inscription on your arm reads First Cavalry, and that's one of the most famous combat divisions of the US Army, isn't it?'

'I think so,' Ruth said, 'but my tattoo reads First Calvary. It's the name of the church I attend.'

'Are you sure?' I said, squinting at the inked calligraphy.

'I'm sure, I'm sure, Rod. I've been going there for thirty years.'

'Yes, it says First Calvary, all right,' Donald said. 'You're reading it wrong, Rod.'

I immediately apologised and allowed Ruth to tell us what she had been doing in the years when she hadn't been in the army.

'I was a kindergarten teacher,' she said. 'And you wouldn't believe how cruel children of that age can be...'

Despite this hiccup the evening was a resounding success, and one that I'm sure Ruth would remember for the rest of her life. The restaurant was named after the same Duke that the International Surfing Museum was dedicated to, and the maître d' had seated us at a window table overlooking the ocean. Our waiter was called Anthony and he gave us his best attention. We toasted Ruth with Mai Tai cocktails, ordered crab cakes, prime sirloin steaks and slices of Key lime pie, and drank two bottles of red wine, though the second bottle, because Ruth was driving, was consumed by Donald and me.

Donald let slip that I was in Huntington Beach to meet the girl of my dreams, which was something I hadn't intended mentioning. Once acknowledged, though, and because Ruth was a person I liked and trusted, I told her the full story and how, on Monday evening, I would be meeting Daisy for the very first time in this very same restaurant.

'Oh my, that's so romantic,' Ruth said. 'I'd be swept off my feet if a man went to all that trouble to find me. I can't see that happening, though,' she laughed. 'I've been blessed with many things in life, but not a beach body. Mine's for the shadows, for the corners of life, and I'm content for it to be that way.

'Daisy's a lucky woman, Rod, and she'd be a chump to turn you down. I have a feeling that it's going to work out just fine for you, though, and when I get home tonight I'm going to pray to God that it does.'

At the end of the evening we walked Ruth to her mobility scooter. She thanked us for the most wonderful evening and said that she hoped to see us at the Blessing of the Waves ceremony on Sunday.

'Now, before I go, do you have any last questions for me? Is there anything I can do to make your stay in Huntington Beach more enjoyable?'

'Well, there is one thing, Ruth,' I said. 'Would it be possible to borrow your mobility scooter tomorrow?'

Continuation 10

D-Day

The next morning we ate a light breakfast at the Coffee Bean and Tea Leaf and then headed for a franchise on the boardwalk that rented bicycles by the hour. Rather than ride the bicycle to the International Surfing Museum, Donald chose to wheel it there, and we walked to Olive Avenue side by side.

'Now you know where you're going, don't you?' Ruth asked. 'You turn left on Main and then just follow the road.'

'We do,' I said, 'and thanks again for lending me the scooter. I'll have it back to you by two.'

'And when we get there, I'll send you a postcard of a penguin in the Falkland Islands,' Donald laughed.

I don't think Ruth understood Donald's joke, which barely registered with me, but she smiled nevertheless.

'You're sure you understand the controls, Rod – how to start the scooter, and how to accelerate and brake?'

I assured her I did, and that it was a model I was familiar with. I think Ruth had difficulty understanding why I drove a mobility scooter at home but was polite enough not to ask, and when a young couple walked into the museum with a small child in tow, we left her to take their admission fees and no doubt apologise for having to do so.

We'd set the day aside for exploring the neighbourhood Daisy lived in and to visit her place of work at Seacliff Village, both of which, according to Mr Seymer, were either on or just off Main Street. Although the downtown section of Main – where the shops and restaurants are – was no more than three short blocks, the street itself extended for miles inland and terminated at Beach Boulevard, which was one of the city's main arteries and the route taken by the taxi that brought us from the airport.

It would have been difficult walking the length of Main even in the winter months, but in the heat of summer, when the sun was unbreakable, it was well-nigh impossible. That Ruth had a mobility scooter she'd been prepared to lend me was providential for the day's activities, as was Donald's resolve to ride a bicycle again after a break of forty years. We could, of course, have taken a taxi that day, but without explaining the nature of our journey to the driver – which I was reluctant to do – it would have probably drawn suspicion, and a possible phone call to the police, if I'd asked him to drive by a particular house several times and then to idle at a discreet distance while Donald and I went on foot to take a closer look.

I drove slowly while Donald familiarised himself with the bicycle, and increased my speed as he grew in confidence.

'It's just like riding a bike!' he shouted.

The lower reaches of Main were largely nondescript – dry cleaning stores, dental suites and repair shops – and it was only after we'd passed the library that it became more residential. The houses here were old and expensive-looking, largely detached and built in a Spanish architectural style, but further out they became smaller and more affordable, ranch-style in appearance and constructed from a mixture of brick and wood.

When we reached Farquhar Park, a green space close to where Daisy lived, I gestured for Donald to follow me to one of its picnic tables. We were the only ones in the park, and it seemed safe to leave the scooter and bicycle under a tree while we reconnoitred the area.

'So where is it she lives?' Donald asked.

'On 12th Street,' I said. 'It runs along the top of the park.'

We walked nonchalantly, as if we'd lived in the neighbourhood our whole lives and were now bored to tears by it, glancing at the houses we passed and looking for one with the number 1232 on its door.

'They're all odd numbers on this side, so I suggest we cross the street when we get to 1233,' Donald said. 'That last house was 1217, so it can't be too far.'

We did as Donald advised and crossed to the other side when we reached 1233. Daisy's house was three doors further down: a one-storey bungalow with a brick base and wooden sides painted yellow. The drive was wide enough for one car and long enough for two, but there was no garage. The lawn, I was pleased to note, was neatly mown and the flower beds were well maintained.

It's said by many that the windows to a person's soul are their eyes, but in my experience it's their front garden. Of all the friends I've had over the years, not one of them has had an untidy front garden, and though I can't say this for a fact – because I've never been to his house – I strongly suspect that the landlord of the Lansdowne has a front garden that is overgrown with weeds and strewn with crisp packets and a source of discord with his neighbours.

If Daisy's garden had been like this I would have worried that her personal values were similarly compromised, but I was pleased to see that it wasn't. Her yard was neat and tidy, structured and symmetrical and in keeping with the other gardens in the street, and it was therefore safe to assume that the inside of her house was equally cared for and that she was a fit parent and a dutiful daughter and a reliable friend and a good neighbour and a concerned citizen and a trusted employee and a considerate motorist and – if everything went to plan – the future Mrs Herod S Pinkney.

'Keep moving, Rod' Donald said, taking my arm. 'We can't be seen taking an interest in this house when we've passed all the others by. And we need to keep heading west for a few more blocks. If we turn back now, it will be obvious to anyone watching that this was our intended destination.'

Donald was right, of course, and also correct in insisting that we return to the park on the other side of the street. My curiosity, however, had been satisfied, and I left the neighbourhood reassured.

We retrieved the scooter and bicycle from the park and continued north on Main; me riding on the sidewalk and Donald cycling beside me on the road. There were banners hanging from the street lamps paying tribute to the men and women of Huntington Beach serving in the armed forces. Each banner had the name and photograph of a different person on it, and the details of the branch of the armed forces they served in.

Donald responded well to these banners, and lamented that no one in Brierley Hill had given a fig when he'd gone off to fight in Vietnam on behalf of the western world, which had, so far as he knew, included the West Midlands at the time, and he wished he'd been shown some of the appreciation on display here. He also liked the profusion of national flags in the gardens and on the house porches and he laughed at a bumper sticker reading: *if you can't stand behind our troops, feel free to stand in front of them.*

'God bless America!' he said. 'Love it or leave it!'

Both sides of the street were lined with houses, but there was a church at the corner of 14th with a tall steeple and a giant cross in its grounds offering relevant teaching and upbeat music and the opportunity to follow Jesus recklessly. At 17th Street we drew level with Daisy's old high school and the Civic Centre, and then, at the point where Yorktown Street crossed Main, we arrived at Seacliff Village, a free-standing development of shops and restaurants.

'How do you want to play this?' Donald asked. 'There was a courtesy code posted by the entranceway, and a sign like that tells me we shouldn't leave the bike and scooter unattended. If you're happy to go into Albertsons alone, then I'm happy to stay here and keep an eye on them. I could get an ice cream while I'm waiting.'

Donald was proving to be a master tactician this day, and I agreed to the idea. I went with him to the ice-cream parlour and waited with his bicycle while he went inside and ordered a large cone of Rocky Road.

'I'd offer you a lick, Rod, but it's probably best if you don't accept one. I don't know what the courtesy code is for Albertsons, but there's a good chance they don't allow people in with chocolate on their chin. Now remember, play it cool in there and don't gawp if you see Daisy.'

I have to admit that I was a bit nervous walking into the store – which, incidentally, was a cut above most other supermarkets I'd patronised – but it was a good kind of nervousness and one similar, I supposed, to that experienced by an explorer who, having discovered an ancient tomb, was on the threshold of unearthing its treasures. I took a hand basket by the door for purposes of show, and then set off down the central walkway that bisected the aisles and gave a view of the staff serving behind the delicatessen counters to the left and the checkouts on the right.

About a third of the way down, and where the walkway divided the aisle dedicated to coffees and teas from the one devoted to detergents and fabric softeners, I came to an abrupt halt and was immediately hit from behind by a trolley. The woman who'd pushed into me was overly apologetic, but as no harm had been done – and my goal in the store was to remain anonymous – I side-stepped her concerns and escaped into the aisle displaying the coffees and teas, even though I was more interested in looking at the detergents and fabric softeners in the aisle opposite – or, to be more precise, at the woman sitting at the far end of the aisle whose image had brought me to a standstill in the first place.

I was about to retrace my steps when the woman with the trolley started to head my way. I thought it would look odd if I just scurried away from her empty-handed, and so I took the nearest can of coffee from the shelf and placed it in my basket. I spent a minute or so at the delicatessen counter, eyeing the cheeses and the cured meats on display, then returned to the aisle where I'd seen the detergents. I went as close to the end as I dared and then took a bottle from the shelf and pretended to read the label, holding it to the light and in the direction of the young cashier at the checkout.

Daisy was just as beautiful standing behind the checkout counter as the day she'd stood before Judge Judy's bench. It was as if an angel had descended from heaven and disguised herself in an Albertsons uniform. She was wearing a short-sleeved blue polo shirt with a logo on the arm and over it a black bib apron with the name of the store written on the front. She smiled at the customers she served, engaged with them, and made them feel more special than they were.

Daisy's black hair was cut shorter, but her skin was as pure and unblemished, and testimony, no doubt, to the wisdom of wearing a wetsuit in a hot clime. More importantly – so far as my own prejudices were concerned – her arms were completely free of tattoos, and it was therefore safe to suppose that so too were her legs, which, I surmised, would have only been a destination for the tattooist's needle if the arms had been fully inked. In this respect, I should have never questioned Daisy.

I'm not sure how long I stood there, certainly no more than a few minutes, but when the same woman with the trolley appeared at the top of the aisle and gave a friendly wave, I hurriedly dropped the detergent into my basket and made my way to the express checkout (10 items or less), picking up a tube of toothpaste and a box of tissues on the way to give my shopping expedition an air of credibility.

'So, how did it go? Did you see her?' Donald asked when I rejoined him outside the ice-cream parlour.

I told him I had, and that I was more convinced than ever that travelling to Huntington Beach had been the right thing to do.

'What have you got in the bag?'

'I bought some toiletries while I was there, but the big items were panic buys and I'll give those to Ruth.'

I then emptied the contents on to the table: a 48 oz canister of Folgers Classic Roast coffee, a large bottle of Tide Liquid Laundry detergent, a tube of Colgate toothpaste and a box of Kleenex tissues.

Donald looked puzzled when he saw my purchases.

'What made you buy sanitary towels?' he asked. 'I can't see Ruth needing those at her time of life, and it's too personal an item for a man to buy a woman – especially one he only met yesterday. She might well favour another brand.'

I had no idea what Donald was talking about, but when he pushed the box of tissues towards me and I looked closer, there was no mistaking that I'd bought a large packet of Kotex sanitary towels and not the Kleenex tissues I'd intended to buy. No wonder the cashier had given me a strange look.

We went to a fast food restaurant called Del Taco for lunch, and I slipped the Kotex into the same bin we emptied our trays. It was a waste of a no doubt fine product, but I couldn't think of what else to do with them.

'Tell me all about it,' Ruth said when we returned to the museum, 'and I mean everything.'

I recounted the morning's events and explained the reason for giving her a 48 oz canister of Folgers Classic Roast coffee and a large bottle of Tide Liquid Laundry detergent. I told her that Daisy was the same girl I'd seen on television and was just as beautiful in person; that she lived in a nice house with a nice front garden and had matured into a fine young checkout operator; and that she was a woman you could introduce to your parents, if you had them, and take to the finest restaurants and to the best hotels.

'And I'll bring her to the museum as well, Ruth. I think you two would hit it off.'

'I'll look forward to it,' Ruth smiled. 'Did you see her, Donald?'

'No, Rod made me wait outside and eat an ice cream.'

'He was watching the scooter and bike,' I explained. 'We didn't want anything to happen to them.'

We didn't stay long at the museum. Ruth had an appointment with the dentist and the woman who owned the museum was going to stand in for her. We arranged to meet at the Blessing of the Waves ceremony on Sunday, and then Donald and I went to ask about bus timetables at the information kiosk on Pier Plaza. We were going to Yorba Linda the next day and we'd decided to go there by bus, which would be a way of meeting more people.

'So, like, how can I help you guys?' the man at the kiosk asked.

The man appeared to be in his early forties and had long, sun-bleached hair and a dark tan. It was difficult to know if he'd just woken up from a deep sleep or was about to enter one, because his eyes occasionally closed and he kept forgetting to open them. At the time, I supposed his behaviour to be representative of California's laidback beach culture, but I later accepted Donald's judgement that it was more likely to have been the effects of marijuana.

'So, yeah, Nixon's pad, man, that's Yorba Linda all right. And you want to take a bus, right? Okay, let's figure out a way of getting you there.'

He then appeared to fall asleep and Donald wondered if we should prod him.

'Sir... sir,' I prompted, 'you were looking for a bus to take us to Yorba Linda.'

'Right, right, a bus to Yorba Linda, no problem...'

It took him about ten minutes to figure things out, but eventually he got there. There was, in fact, no bus that went to Yorba Linda, but if we rode the 29A to the intersection of Beach and La Palma and then caught the 38 bus to Old Canal East Park, we could get off at Yorba Linda Boulevard and from there walk to the Richard Nixon Presidential Library and Museum.

'It's no distance, man – the breeze will carry you. You guys here on holiday?'

We told him we were and then, for the sake of politeness, I asked him if he'd lived here long.

'My whole life, dude, and I wouldn't live any place else. HB's got the four Ws, man!'

Neither of us understood what he meant by this, and although I was content to live in ignorance, Donald asked him to explain.

'It's got the waves...' the man started to enumerate on the fingers of his left hand, 'it's got the weather... it's got the women... and it's got the...' He paused for a moment here, recounted the previous three and then remembered the fourth. 'Weed – it's got the weed!'

He then looked behind him, even though there was room only for him in the kiosk, and lowered his voice.

'I don't know how cool you dudes are, but if you want to catch a buzz while you're in town just say the word.'

It was kind of him to think of us, and flattering to be called cool, but in the circumstances it seemed wiser to settle for a printout of the bus timetable.

'There was something familiar about that fellah,' Donald said as we walked to the franchise to return his bicycle, 'something about his voice that rang a bell.'

It was over dinner that night, at a Japanese restaurant in Pacific City, that the penny dropped.

'The man in the information kiosk, Rod, the one I said looked familiar? It was Clay Miller – the fellah who took Daisy to court!'

*

The journey to Yorba Linda wasn't as straightforward as Clay had led us to believe. The 29A made a lot of stops as it travelled north on Beach Boulevard, and we had to wait a good twenty minutes on La Palma for the connecting bus to Old Canal East Park. Donald, out of respect for Richard Nixon, but with no thought for the day's temperature, had worn his suit for the trip and was perspiring heavily by the time the 38 bus arrived. This too made a lot of stops as it journeyed eastward, and when it finally drew to a halt at the foot of Yorba Linda Boulevard we'd been on the road for two and a half hours and not talked to a single person, which had, after all, been the prime reason for taking the bus.

You meet a cross-section of society riding a bus in London, but not in California. Here you encounter those left behind, the dispossessed and the troubled – America's car-less population – and we were as wary of them as they were of someone wearing a suit. We were reluctant to fall into conversation with the likes of a man who had blood running down his leg or with a woman who refused to touch any part of the bus with her bare hands, and we were equally unwilling to engage with people who talked loudly to themselves or got into arguments with the driver.

'Pardon my French, Rod,' Donald whispered, 'but this bus is like a fucking zoo!'

Donald rarely used the F-word, and although we'd paid for return journeys – at no more than $5 per head – I decided it would be better, and probably safer, if we returned to Huntington Beach in a taxi.

'What kind of breeze do you suppose Clay had in mind when he said it would carry us to Yorba Linda – a tornado?'

Donald asked a good question.

We were standing at the very bottom of Yorba Linda Boulevard and the avenue rose steeply to the horizon. Considering the lengths of Main Street and Beach Boulevard, and the inclination of Americans to get their money's-worth from any name they coin for a road, it was impossible to tell if Yorba Linda was at the crest of the hill or a good distance further down. There were no signposts to guide us or pedestrians to ask, and so we walked to a nearby car dealership, which was the only life in the area. And it was fortunate that we did because the centre of Yorba Linda, and the location of the museum, proved to be nowhere near where the bus had dropped us and was, in fact, seven miles distant.

The receptionist was kind enough to call a taxi, and while I waited outside for it to arrive Donald paid a visit to the men's room. He joined me a few minutes later with a row of medals pinned to his breast pocket and an Australian Army cap in his hand.

'First time I've had a chance to wear these in years,' he said. 'Feel free to salute me, Rod.'

The Richard Nixon Presidential Library and Museum, unlike the International Surfing Museum, looked and acted like a real museum, and was there to inform and educate any person willing to spend $16 on the admission fee about the life, legacy and times of the 37th President of the United States. It was located on the site of a small lemon farm once owned by the Nixon family, and Richard and his wife Pat, who were born and died within a year of each other, were buried near the original house and a short distance from a grounded helicopter.

Although Donald and I were intending to tour the museum together, we found ourselves interested in different things and it seemed sensible to go our separate ways. Donald spent most of his time in the rooms devoted to the Vietnam War, and most of mine was spent reading about Watergate and the events leading to his resignation.

Richard Milhous Nixon was Donald's hero and, in his opinion, the greatest of all American presidents. He was the man who'd stood up to communism and this was all that mattered to Donald and not the break-ins and the dirty tricks. To his way of thinking the means justified the end, and if others didn't see it this way then too bad. And if people wanted to denounce Nixon for his occasional misjudgement and make mountains out of molehills, then they should also condemn the hoteliers who'd given him freshly painted rooms when he came to their cities, and consider how well their own decision-making processes would have been functioning if they'd had to breathe paint fumes for eight hours straight.

I never argued with Donald about Richard Nixon because there'd have been no point. He cherry-picked the best parts of the man's life and ignored the uncomfortable truths. He hailed Richard Nixon as a great friend of Israel, for instance, but overlooked his overt suspicion of Jews living in his own country, especially those working in the Justice Department and the civil service and the ones he accused of controlling the media. Heroes can be as fallible and contradictory as the next person and perhaps Donald knew this. It certainly suited him not to scrutinise the life of his idol too closely.

In my opinion, and for what it's worth, Richard Nixon was a man who could only climb ladders by leaving the rails. He believed that if a person was to get anywhere in life then he had to lie, and that to win you had to defeat someone else and it didn't matter how you did it. You could unfairly undermine them and you could harass them, and if this involved bugging their offices and stealing their campaign workers' shoes, then so be it. And oddly, considering the ladders he'd chosen to climb, he was a man uncomfortable with people and thought that politics would be better off without them. He didn't even let his hair down among friends and he always wore a suit and tie in their presence. He was, in fact, at best in his own company, and the one thing he liked most about himself – unfortunate, in the circumstances – was the sound of his own taped voice...

'I wrote him a letter once,' Donald said after we'd met in the garden close to the fountains. 'I told him what a great man he was and that it had been a privilege to serve under him in Vietnam. I didn't expect to hear anything back, but he wrote me a short note thanking me for my letter and saying it had made his day. He also sent me a copy of a book he'd written that's on sale here. I suppose I should read it sometime.'

'How come you haven't read it already?' I asked. 'It's not every day a president sends you a gift.'

'I'm not really one for books, Rod. I never have been. I read the paper every day but that's about it. I can lend it to you if you like and you could tell me about it. There's no point in us both reading it, is there?'

We arrived back at the hotel shortly after five and arranged to meet at seven. It was odd how complete strangers passed us in the street and said hello, while the ever-changing receptionists behind the desk did no more than raise and lower their eyes whenever we walked into the lobby. Rudeness, I'm afraid, breeds rudeness, and I now made a point of ignoring them. The only people I acknowledged in the hotel were the maids who made up the rooms, and every morning I would leave three one-dollar bills on the pillow as a token of my appreciation and as a quid pro quo for them not stealing my passport and travel documents, which, in the absence of a room safe, I'd had to leave in the same drawer as my handkerchiefs and cravats.

I'd grown used to my room, and the maids always left it

clean and tidy. It had a king-size bed, a table and two chairs and a chest of drawers with a small fridge and microwave built into it. It was cooled by a large, old-fashioned air conditioner attached to the wall, and when it was on I had to turn up the television. The room was also soundproof and I never heard the people in the next room, who were probably paying half the rate I was.

I lay on the bed for a while and flicked through the television channels and then took a shower. It was Saturday night in Surf City and I dressed for the occasion. I wore linen trousers, a loose-fitting shirt and a cravat made from yellow silk and patterned with green lobsters. Donald, however, chose to dress down for the evening, and when I met him in the lobby he was wearing a pair of faded blue jeans and a red T-shirt he'd bought at the museum that afternoon.

The only problem with Huntington Beach on a Saturday night is that it's impossible to get a table in a restaurant without having previously made a reservation, which I hadn't thought to do. We were either turned away at the door or offered tables too late in the evening to be of value and so we reluctantly returned to the Pizza Press, not because the food there was bad, but because its ambience was as far from a Saturday night as it was possible to be.

'I never thought to mention it,' Ruth said the next day. 'We get a lot of visitors on a weekend and the restaurants are always full on a Saturday night. It's a bit like the days of the Wild West when cowboys rode into a town and drank the saloon dry.'

'You know where the Wild West is now, don't you?' Donald asked.

Ruth thought about it but eventually gave up and said she didn't.

'The Middle East,' Donald said. 'Ha!'

He then wrote the joke on the back of the programme he'd been given when we'd arrived at the plaza.

'I make up jokes all the time, Ruth, but if I don't write them down I forget them – even good ones like this. Edmundo's sure to get this one,' he said turning to me.

I think Donald was being over-optimistic, and that the joke would make as little sense to Edmundo as all his other jokes did. Edmundo was a literalist and would doubt the possibility of any place known as the Wild West being located in the Middle East when it was a well-known fact that the Middle East was in the east and not in the west. I think Edmundo had a different sense of humour to Donald, and, judging by the expression on her face, so did Ruth.

A small man stepped to a podium at the side of the plaza and gave the microphone a tap with his finger. I've always found it puzzling why speakers never trust that a microphone's been turned on, yet are quite happy to accept that one has been turned off. Someone should write a book about the things people say when they think no one can hear them and the trouble it causes when their words are unintentionally broadcast. I think this is a book that Ric might be interested in and I'll mention it to him once he regains his senses. I'll say it's a welcome-home gift.

'You wouldn't believe the difficulty Jim had finding a podium he could see over,' Ruth whispered. 'It took him weeks!'

Jim was the small man tapping the microphone and the emcee of the Blessing of the Waves ceremony, which was a yearly event organised by the local interfaith council.

'The water is our link to life...' he began.

The rest of what Jim said was a bit more complicated and

I didn't really understand it. I don't think he said the ocean was God – which would have been a hard sell to all but the Pantheists in the audience – but I'm also not sure that he didn't. I was without coffee and suffering from a slight hangover that morning, and I would have readily accepted that Jim was delivering his address in Swahili if someone had mentioned it.

The ceremony was a lot longer than I'd anticipated, and if we hadn't been sitting with Ruth and her friends I'd have probably left early. There were all kinds of religious and community speakers and then awards were handed out and the people presenting them and the people awarded them all made speeches and then the mayor came to the microphone and spoke at length because she was the mayor and the most important person there and liked the sound of her own voice and then Jim started talking in Swahili again and all the while the sun was growing hotter and the concrete seats more uncomfortable. When Donald fell asleep and his head lolled on to my shoulder, I looked to Ruth for help and found her missing.

'She had to go and open the museum,' one of her friends told me. 'She didn't want to spoil your enjoyment of the ceremony, and so she asked me to wish you well for tomorrow and ask that you stop by the museum when you get a chance.'

Ruth had introduced us to her friends when we'd arrived at the plaza, but I couldn't remember either of their names. I remembered that one was a member of the local historical society and the other a fellow congregant of First Calvary, but no more than that.

'Well, it's been very nice meeting you both,' I equivocated.

'It's been a pleasure meeting you, Rod – and you too, Donald. Enjoy the rest of your visit here.'

I felt bad that I couldn't remember their names when they remembered ours, and I asked Donald if he knew them.

'I'm no good with names, Rod,' he said. 'I wouldn't remember Lydia's if she didn't wear a nametag around the house. Now, where are we going to eat? I'm hungry!'

It made sense to avoid the crowds on Main Street and the pier, so we walked to Pacific City and ate in the Old Crow Smokehouse that had turned us away the previous night. We ordered steaks with baked potatoes and side salads, and drank coffee while we waited for the food.

'How about we have a lie-in tomorrow,' Donald suggested, as if reading my thoughts.

We'd been up early every morning since arriving in the city, and I was unused to such long days and covering extended distances on foot. It had been necessary to get a feel for the area before I met Daisy, but now that the spadework was done we could afford to move at a more leisurely pace, and I was pleased that Donald was of a similar mind.

I was expecting the rest of my time in Huntington Beach to be dictated by Daisy's schedule rather than be of my own making. I was hoping that she'd be able to take time off from work while I was here, and I anticipated spending most of my time with her and her daughter in the days ahead rather than with Donald. I wouldn't, of course, abandon my friend – and I would certainly include him in as many of our activities as possible – but it was important that Daisy and I spent time alone together. Over the meal I broached the subject with Donald and I was pleased that he understood the situation.

'Don't worry about me, Rod,' he said. 'I don't mind eating alone at night and I've got my days planned. I'm going to go cycling and ride the boardwalk as far north and as far south as it goes, and maybe go whale watching, too. It would be good to see a whale in the flesh or the blubber or whatever you call it when you see one up close.

'I'm going to learn how to surf before I go home, too. There are places on the front that teach you how to do it, and it would be a waste not to give it a try while I'm here. If Donald J Walker can survive Vietnam, then it's not likely he's going to fall victim to a rip current or an inshore hole. That's the way I'm looking at it.'

I admired Donald for his sense of adventure – which was head and shoulders over mine – and I was relieved that he wasn't expecting to spend his time with Daisy and me, though some of it I would ensure that he did. If Daisy took to me, as I expected she would, then there was no reason to suppose that she wouldn't take to Donald. And it would be good to have another person tell her what a nice man I was and vouch for my integrity and describe the beauty of Battersea and the advantages of living there, without me having to hammer these points home to her.

We spent the afternoon sitting on a bench overlooking the ocean and enjoying the sun. We'd been careful to use a high-factor sunscreen during our visit and had avoided getting burnt. Although my features speak for themselves, I would, nonetheless, have been reluctant to meet Daisy with a reddened face and a peeling nose. We moved to the shade of a palm tree when the sun grew too hot, and we spent the rest of the afternoon asleep on the grass.

Having decided on an early night and to forgo the bottle of bourbon we'd bought the previous evening, we went to the bar area of Dukes and ordered pints of what passed for lager and a large plate of nachos. We were back at the hotel by eight, and an hour later I was in my bed thinking of the day ahead.

Tomorrow wouldn't be just another day in my life; it would be D-Day and the start of my new life. Daisy Day!

*

I slept well that night and stayed in bed until mid-morning. I showered and dressed and then decided to call Edmundo. His former life had prevented him from joining us on the trip, but I wanted him to be as much a part of this special day as Donald. Although it was only eleven in the morning in Huntington Beach, it was seven in the evening in London and he and Nelly would be home. Edmundo picked up on the third ring.

'The Pinkney residence,' he answered.

'Edmundo, it's Rod. How are you?'

'I am well, Señor. It is good to hear your voice. How is life treating you in the land of the presidents?'

'It's treating me well, Edmundo. I just wanted you to know that today's the day.'

'It's Monday,' Edmundo said, 'and tomorrow is Tuesday.'

'Yes, I know what day of the week it is. I'm calling to say that today is the day I'm meeting Daisy. Eight hours from now I'll be sitting in a restaurant called Dukes and I'll be actually talking to her. I just wanted you to share in the day.'

'This is good news indeed, Señor Rod. I will set my alarm for three in the morning and I will rise from my bed and think of you. Is this what you want of me?'

'Well, only if you happen to be awake at the time or on your way to the toilet,' I said. 'I don't expect you to get out of bed in the middle of the night especially. I just wanted you to know that it's happening today.'

'No, Señor, it is happening tomorrow. You will be meeting

Daisy at three o'clock on Tuesday morning. I am surprised the restaurants are still open in America at this time. Perhaps it is only in California where these things happen. California is a strange place. It is the land of hippies and Ronald Reagan, if I am not mistaken.'

The conversation was becoming muddled and it seemed easier to change the subject and ask about the house.

'The house is fine, Señor Rod. There have been no break-ins and your electric toothbrush is safe. Lydia has been banging on the door but we choose not to open it. I believe that this is the prerogative of a householder, is it not? I am happy to pour a bucket of water on her head from an upstairs window if this is what you would like me to do. All you have to do is say the word, my friend, and I will give her a good piece of your riddance.'

I was beginning to wish I'd never called, or that Nelly had picked up the phone instead of Edmundo. It was a lot harder getting through to him on a phone than it was in person, and Donald was in enough trouble as it was with Lydia without him pouring a bucket of cold water on her head. I made it as clear as I possibly could to Edmundo that in no circumstances should he carry out such an act, and I hoped to the God I no longer believed in that he understood this.

I drew the conversation to a close and asked him to give my regards to Nelly.

'I will, Señor Rod. And good luck tomorrow!'

Edmundo then hung up and I was left listening to the sound of a disconnected line that made a lot more sense than him.

Donald laughed when I told him about the conversation, and was unworried by the thought of Edmundo dousing his wife with water.

'If he did do that, Nelly would make sure that he was the next thing out of the window. She's as tough as Lydia in her own way, just a lot nicer. How is it that a drongo like Edmundo ends up with her and I end up with Lydia?'

We didn't have to meet Mr Seymer until three and so we walked to the pier and ate a leisurely lunch of burgers and fries at Ruby's. I liked spending time on the pier and I wished there was something like it in Battersea. I was beginning to warm to Huntington Beach, and though I was still hoping that Daisy would agree to move to England, it wouldn't have been the end of the world if I'd had to live here.

'It's a nice-enough place all right,' Donald said when I mentioned this to him, 'but wouldn't you miss the robins and the hedgehogs? That's what I'd miss most about not living in England.'

I thought Donald was in danger of missing what was no longer there, because I couldn't remember the last time I'd seen a hedgehog – it was almost an endangered species these days. And, as for robins, well, you could see those on Christmas cards every year and there were sure to be American birds just as nice.

In fact, when I thought about it now, I wasn't sure there was anything I would miss about England if I moved to California. I'd miss my friends and the royal family, of course, but I certainly wouldn't miss Helen Mirren. No, if push came to shove, as Donald had once phrased it, I could be equally happy living in Huntington Beach with Daisy. And I was pretty sure that the people of the United States would be glad to have someone of my standing living amongst them, too. It would, in fact, be a win-win situation for everyone – for America, for Daisy and for me – and I couldn't see the government refusing me a visa.

I don't like being late for appointments, and I certainly wanted to arrive in good time for my meeting with Mr Seymer. Pacific City was a good walk from the pier and I suggested to Donald that we start heading that way. The weekend crowds had thinned and the sidewalks along the Pacific Highway were now largely empty. It was a hot day and we walked slowly.

'What does this Seymer fellah look like?' Donald asked.

'I don't know.'

'Does he know what you look like? Did you send him a photograph?'

'No, I didn't see the need. I told him I'd be the only person in the restaurant wearing a cravat.'

Donald looked at me. 'You're not wearing one,' he said.

Instinctively I felt for the cravat and was shocked to find it missing. I had a clear recollection of putting it on before I left the hotel that morning and I was momentarily confused by its disappearance. But then I remembered spilling ketchup on it at Ruby's and taking it off, wiping the tomato sauce with a napkin and dabbing it with water and then...

'I've left it on the window shelf at Ruby's,' I said. 'I put it there to dry and forgot all about it. Of all the stupid things to do – and on this of all days! I could kick myself!'

'Tie a paper napkin round your neck,' Donald suggested. 'You'd be the only person wearing one of those.'

'Apart from the other diners, you mean?'

'Hmm, I never thought of that,' Donald said. 'Arranging to meet the fellah in a restaurant mightn't have been the best idea you've had.'

'It wasn't my idea, it was his,' I said. 'It was Mr Seymer who suggested we meet at Lemonade. He sent me a text this morning confirming the venue.'

'Problem solved then. He's got your phone number and

you've got his. You didn't leave your phone at Ruby's, did you?'

Fortunately I hadn't, and I breathed a sigh of relief when I found it in my pocket. The crisis was over and I would compose myself over a large glass of wine once we reached the restaurant.

Donald and I arrived at Lemonade fifteen minutes early, and we took our glasses to an outdoor table that was shaded from the sun. Even in the mid-afternoon the terrace was crowded, a few eating a late lunch but most drinking the house lemonade or wine. Our backs were to the restaurant's plate-glass windows and we had a good view of the outside area where I was supposed to meet Mr Seymer. Three o'clock came and three o'clock went, and then, at 3:10, my phone rang.

'Hi, Mr Pinkney, it's Phil Seymer. What time do you expect to be here?'

'I'm already here, Mr Seymer. I'm sitting on the terrace.'

'That's where I'm sitting,' he said. 'Hang on a minute and I'll stand up. Okay, I'm standing. Can you see me?'

'No, but if I stand up, maybe you'll see me.'

'No, nothing yet, Mr Pinkney...'

I turned to Donald and asked him if he could see anyone standing.

'The fellah at the next table is on his feet, but he's on the phone to someone,' Donald replied.

I'd been looking outward rather than to my immediate right, and the man on the phone was doing the same thing and ignoring his left.

'Are you wearing a dark suit, Mr Seymer?'

'The tailor described it as charcoal grey, but I guess you could call it dark. Where are you?'

'I think I'm standing next to you.'

Mr Seymer turned to his left and continued to talk into his phone when he saw me.

'I thought you said you'd be wearing a cravat.'

'I was when I left the hotel, but it's on a shelf at Ruby's Diner now. Do you think we should hang up?'

Mr Seymer gave a sheepish grin and held out his hand.

'I was expecting you to look different, Mr Pinkney,' he said. 'You are Herod S Pinkney, aren't you?'

'I am,' I said, taking his hand. 'And this is my friend Donald Walker.'

Donald shook Mr Seymer's hand and said that he could vouch for me because he was my next-door neighbour and had known me for years.

'I can believe that,' Mr Seymer said, looking at me curiously.

He then joined us at the table and we agreed to call each other by our first names. He then showed me a copy of the letter I'd sent to Mr Stenger and asked me to check its details. I knew the letter by heart and I skimmed through it: *mortgage-free house... non-smoker... contributor to the Conservative Party...* yes it was all there, Herod S Pinkney present and correct.

I offered to buy Phil a drink but he said that he'd pass. He had to serve papers on someone at four and he didn't want to smell of alcohol when he did this.

'I'll have a drink with you at Dukes, if the offer's still open. Will we be toasting anything in particular?'

'I hope so, but I'd like Daisy to hear the news first. I hope you don't think I'm being rude for saying this.'

'For the money you're paying us, Rod, you could poke me in the eye with a pencil and I wouldn't take offence. I'm just glad we've been able to bring the two of you together – for whatever reason.'

I liked Phil. He was professional in manner but not stand-offish, and his humour was self-deprecating. He took his job seriously but not himself, and I like this in a person. He appeared to be in his early forties and had the build of an athlete and the chiselled good looks of a comic book hero. If I'd met him in Battersea, I would have become his friend and invited him to our Thursday night gatherings.

We chatted for about an hour and then Phil left to serve the papers he'd mentioned.

'I've reserved the table at Dukes in my name, Rod, and it's available from 6:30,' he said. 'If Ms Lamprich is ready on time, I should be there by seven. Take it easy, bud.'

Donald and I walked back to Ruby's and I found my cravat where I'd left it. There was still a trace of the sauce on the fabric, and the necktie would have to be dry-cleaned before I could wear it again, but I was relieved to have it back in my possession.

'Do you want to stay for a drink?' Donald asked. 'It's only 4:30.'

'I'd better not,' I said. 'I need to be at my best when I meet Daisy and I also need to take a shower.'

'There'll be nothing left of you,' Donald said. 'I bathe once a week and that's enough for any man.'

We returned to the hotel and I arranged to meet Donald in the lobby at 6:30. I took a short nap and then readied myself for what I expected to be the most defining evening of my life. I dressed in my best linen suit and wore a light cotton shirt and a plain blue cravat.

'You're looking very dapper,' Donald said when we met in the lobby.

He was wearing his suit and tie and I complimented him on his appearance, too.

'I have a good feeling about tonight, Rod. The way I see it, Daisy has everything to gain and nothing to lose by becoming your wife. She's a single mother living in a rented house, doing a menial job and without prospects. And then, out of the blue, a rich fellah like you turns up and offers her the world. It's like that Sheila who goes to the ball and meets Prince Charming: one minute she's a skivvy and the next she's a princess.'

I appreciated Donald's words of encouragement, but I wanted Daisy to fall in love with me for the right reasons and not for my money. I'm sure that money does buy love, but it's not a concept I'm comfortable with and I doubted that Daisy was either.

We arrived at Dukes at 6:45 and were shown to the table reserved by Phil. We ordered small glasses of white wine, and I asked the sommelier to put a bottle of champagne on ice. The table had a view of the ocean and Hawaiian music played in the background. It was the perfect setting for a romantic evening with Daisy, Donald and Phil.

'I'm surprised you're not more nervous,' Donald said. 'I was nervous around Lydia for months when we first started going out. In fact, I only stopped being nervous once I became scared of her.'

I think Donald was joking but I couldn't be sure. There was always a grain of truth to the jokes he made about Lydia.

'At one time of my life I would have been,' I said. 'I didn't know how to behave around women then and I used to get tongue-tied a lot. But once I grew comfortable in my own skin I became more confident, and I've never lost that confidence.'

'Have you rehearsed what you're going to say?'

'Not really. I know what I want to say, but I want the words to flow naturally and not sound too practised. It's always best if...'

'They're here!' Donald said. 'They've just walked in.'

I looked up and saw Phil guiding Daisy towards me, his hand resting on the small of her back. I stood up and Donald stood too.

'Hi Rod, sorry we're late but there was a problem with the babysitter. Daisy, this is Herod Pinkney.'

Daisy held out her hand and gave me the most beautiful smile.

'I'm very pleased to meet you, Mr Pinkney,' she said.

Her hand was as soft as silk and as warm and dry as the Saharan desert. I held on to it for as long as I dared and asked her to call me Rod. I then introduced her to Donald.

Phil had introduced me as Herod, and I think this confused her.

'Is it Rod or Herod?' she asked.

'It's Rod,' I assured her. 'My parents christened me Herod, but I've gone by the name of Rod ever since my mother committed suicide.'

'Oh, how awful,' she said. 'That must have been a difficult time for you.'

'It was,' I admitted. 'The boys at school used to tease me about it.'

'They teased you about your mother's death!'

'No, they made fun of my name,' I clarified.

I asked Daisy and Phil to take a seat and signalled for the sommelier to bring the bottle of champagne.

Daisy was wearing a black dress, cut low to reveal her cleavage, and she had a silver evening shawl draped over her shoulders that would have been the envy of young Roy Danter. She was more beautiful in person than she had been on television, and even more becoming than when I'd seen her at the checkout at Albertsons. I was so taken with her, in fact, that I forgot all about the sommelier hovering next to me and Donald had to nudge me.

'Hey, Rod, the fellah wants to know if you want him to pour the champagne?'

Well, of course I wanted him to pour it. The evening was a celebration and I had a toast to make.

'To Daisy,' I said, once our glasses were filled.

'To Daisy,' Donald and Phil responded.

Daisy, who wasn't sure why she was being toasted, or if etiquette allowed her to join in, simply raised her glass and thanked us.

'I don't mean to be presumptuous, Rod, but Phil said you wanted to discuss something that might be of benefit to me. Is this what we're toasting? We're not related, are we?'

'No, at least not yet, we're not,' I smiled.

I explained that it was a long and unusual story and asked her to bear with me.

'I met you for the first time a few months ago when you were twenty-five,' I said. 'Two years prior to this event I'd bought a new television...'

'It was a Bang & Olufsen,' Donald interjected, 'one of the best on the market.'

I touched Donald's sleeve as an indication that he shouldn't interrupt, and then continued.

'I spend Thursday evenings with Donald and a friend of ours called Edmundo...'

'He used to be a terrorist and so he couldn't travel with us to the United States,' Donald cut in again. 'Otherwise he'd have been here tonight too.'

'Please, Donald,' I said.

'Sorry, Rod, I was only trying to fill in some of the details for Daisy.'

'Anyway,' I continued, 'Donald and Edmundo wanted a demonstration of the television, and because Donald had already seen the evening news he suggested we turn to channel 66 and watch the *Judge Judy Show*. It was Donald's favourite programme and it quickly became mine and Edmundo's too, and for the next four years we watched it every Thursday night. The episodes they show in England are usually old ones, but we're seeing them for the first time and so it makes no difference to us. And then, earlier this year, we saw a case involving you that had first been broadcast thirteen years ago.'

Daisy rolled her eyes as if discomfited by the memory.

'It wasn't my proudest moment,' she said. 'I wish I'd never agreed to appear on the show.'

'On the contrary, Daisy, you acquitted yourself well and you left the courtroom with your dignity intact. In my opinion, Judge Judy wronged you that day and she should have ordered Clay to pay you the back rent.'

'We met him down by the pier the other day,' Donald said. 'He's working at the information kiosk.'

'He'll be working there ten years from now,' Daisy said. 'I don't know what I ever saw in him.'

'And he's not very good at his job, either,' Donald said. 'Rod and I were trying to get to the Richard Nixon Museum in Yorba Linda, and if we'd followed his advice we'd have had to walk seven miles from where the bus dropped us.'

'You went there by bus?'

'It was Rod's idea. He's not short of a bob or two, if that's what you're thinking – and we flew here business class – but he thought it would give him a chance to get to know the people before he decided to move to Huntington Beach.'

'You're thinking of moving here?' Daisy asked.

I knew Donald was trying to help me, but the conversation

was getting out of hand and I needed to finish telling Daisy about the chain of events that had led us to Dukes.

'Maybe we can come to that later, Daisy, but first I'll finish my story, which might start to sound a little strange now.

'I was moved by your appearance on television, and I instantly felt connected to you. I believe in fate, Daisy, and have done ever since a young girl blew her nose on my dress handkerchief. And I think we – yes, you and I, Daisy – were fated to meet and are meant to be together. The truth is that I fell in love with you the moment I saw you on television and I've never stopped loving you. I'm hoping that once we've spent time together you'll feel the same way about me and agree to be my wife.'

'You'd be a fool to pass up an opportunity like this,' Donald said.

Daisy stared at me and it was difficult to read her expression.

'I hope you don't mind me asking you this, Rod,' she said, 'but how old are you exactly?'

'I'm eighty-four,' I smiled. 'I know. It's hard to believe, isn't it? I...'

And then something strange happened. Daisy's face started to blur and then it completely disappeared, and the next thing I knew I was lying on a trolley in a hospital emergency room with a woman I didn't recognise hovering over me.

'Mr Pinkney,' she said, 'I need to see some proof of insurance.'

10 April 2020

It's funny growing old. You know it happens, but you only see it in others. I didn't look upon myself as an eighty-four-year-old man – just as I'd never looked upon myself as a forty- or a sixty-year-old man at previous stages in my life – and I certainly didn't identify with people of my own age. I didn't introduce myself to others and say hello, my name's Rod and I'm eighty-four years old and expect a round of applause, because I've never felt defined by my age or a need to mention it. I was simply a man called Herod 'Rod' Pinkney, neither child nor grown-up.

I'd been cushioned from the real world by financial independence and lived in a continuum that wasn't anchored by time. I'd avoided the responsibilities of employment and parenthood borne by most and been oblivious to the milestones that contextualised time for them. I was never prompted by events to consider my age or to think that I was old, and neither did I have any nagging aches and pains that might suggest that I was. I rarely visited the doctor, and I suffered from no chronic conditions that demanded a repeat prescription. And because I'd always been of a sedentary nature, it was difficult to know if my energy levels were any less vital – especially when I'd taken the precaution of installing stairlifts in the house and buying a mobility scooter.

I was old, but at the same time not old. Rightly or wrongly, I'd supposed myself to be in the prime of life when I met Daisy, and I expected her to think the same. Although it might have occurred to others that my mind and body had been living separate lives for too many years, the thought had never occurred to me. What did strike me at Dukes, though, and something I hadn't anticipated, was a transient ischaemic attack.

*

It was Ric's idea for me to write the addendum that follows. I'd finished the final continuations two months after returning from Huntington Beach, placed them in a drawer and forgotten all about them. But then, four months later, Ric came by the house and asked me about the manuscript. I was more concerned with his welfare than discussing my book, and I first asked him about himself and if his troubles were behind him.

He assured me they were. He'd been on a journey, he said, which is usually a claim too far when most people say this and amounts to little more than them crossing a road at rush hour, but in Ric's case the word did have meaning. He'd been released from the psychiatric unit after an enforced stay of three weeks, and become either a new man or the same man he'd been before he'd decided that barbecuing books on Charing Cross Road was a good idea.

There are newspapers and television channels that take an interest in the stories of people rising to the top or falling from grace and Ric's protest had caught their imagination. He became a cause célèbre for a short time and he was interviewed by the press and invited to appear on television programmes both light and serious. Considering that few people read books these days, it was surprising that the health of the publishing industry was of such interest in these quarters, but apparently they have column inches to fill and schedules to populate and are in constant need of subject matter.

On the back of this exposure, Ric had been offered a position with a small but prestigious literary agency that was prepared to give him greater freedom in commissioning books than most other agencies allowed their associates. With no other offers on the table, and reluctant to clear glasses for the rest of his life, he'd accepted their proposal and was now working on a series entitled *The Wonder of Meat*. He'd already commissioned books on the wonder of the pork chop and the wonder of the lamb cutlet and he was about to sign off on the wonder of sausages, which was his personal favourite.

With the help of his psychiatrist, Ric had also reconciled with his wife and was now allowed to eat meat outside the house and without having to conceal the fact from his family. Ric, the psychiatrist explained to Suzie, was as dependent on meat as a diabetic was reliant on insulin, and if doctors had been allowed to write prescriptions for meat on the NHS then Ric would have been the first to qualify for such treatment.

After telling me all this, and drinking four cups of coffee, Ric returned to the question of my book and wanted to know if I'd finished the manuscript or if I was still writing it. He'd discussed the story with several publishers, and there were three that were definitely interested. I told him that I'd finished the book, but that it didn't have the happy ending we'd been hoping for. I took it from the desk drawer and handed it to him, and we arranged to meet the following week once he'd had a chance to read it.

Ric, I'm glad to say, liked the book, and he suggested I

include the journal entries I'd previously kept from him. He did, however, think that continuation 10 ended too abruptly and might lead the reader – whose average IQ he estimated to be about 45 – to believe that I was dead. He said that I had to gather all the loose ends together and tie them into a nice bow, because that's what readers with an IQ of 45 expected from an author.

And so, at Ric's insistence, and for a short time only, I'll return you to Huntington Beach.

The Finish

I was formally admitted to the hospital after Donald brought my insurance documents from the hotel, and I remained there for five days. The room was nicer than the one at the Huntington Beach Inn, and it was consoling to know that I was being charged the same daily room rate as every other patient in the hospital. Although by morning the symptoms of the attack had largely disappeared – the numbness and confusion gone and my vision restored – the doctor insisted on keeping me under observation for a few days and running a series of tests.

He later explained that I'd experienced what in their book was termed *a brief episode of neurological dysfunction caused by a disruption in blood flow to the brain*, and that in mine would be known as a mini-stroke. The word stroke hit me as hard as when Miss Wimpole had told me I had a disability when I'd approached her about my dyslexia, and the doctor took note of my reaction.

'Your brain hasn't suffered any permanent damage, Mr Pinkney – the MRI scan proved that – but the episode you've just had was a wake-up call. You have high blood pressure and raised cholesterol levels, and if you don't address these conditions you'll be in danger of suffering a major stroke. I'm surprised your own doctor hasn't told you this.'

I told him not to be, because apart from the time I'd gone to see him about my eye, I couldn't remember the last time I'd visited him and wasn't even sure of his name.

Bearing in mind that I'd been in Huntington Beach for less than a week at the time of the stroke, I was never short of visitors. Ruth came by three times, and on one occasion brought the two friends she'd introduced me to at the pier and whose names I still can't remember. She was sorry to hear that things hadn't worked out with Daisy, but wondered if it was for the best.

'If you had a small stroke just talking to her, then you have to wonder what might have happened if you'd been doing anything more physical,' she said. 'I couldn't have prayed harder for you and Daisy, Rod, and so I'm wondering now if the stroke wasn't God's way of encouraging you to be more careful. I think it was His way of watching over you and prolonging your life.'

Well, if it was God's way of watching over me and steering me away from Daisy, He certainly didn't have any objections to her visiting me in the hospital. She'd accompanied me to the emergency room on the night of the attack, and she came by every day afterwards, and most days she brought her daughter.

Amelia was a beautiful child and looked a lot like Daisy. She'd sit quietly on the bed while her mother and I talked, and she'd draw pictures in a ruled exercise book and show them to me before she left. The one I remember most is the one she drew of me. It portrayed me as an old man with a walking stick and with wings on his back and floating in the air.

'That's you dying and going to heaven, Mr Pinkney,' she explained.

'But a long time from now,' Daisy hastened to add.

Amelia didn't say anything and just shrugged.

The first time Daisy came to see me, and without Amelia, was the time she laid her cards on the table – or, in the circumstances, my hospital food tray. She told me she was flattered by my attentions and the efforts I'd made to find her, but that for her the age difference was just too great.

'You're a good-looking man, Rod, and if we'd met thirty years ago I know things would have been different.'

Daisy hadn't meant this literally of course, because thirty years ago I'd have been fifty-four and she'd have been eight, and the only difference then would have been the involvement of the police. I knew what she meant, though, and I appreciated her words.

The thing that puzzled her most, though, was my reason for saying I was forty-eight in my letter to the Turnipseed Agency – the key points of which had been communicated to her – and this was also a matter that intrigued Phil when he came to visit. He told me he'd been looking for a forty-eight-year-old man on the terrace of Lemonade the day we met, and had been surprised when someone my age had come forward claiming to be Herod Pinkney, and that was why he'd asked me to check the details of the letter I'd sent to Mr Stenger. After I'd confirmed that everything in the letter was correct, he'd naturally assumed that I had an ageing disorder that made me look older than I was, but didn't like to ask about it because if you asked questions like that in California you usually went to prison.

I explained to them both that I'd made a stupid but unintentional mistake when I'd written the letter, and that instead of recording my age as 84, as I'd intended doing, I'd unknowingly transposed the digits but continued to read the number as 84 because that was the number I was expecting to see there. It was a consequence of my lingering dyslexia, I added, and also spoke to the limitations of a spellchecker!

Ric told me later that it was a pity he'd been unavailable to proofread continuation 6 before I left for California, because he'd have spotted the mistake and probably saved me a lot of trouble. He also told me in this conversation that he'd never actually described my book as *a quest for love in an uncertain age*, as I'd written in continuation 2, but as a quest for love *at* an uncertain age, which was a reference to my years he said, and he claimed to have circled the offending word in red ink.

'What I liked about your story, Rod, was its potential futility,' he told me. 'I liked the idea of an old guy looking over his shoulder as the years crept up on him and having one last hurrah at finding love. The odds were against you from the start, but there was always a chance – a *small* chance – that you might have succeeded and that would have made one hell of a story. That you failed doesn't really matter because it's still a good story. The important thing is that you tried and went searching for the impossible, and there are plenty of losers out there who'll identify with your tale.'

Donald, of course, was my chief mainstay during my time in hospital, but I eventually insisted on him limiting his visits to the evening and making the most of his remaining days in Huntington Beach. And so he hired a bicycle and rode the boardwalk as far north and as far south as it went, and one day went whale watching and saw two dolphins. He also tried learning to surf but gave up after the first lesson.

'It's not going to happen, Rod,' he said. 'I can't hit golf balls and I can't keep my balance on a surfboard. It's as simple as that.'

Instead of learning to surf, he'd spent his time on the pier and made friends with a man called Chinh who fished there every day. Chinh loaned him a rod and Donald gave him the fish he caught, and Chinh then sold them to a store in Westminster and bought Donald the occasional ice cream in recompense. Donald said that Chinh had left South Vietnam in a boat and had no intention of ever climbing back into one. I don't know what else they talked about because Donald never said, but I'm sure that the war and Richard Nixon were a part of their conversations.

I was discharged from the hospital on Saturday morning and given four blister packs of pills and a letter to give to my doctor, once I'd remembered his name.

I'd booked a table at Dukes while recuperating in the hospital and I invited Daisy, Amelia, Phil and Ruth to join Donald and me for Sunday lunch. It would be a way of thanking them for their kindness and of saying a fond farewell to Huntington Beach. I also gave Donald leave to invite Chinh to the meal, but he declined to take me up on the offer. He said that Chinh was a nice enough fellah but smelled of fish all the time and wouldn't be able to join in the conversation because he didn't speak English all that well. He could hold his own in Vietnamese if the subject was fish, he said, but that was about it.

As hosts of the meal Donald and I arrived early, and I ordered a glass of wine for Donald and an orange juice for myself while we waited for the others. The doctor had suggested I cut down on alcohol and I followed his advice for two weeks.

Ruth was the first to arrive, and shortly afterwards Phil,

Daisy and Amelia came together. They looked like the perfect family when they walked into the restaurant, and when I mentioned this to Daisy she blushed. Amelia told Ruth that she looked funny and asked if she was my girlfriend and Ruth smiled and said that she wasn't and Daisy told Amelia to mind her manners. The waiter came to the table and we ordered our food and over the meal Donald talked about fishing on the pier and Phil about an old case he'd worked on in Los Angeles and Daisy about Albertsons and Ruth about the International Museum of Surfing and the local historical society. After she'd finished her meal Amelia asked Ruth if she wanted to go outside and play and Ruth said that she did and promised to let Amelia sit on her mobility scooter.

After they'd left, I pushed an envelope across the table to Daisy and when she asked what was inside I told her it was the money Clay owed her in back rent and hoped that she'd accept it. She politely pushed it back to me and smiled and shook her head and I knew then that Daisy was the woman I'd always believed her to be.

When we left the restaurant, I shook hands with Phil and thanked him for his help. He said he wished he could have done more and that the Turnipseed Agency would send the final bill to my home address in England. Ruth hugged me and thanked me for the best birthday she'd ever had and asked me to keep in touch and Amelia said that she hoped I wouldn't die and I said that I hoped this too.

And then I said goodbye to Daisy. She gave me a long hug and kissed me on the cheek and wrote down her email address and told me not to give up hope and that – as Nelly had said only two weeks earlier – there were plenty more fish in the sea and Donald said that most of them were mackerel and the next day Donald and I flew home to England.

On the flight home Donald said that he'd missed Lydia and looked forward to a new beginning with her. He was optimistic that her heart would have grown fonder of him during his absence, but it turned out that it hadn't and she refused to speak to him for two weeks, which Donald still thought of as an improvement.

Edmundo and Nelly fussed over me for a few days, but when it became clear that I wasn't about to die things quickly returned to normal. I enjoyed sharing the house with them and I persuaded them to forgo their flat and live with me on a permanent basis. In light of the ischaemic attack and the possibility of something more serious to come, it was advantageous to have people at hand that I trusted.

The attack had also incentivised me to put my affairs in order and to write a will, which was something Graham had been encouraging me to do for some time. I'd never given much thought to dying because I could never contemplate not being alive, but now that I realised I was no more immune to death than the next person, I decided it was time.

I've left the house and a substantial sum of money to Edmundo and Nelly, and another substantial sum to Donald. I've also remembered Clarence and his family in my will, and I've left money in trust for Amelia's college education. The rest will be divided between various charities once Graham has found a way of ensuring that all monies will be used for the actual causes.

The Donald Walker Experience continues to practise in my basement and Henry, who's decided to pursue a career in music for the time being, has joined them on tambourine after Nelly suffered repetitive strain injury. I still see Lorna from time to time, but she no longer invites me to accompany her to dinners. She had no idea how old I was and she now holds this against me.

'I just hope to God that no one else knows this, Rod. Do you know how embarrassing it is to know that I've been accompanied to dinner parties by a man who's fucking eighty-four? They'll have been thinking I was fucking desperate! I don't know how you could have been so selfish!'

I keep in touch with Ruth and Daisy, and Amelia occasionally sends me drawings. I'm glad to say that all is well in Huntington Beach, and I received news yesterday that Daisy and Phil are to be married in June and that Donald and I are invited to the wedding. I'm happy for Daisy and I'm glad that she's marrying Phil, who will be a good father to Amelia.

Edmundo, Donald and I still meet on a Thursday night and I enjoy these evenings. It's a Thursday night now, in fact, and Donald has just returned home and Edmundo gone to bed. I'm sitting at my desk in the library surrounded by books, and I have just brought my own story to an end.

Eventually, my life will also draw to a close and a full stop placed after the name of Herod S Pinkney. Until that moment comes, however, I will continue to live in hope.

It's enough to be going on with.

THE END

For Esther
1951–1997

Acknowledgements

The author would like to thank John Lea for sharing the story of his early life and the only time he was interesting; the Naylors for a name; and himself for writing a book in the first person. He would also like to express his gratitude to Val Henderson and Trevor Armstrong and to the NEPers of Harpenden: Claire, CQ, Ellie, Ion, Katherine and Lisa.